NOT HIS FAVORITE SONG

The phone rang again. Berenger quickly picked up the receiver and was bombarded by loud, distorted Punk music coming through the earpiece. He winced and held the phone away from his head. Then someone on the other end added "vocals." Screaming into the phone in Punk Rock fashion, the caller shouted in rhythm—

"You're going to DIE tomorrow night, mister mister mister, you're gonna DIE DIE DIE,

you're going to DIE tomorrow night, mister mister mister, you're gonna DIE DIE DIE!"

And the phone went dead.

A HARD DAY'S
DEATH

A Spike Berenger Hit

RAYMOND BENSON

LEISURE BOOKS   NEW YORK CITY

A LEISURE BOOK®

April 2008

Published by

Dorchester Publishing Co., Inc.
200 Madison Avenue
New York, NY 10016

ISBN 10: 0-8439-6063-9
ISBN 13: 978-0-8439-6063-1

The name "Leisure Books" and the stylized "L" with design are trademarks of Dorchester Publishing Co., Inc.

Printed in the United States of America.

10 9 8 7 6 5 4 3 2 1

Visit us on the web at www.dorchesterpub.com.

For Randi

LINER NOTES

Although real-life rock stars such as John Lennon, David Bowie, and others appear or are referenced in this book, it is a work of fiction. The characters of Flame, his family, and fellow musicians are not meant to represent any persons, living or dead. Needless to say, John Lennon and David Bowie never knew a musician named Flame.

The author and publisher wish to thank Kenny Wylie, Dean Zelinsky, James McMahon, and Lieutenant Gene White for their help in the preparation of this book.

TRACK LISTING

1. Rock 'n' Roll Suicide *(performed by David Bowie)*
2. Mood for a Day *(performed by Yes)*
3. L.A. Woman *(performed by The Doors)*
4. Roll With the Changes *(performed by REO Speedwagon)*
5. Morning Has Broken *(performed by Cat Stevens)*
6. Jailhouse Rock *(performed by Elvis Presley)*
7. Family Affair *(performed by Sly and the Family Stone)*
8. Jesus is Just Alright *(performed by The Doobie Brothers)*
9. Mother *(performed by John Lennon)*
10. Trouble Every Day *(performed by Frank Zappa and the Mothers of Invention)*
11. Son of Your Father *(performed by Elton John)*
12. Band on the Run *(performed by Wings)*
13. Boys Don't Cry *(performed by The Cure)*
14. Angry Eyes *(performed by Loggins and Messina)*
15. Wild in the Streets *(performed by The Circle Jerks)*
16. For What It's Worth *(performed by Buffalo Springfield)*
17. The Wicked Messenger *(performed by Bob Dylan)*
18. Legend in Your Own Time *(performed by Carly Simon)*
19. Prove It All Night *(performed by Bruce Springsteen)*
20. Free Fallin' *(performed by Tom Petty)*
21. Something to Believe In *(performed by The Ramones)*
22. Night Moves *(performed by Bob Seger and the Silver Bullet Band)*
23. Dead Man's Party *(performed by Oingo Boingo)*
24. Stir It Up *(performed by Bob Marley and the Wailers)*
25. Black Limousine *(performed by The Rolling Stones)*
26. Doctor Rock *(performed by Motörhead)*
27. Higher Ground *(performed by The Red Hot Chili Peppers)*
28. Nothing is Easy *(performed by Jethro Tull)*
29. Danger Zone *(performed by Kenny Loggins)*
30. Barrel of a Gun *(performed by Depeche Mode)*
31. Run Like Hell *(performed by Pink Floyd)*
32. Watching the Detectives *(performed by Elvis Costello and the Attractions)*
33. A Hard Day's Night *(performed by The Beatles)*

"I believe rock 'n' roll is dangerous . . ."
—DAVID BOWIE, in *Rolling Stone*, 1976

1

Rock 'n' Roll Suicide

(performed by David Bowie)

There was death in the air.

It was a comment that Gina Tipton had made before the show and Kenny Franklin had thought nothing of it. "Gina the Gypsy," as she used to be called back in her hippie days, had a reputation for making spooky predictions. A day later Franklin would remember Gina's words and what they portended, but he currently had other things on his mind.

Franklin, who held the all-important job of acting as Flame's tour manager, signed off on the union time cards and sent the crew home. The stage was clean and the tour was done. The show had been a success, such as it was, and the meet and greet had gone smoothly, more or less. Flame, of course, had gotten into volatile arguments with no less than three different individuals before and after the show. But all things considered, the tour ended on an upbeat note.

"Hey Kenny," called Louis, the band's monitor and guitar tech. He held up a bank money bag. "What do I do with this?"

Franklin frowned. "Oh shit, didn't Al take that with him?"

Louis shrugged. "I guess he didn't. I have it."

"Damn." Franklin took the heavy bag from his assistant. The bag held the night's receipts and concession money. "I'm flying to Nashville tomorrow morning. I don't want to be stuck with this. Can you take it to Flame's office tomorrow?"

Louis shook his head. "I'm driving out to my folks' place in Jersey as soon as I get out of here. I'm on vacation now."

Franklin cursed. "That means I have to drop it by there tonight. All right, Louis, see you next time. Stay out of trouble."

"You too, Kenny."

Franklin held on to the bag and turned the theater over to the venue's stage manager to lock up. He went out the stage door and walked toward Broadway, where he hoped to catch a cab. It was nearly two in the morning but surely there would be some taxis on such a major thoroughfare. New York City never slept.

He waited only two minutes. He flagged down a cab heading north and got in the backseat.

"Turn her around, we gotta go to Greenwich Village," he told the driver. Without a word the driver slapped the meter and took off. At the light he made an illegal U-turn and drove south on Broadway. The going was smooth until the cab reached Columbus Circle, where several NYPD patrol cars sat with lights flashing. An officer slowly waved cars through a roadblock and prevented any from turning east on Fifty-seventh Street.

"What's going on?" the cabdriver asked the officer as he moved past him.

"The Jimmys pulled another show at the bottom of Central Park. Keep moving, sir."

The cab moved on and continued south.

"Those lunatics," the driver said. "Them and those nutty Cuzzins oughta be shot on sight."

Franklin came close to agreeing. The Jimmys and the Cuzzins were relatively new phenomena in New York City. Technically they were mysterious, ruthless, and violent rival gangs that vied for control of the illegal drug trade in the metropolitan area. And, like most gangs, they had their share of responsibility for thefts, vandalism, and murders. On the other hand, they were rock bands that kept their identities secret. The Jimmys were punks that made the Sex Pistols look like the Partridge Family. They wore grotesque masks supposedly made from the skin of corpses—patterned after the "Leatherface" character from the *Texas Chainsaw Massacre* movies. The Cuzzins fashioned themselves after the black leather-look of the Hamburg-era Beatles. Beneath their greasy, slicked-back hair, the Cuzzins wore black face masks, and specialized in 1950s rock 'n' roll. Both bands occasionally held impromptu "guerrilla" concerts around the city, using stolen portable equipment that they destroyed and left behind when the police arrived. These happenings attracted a rough crowd and a riot almost always ensued during and after one of these bands' so-called performances. They frequently started fires and damaged public property. Sometimes there were deaths. Thus the bands' sets were never very long. By the time the Jimmys or Cuzzins had played three songs, the police were already on the way. The gangs then enjoyed leading the cops on wild and reckless chases through the city streets, usually on motorcycles. To date none of the major players in either group had ever been caught, and no one knew who the leaders were. Any arrests made were usually of street soldiers who were bailed out quickly by high-powered attorneys—just like in the old days of the mafias.

Franklin forgot about the Jimmys and the Cuzzins as soon as the cab entered Greenwich Village. Flame lived in a three-story town house on Charles Street between Seventh Avenue and Bleecker Street. The bottom floor was the office of Flame Productions and it had a separate entrance from the living quarters on the top two floors. It was one of Flame's three homes. Franklin had spent some time at the mansion in Hollywood but had never been to the flat in London. He considered the huge place in Hollywood to be a waste. Flame was rarely there. For some reason the rock star preferred Manhattan to L.A. and when he wasn't on tour he stayed on the East Coast. There had been talk of selling the Hollywood home and buying a large estate near New Rochelle.

Traffic was light at that time of night and the streets in the Village were dark and empty. But as the cab pulled onto Charles Street, a figure darted in front of the vehicle from out of the shadows, causing the driver to brake hard and startle his passenger.

"Damn!" Franklin blurted. The pedestrian, caught in the glare of the headlights, stared wide-eyed into the cab.

It was Flame's son from his first marriage. Adrian Duncan.

"What the . . . hey, wait a second," Franklin said. Duncan started to run as Franklin rolled down the window.

"Adrian?" he shouted, but the figure was already around the corner.

"You know that guy?" the driver asked.

"Yeah. Never mind, just go on."

That was odd, Franklin thought. What was Adrian doing down in his father's neck of the woods? Franklin remembered seeing Adrian with his mother, Gina Tipton, at the venue before and after the concert. Adrian had appeared very upset with his father, but that was nothing new. Adrian Duncan and Flame never got along and apparently there had been some unpleasantness between them in Flame's dressing room before the show.

"The town house is up there on the right." Franklin had the cabdriver park in front of the building and wait. "We're going back to midtown after I drop something inside," he said. "Keep the meter running."

Franklin got out of the car and used his key to open the door marked FP INC. As soon as he was inside, he shut the door and turned on the lights.

He immediately felt a chill run up his spine.

The office was a mess. Papers had been flung all over the room and the frames holding Flame's gold records had been smashed. Broken glass lay everywhere. A bottle of Jack Daniel's was overturned on top of the mahogany desk, its contents spilled in a large puddle, dripping onto the wood floor.

"Flame?" he called. The door that led to the private quarters upstairs was wide open. Lights were on in the stairway. Franklin poked his head through and called again toward the second floor. "Flame, are you there?"

Then he heard it. Music, coming from above. The song was vaguely familiar. Franklin slowly moved up the stairs, the money bag still clutched in his hand. As he reached the second floor, he recognized the music. It was Flame's big hit, "Forever Hot," only it was skipping, over and over. Flame must have put the old vinyl LP on a turntable but the record was scratched. The music drifted down from the bedroom on the third floor.

"Flame? It's me, Kenny!" he called again.

This time he went up the stairs at a brisker pace. He hoped nothing was wrong—it could be that Flame had just gotten drunk, broke up his office and gone to bed. Franklin was slightly concerned that he might walk in on Flame and his weird girlfriend, Brenda, doing the nasty. That would be truly embarrassing.

When he got to the third-floor landing Franklin saw that the bedroom door was ajar. The skipping record was getting on his nerves, the chorus not quite resolving—

"You make me forever hot baaaby yeah, don't y—
You make me forever hot baaaby yeah, don't y—
You make me forever hot baaaby yeah, don't y—"

Franklin knocked loudly on the door. "Flame, what's going on in there?" The door swung open and Franklin's heart nearly failed.

An overturned stepladder lay on the carpet beneath a pair of dangling feet that belonged to Peter Flame, his face purple and bloated and his head cocked at a freakish angle by a noose. He hung like a rag doll from a rope that had been tied to a light fixture in the ceiling.

Forever dead.

2

Mood for a Day

(performed by Yes)

"Sharp! Distance! How can the wind with so many around me?"

Jon Anderson's soaring voice pierced the air as Spike Berenger finished the last of three sets of bench presses. He eased the handles to his chest and then reached for the towel that lay at his feet. The sweat might as well have been coming from the tap. He swung a leg over the bench and stood away from the Nautilus machine as the powerful rhythm section of Bill Bruford and Chris Squire blasted away on one of Berenger's favorite Yes songs, "Heart of the Sunrise." Music—especially loud music—certainly made a workout a much more pleasurable experience. Considering that the CD collection in the room—a makeshift gym and recording studio—was massive, Berenger was never without something to play. There were so many CDs that if he played three a day for the rest of his life, he'd never get through them all. Of course, there was no telling how long he was going to live. Once one passed the age of fifty, as he had done a couple of days ago, all bets were off.

The CD faded out with the reprise of "We Have Heaven" and one of the great progressive rock albums of the early seventies was over. Time for a shower and perhaps a little work.

Berenger removed the compact disc from the player and carefully replaced it in the jewel case. Hopelessly compulsive, he filed it in his collection exactly where it should go—in the fourth slot under "Yes." All of his CDs were in alphabetical order by artist and chronological order *within* artist. It was the only way he could find something quickly. He knew guys that didn't have a system and they invariably either lost or damaged their beloved discs. His son, Michael, liked to tease him by calling his father a neat freak, but Berenger always countered by pointing out that he couldn't perform his job any other way.

For Spike Berenger was a private investigator. A PI, a detective, a gumshoe, a private eye, a troubleshooter—whatever you wanted to call it. Sometimes he was a damned fool, too, but luckily that was a rare occurrence.

The overhead intercom clicked on and Danny Lewis asked, "Are you *done* playing that prog shit in there?"

Berenger laughed. "It's a helluva lot more interesting than the garbage *you* listen to, Remix."

"I resent that remark. You know Rage Against the Machine could whip Yes' ass anytime, anywhere."

"We're not talking about a street brawl, Danny, we're talking about making music," Berenger said.

"Yeah, right. Tryin' to make sense out of them Yes lyrics is enough to make *me* wanna start a fight. Are you comin' to work today?"

"I'm here, ain't I?"

"You in *there,* sweatin' like a motherfucker. *We* are in *here* waitin' on your sorry ass."

"What, you need me to give you something to do? Don't you have that list of tasks I gave you at the beginning of the week?"

"I done all that, Spike! We're in here twiddlin' our thumbs!"

"All right, I'll be in after my shower."

"Oh, well thank God for *that*. We wouldn't want you to come in *before* you shower."

"Turn off the intercom, Remix."

"Yes, sir."

It's too bad rap-metal played such a huge part in Danny's musical vocabulary, although Berenger respected that the kid was occasionally into jazz artists like John Coltrane and Miles Davis. Rap, rap-metal, and death metal were not high on Berenger's list of favorite types of music. Call him a dinosaur. He enjoyed the "classic" rock of the sixties and seventies the most. Especially prog rock, a style of music that was frowned upon by music critics but enjoyed by a devoted legion of fans.

Berenger went through the door that separated the studio from the inner hallway, skirted past his private office, and down to the bathroom. It was a fabulous setup on the second floor of the brownstone that was the headquarters for Rockin' Security Inc. The ground floor contained Rudy's office, the conference room, and other administrative offices that were primarily used to store junk. The second floor, where Berenger hung out the most, held his office, Suzanne's office, and the studio/gym. Berenger liked to spend off-hours in the studio playing the myriad instruments they kept on hand. Sometimes he'd roll some tape for the fun of it, especially when Charlie Potts came over and they hit a nice vibe together. The top floor was reserved for operations—the computer equipment and Danny's hideaway were up there, along with Tommy Briggs's office. Rudy had let Berenger have a lot of say when the building was purchased and gutted so that it could be redesigned from the inside out. Located on East Sixty-eighth Street between Third and Second avenues, the brownstone had needed a major overhaul anyway. Rudy had sunk most of his own money into the remodeling but they had made it back within four years. Rockin' Security was the number one security business in the world of rock music. With branches in L.A. and London, the firm had a database of security personnel that could be called in for a single gig or a major tour at a moment's notice. Bodyguard service was a specialty as well. Not many people knew about the private investigation operation, which belonged exclusively to Berenger, and he was happy about that. If he had to work undercover it was best that the rock 'n' roll world thought of him as an expensive bodyguard rather than a PI. All in all, the partnership of Rudy Bishop and Spike Berenger worked like a dream. As long as Rudy handled the money and the dealings with Uncle Sam and let Berenger handle operations, it was the best job he could hope for. Except perhaps being a major rock star, but that prospect went out with the bathwater at least two decades ago.

Berenger stripped and looked at himself in the mirror. He frowned at his bulky physique. No matter how hard he worked at it, he'd never get rid of that extra twenty-five pounds that had attached themselves to him in his forties and never let go. "Heavyset," was how he'd characterize himself if he had to provide a description. Still, there was very little fat on his body. Most of the bulk was pure muscle. His daughter, Pam, once told him he looked like a wrestler. That was probably too true.

He was a rather hirsute guy as well. The long salt-and-pepper hair he had worn in a ponytail since coming out of the army reached to the middle of his back. His facial hair was slightly darker but the gray and white patches complemented his blue eyes. The carpet of thick, curly chest hair was nearly all white, oddly enough. Berenger wondered why that would be the first area to grow completely middle-aged.

All in all, he was a good-looking man. At least the women he dated told him so. Of course, it had been months since he'd dated anyone, but who was counting? For a fifty-year-old, middle-aged, twenty-five-pound-overweight private investigator he could be a winning beau.

Berenger tried to exude sexual intensity into the mirror but ended up laughing at the absurdity of the idea. He quickly turned on the shower and got inside the stall. As the hot water washed away the sweat, he thought back to the birthday party that had taken place in the studio. It hadn't been a particularly happy occasion for him. He wanted to turn fifty about as much as a cat wants to lose its eighth life. Berenger wasn't much of a believer in birthday parties but his staff had insisted on celebrating. They had invited his ex-wife and kids, too, and that was a little weird. Berenger loved Michael and Pam, both of them pushing the tail ends of their teens, and he still had a warm fondness for Linda, the woman he had married rather abruptly in 1984. Michael and Pam were born minutes apart in 1985 but by 1987 the marriage was kaput. Berenger just wasn't the go-to-work-and-then-come-home kind of husband. There were too many pulls on his life and he had to satisfy each one. Apparently he hadn't satisfied Linda's. He had to hand it to her for not remarrying, even though she had changed her name back to Steinman.

Turning fifty was similar to turning forty, although Berenger had to admit it wasn't as bad. This time he merely went on a three-day binge of Southern Comfort and marijuana, out from which he had decided to climb that very morning and come to work. Ten years ago he had disappeared for nearly two weeks.

That was a hangover for the record books.

Dressed and refreshed, Berenger was preparing to leave his private quarters and join the rest of his staff when his phone buzzed. It was Rudy, calling from the ground-floor office.

"Yeah?" Berenger answered.

"Get down here," Rudy said. "We have a client."

"You don't say?"

"I do say."

"Who is it?"

"Does the name Gina Tipton mean anything to you? She's in my outer office as we speak."

Gina Tipton!

"Flame's first wife?" Berenger blurted, unable to mask his amazement.

"Yeah, Flame's first wife!" Rudy answered with enthusiasm. He obviously thought there was money to be made.

Peter Flame had been the number one topic in the music news for the past two weeks. Ever since his apparent suicide after the New York performance of his American tour, the tributes and testaments to the rock star's life had been flooding the airwaves. Not since the death of John Lennon had the world been so mournful over a musician.

"She's here with her lawyer," Rudy added.

Berenger asked, "Has something happened I don't know about?"

"Haven't you heard the news? The police arrested Flame's son for murder."

"What?"

"Yeah. Can you believe that?"

"Which son?"

"Adrian."

"I thought Flame hung himself. It was a suicide."

"That's what they thought at first. Now they're saying it was murder. Last night they picked up Adrian Duncan and booked him."

Berenger was surprised. "Well, hell, I didn't hear that. I didn't turn on the news today. In fact, I haven't heard any news for the past three days."

"So get down here."

"I'm on my way."

Berenger had been a fan of Flame's and had known him personally. Berenger remembered meeting him in 1979. At that time Berenger was the tour manager for Grendel, a prog rock act that had been pretty big in the early seventies but was on its last legs by then. Flame was mates with Grendel's front man and guitarist and as a favor he hired the band to support his solo tour of Europe. Berenger got to know Flame as well as anyone that summer. Later, when Flame's Heat was back together, Berenger ran into Flame again on several occasions associated with the music business. Berenger thought Flame was a decent guy. Hell, the man was a legend, right up there with the greats. Berenger was shocked to hear of Flame's death and couldn't understand why he would have done it. He knew that Flame had converted to a fundamentalist religious cult at the turn of the century and that it seemed to make the star very happy. Why would the guy kill himself? Could Flame have been despondent over the lack of success of his religious material? Berenger didn't care much for the new stuff—he preferred Flame's Heat material to anything else in the rocker's career.

Still, the man was a legend. The superstar's famous "David" stance, the one patterned after Michelangelo's statue, was an indelible image in the annals of rock 'n' roll. Striking the pose was always a clue that he was about to launch into the last song of a concert. Even in recent years, Flame still had the physique for it. For a fifty-five-year-old rock star, he had looked damned good. Tall and lean and with his angelic shoulder-length blond hair showing no signs of graying, Flame was still a groupie's dream.

Until now. Murder? That would certainly explain some things. Berenger had wondered if there was more to the situation than initially reported. The police had interviewed everyone associated with Flame and by all accounts the pop star was "very depressed" that night after the concert. His long-time driver had taken Flame home after the show, dropped him off around midnight, and departed. It was Kenny Franklin, Flame's production and tour manager, who found the corpse. Berenger knew Franklin, too, and he was a real straight shooter.

Well, if it was truly murder that brought down one of the world's biggest stars, then the week was going to shape up to be a lot more interesting than Berenger had first expected.

Berenger went down the stairs to the first floor and knocked on Rudy's office door.

"Come in," Rudy called.

Upon entering, Berenger saw Rudy behind his desk. Seated in front of him were two people—a man in a suit, obviously the lawyer, and Gina Tipton. She turned and looked at him with those fabulous green eyes of hers and he was reminded of just how good-looking a woman she was.

"Well hi there, Spike," she said. "Long time no see, sweetheart."

3

L.A. Woman

(performed by The Doors)

Rudy Bishop blinked. "You two know each other?" he asked.

"Sure," Berenger said. He smiled and held out his hand. "How ya doin', Gina?"

Gina ignored his hand. Instead she stood, leaned over the back of the chair and threw her arms around his neck. "You big bear, I love you! How are *you?*"

Berenger kissed her cheek and gave her a squeeze in return. "I'm doing okay. You look great."

"Yeah?" She let him go and said, "I don't believe you. After what happened last night and this morning I probably look like shit. I sure feel like it."

"I just heard about it, Gina."

"Come on in and sit down, Spike," Rudy said. He gestured to the other man, who stood and shook Berenger's hand. "This is Derek Patterson, the attorney working for Gina and Adrian."

The men exchanged pleasantries and then Spike sat in one of the empty chairs. Gina felt compelled to explain the familiarity to Patterson and Rudy. "Spike and I met, what, early eighties?"

"Seventy-nine, actually," Berenger said. "Grendel supported Flame in Europe and I was their tour manager at the time."

"That's right! I knew it was on a tour. We had some good times, didn't we?"

She had aged a little but she was still gorgeous and had managed to keep her figure. Blonde, with deep green eyes, Gina Tipton had been a flower child in the sixties, a rock star's wife and a mother of a rock star's son in the early seventies, and a party girl in the eighties. From what Berenger had heard, in the nineties she went into the business world and started selling real estate. Today she looked that part, wearing a tasteful gray suit that reminded him of Kim Novak's wardrobe in Hitchcock's *Vertigo*. Gina had cut her hair shorter and now wore it layered, just covering her ears and the back of her neck. Thin bangs hung about an inch on her forehead.

"Seventy-nine?" Patterson asked. "But you and Flame . . . ?"

"Yeah, we were divorced," Gina answered. "Had been for seven or eight years. Flame was married to that other harlot at the time." She laughed to show she was kidding but Berenger knew she wasn't.

"You and Adrian met up with us in Paris, didn't you?" Berenger offered. "Came to the show and saw Flame backstage?"

"Yeah, wasn't that a wonderful moment in the lives of the rich and famous? That bitch Carol threw a fit. Scared Adrian half to death. He was, what, seven? Eight? Spike here happened to step in and calm everyone down. Before you know it, he's taking us to our hotel. The next day was your day off, wasn't it, Spike?"

"That's right."

"And we toured Paris together."

18

Rudy looked at him with an "Oh, I *see!*" expression. Berenger blushed.

"We met again in L.A., gosh, a year later?" she continued.

"I think so," Berenger said. He felt awkward with all this stuff coming out.

"We dated for six weeks," she said, looking at Berenger out the corner of her eye. "And then he *dumped* me!"

Berenger cleared his throat and said, "Uhm, I seem to remember it was you that dumped *me.*"

"I did? Why would I want to do that?" she said playfully. "You were quite the catch."

"Frankly, I don't remember," Berenger said, totally embarrassed. He couldn't imagine how anyone could dump Gina Tipton, even Peter Flame. Berenger looked over at Rudy and saw that the forty-seven-year-old entrepreneur was already bopping in his chair. Extremely hyper, Rudy could never keep still. He was always drumming his fingers on the table or wiggling his leg or bouncing to a rhythm that only he could hear. Rudy knew the music business inside and out but he could be a maniac.

"Uhm, is this, er, *history,* going to affect our working together?" Rudy asked.

"Of course not!" Gina said. She looked at Berenger. "Is it?"

"Uh, no, not at all," Berenger said. "What *are* we doing together?"

"I want you to clear my son," she said. "He was arrested for murdering his father, for God's sake."

"I take it you believe he's innocent?" Berenger asked.

"*Of course* he's innocent!" she said indignantly. "It's the most ridiculous thing I've ever heard. Someone's trying to frame Adrian."

Patterson spoke up. "I'm representing Adrian and we're doing everything possible to make sure this thing doesn't go to trial. We'd like to hire your firm to investigate Flame's murder and at the very least come up with some other suspects that the police aren't considering. Our goal is to get the charges dropped."

"Where is Adrian now?" Berenger asked.

"In jail!" Gina said.

"They're not going to let him out," Patterson continued. "Bail has already been denied and frankly, we're not pushing for it for Adrian's safety. There are Flame fans out there that would lynch the young man if he was seen on the street."

"I believe it," Berenger said. The same thing would have happened to John Lennon's assailant back in 1980. The fans were out for blood.

"They're transferring him to a protective-custody facility at Rikers this afternoon," the lawyer said.

"Okay, let's start at the beginning, as they say. Tell me exactly what happened this morning." Berenger grabbed a legal pad and pen off of Rudy's desk and began to take notes. Rudy began to drum his fingers on the desktop, completely unaware of how annoying it was.

As Gina spoke, Berenger was impressed by her composure but he could see through the façade. She was very upset and her earlier kidding around was merely bravado.

"I came east to visit Adrian a little over two weeks ago," she said. "Adrian lives on the Upper West Side. I have a room at the Empire Hotel, across from Lincoln Center. I had planned to go back to L.A. after a few days, but when Flame died I decided to stay until after his memorial service. Now it looks like I'll be here even longer." She gave a small, sarcastic laugh.

Patterson took over the story. "The police came to Adrian's apartment last night around seven thirty and had a warrant for his arrest. They hustled him out and took him downtown to the Sixth Precinct. The Sixth covers West Greenwich Village, where Flame's townhouse is."

"Had Adrian been questioned or anything before that?"

"Oh yeah," Gina said. "Me too. The police talked to everybody in New York that knew Flame. It was being treated as a suicide until, I don't know, a couple of days ago."

"Actually I have a feeling that foul play was suspected within a day or two after the discovery of the corpse," Patterson said. "The DA is being very quiet about it."

"Who's in charge of the investigation?" Berenger asked.

Patterson looked at his notes. "A detective downtown . . . here it is, Lieutenant Billy McTiernan."

Berenger nodded and smirked.

"You know him?"

"Yeah," Berenger answered. "We've had some dealings with each other. Total jerk. Did you notice he can't say a sentence without inserting the F-word or the GD-word?"

Patterson smiled. "I did notice that."

Berenger made his voice go low and gravelly in a perfect imitation of Lieutenant McTiernan and said, "And he fucking sounds like *this,* goddammit!"

Everyone laughed and Berenger enjoyed his little moment before Patterson continued. "So anyway they took Adrian to the Sixth Precinct and booked him. They had him there in a holding cell all night where he was questioned intensely by the detectives. Adrian said nothing except that he was innocent. The one phone call he made was to his mother."

"Then I got hold of Mr. Patterson," Gina said.

"The DA had Adrian's court appearance expedited and he was in front of a judge at eleven thirty this morning. I had maybe ten minutes to talk to him before that. It was all very irregular, but given that it's such a high-profile crime—" Patterson shrugged. "They're supposed to take him away to Rikers right after lunch today."

"What did Adrian tell you?" Berenger asked.

"That he didn't do it. That the last time he saw his father was backstage at the Beacon Theater two weeks ago, the night he died."

"What can you tell me about that night? You were at the show, right?" Berenger asked Gina.

"Yeah, Adrian and I went together. Al Patton had sent me a couple of tickets. And you know, I felt funny about it all evening, before and during the show. I *knew* something bad was going to happen. You know me, Spike, it was one of those funny premonitions I get. I could *smell* death in the air and I even mentioned that to Kenny, you know, Flame's tour manager?"

"I know him."

"Anyway," she continued, "Adrian was being his usual curmudgeonly self, slumped in his seat and doing his best to show that he wasn't enjoying the music. Everyone else in the theater was on their feet, clapping, hollering, and whistling. Granted, it had taken them a while to warm up to Flame's, uhm, *newer* material. I don't understand Flame. It was obvious that the audience only wanted to hear his old stuff. When the band segued from one of the newer 'religious' songs into 'Keep On Rollin' to Me' the crowd went wild. It is amazing what difference a choice of song makes. The audience put up with Flame's conversion to hardcore religious-cult rock just for a

22

chance to hear one measly song that Hay Fever or Flame's Heat recorded."

Berenger needed to steer her back on track. "You saw Flame before the show?" he asked.

"Uh huh. He wasn't just cool to us—he was cold as ice. But what else is new? Did I expect anything else? After all, I'm only the rock star's *first* wife, the one discarded long ago with a young son to show for our four years of marriage. Anyway, in Flame's dressing room that night, he and Adrian got into another one of their big arguments."

"What about?" Berenger asked.

"The usual," Gina replied. "Adrian's career, mostly. Flame always accused Adrian of being lazy, and I suppose that's true to an extent. It's common knowledge that Adrian didn't get along with his father. Flame disinherited him in 1988. At the time they were *both* doing a lot of drugs and drinking way too much. You know how Flame could get really belligerent when he was drunk? So can Adrian. Adrian resented the fact that Flame wouldn't help him with a career in music. All he had to do was pull a few strings and Adrian could have had a head start, but no, Flame wouldn't do it. Adrian is talented, too. You've probably heard some of his music."

Berenger merely nodded. He remembered that Adrian made a record in the late eighties that was released with fanfare as the album by "Flame's son," but it tanked—big time.

"Wasn't there an incident at one of Flame's concerts that involved Adrian?" Berenger asked.

Gina rolled her eyes. "Yeah. Adrian was drunk. He caused what the police called a 'disturbance,' and he was arrested. Adrian spent two days in jail because I wasn't around and his father wouldn't help him. Look, I know Adrian's got a reputation for being a bad boy. He's been arrested a few times, that's the tabloid truth. But is he capable of *murder?* No. Absolutely not."

Berenger nodded, letting all this sink in. "Well, I'm going to have to talk to him. Can you get me in to see him?"

"Yeah," Patterson said. "Visiting hours are restricted, even with his counsel. But we'll manage something."

Rudy asked, "How did murder enter into this picture, anyway? Didn't the guy hang himself?"

Patterson frowned. "That's what it looked like, at first. I don't have all the details yet, but obviously the post-mortem revealed some things that weren't immediately apparent. Like the fact that Flame was strangled to death *before* he was hung. The crime scene was staged to make it look like he had committed suicide."

Berenger looked at Gina. "So who do *you* think killed him?"

"If you ask me it's probably one of those creepy Messengers that Flame was hanging with. They're definitely involved," she said.

"How do you know?"

"Have you ever met them?" she asked. "They're totally bonkers. They're what the Manson family would have been if they'd been into Jesus instead of . . . well, *Manson*. And that *girlfriend* of his . . ."

"Brenda Twist," Patterson said.

"Yeah. What a phony. I can see right through her," Gina said. "She acts like she's Mother Teresa but I'll bet she's got skeletons in her closet. Those people are just after Flame's money."

"All right," Berenger said. "Anyone else?"

"I hate to say it," Gina said, "but Dave Bristol is high on my list, too."

Berenger was surprised. "Dave? He was Flame's friend and partner for years! The drummer for Hay Fever and Flame's Heat!"

"Exactly. You know they had a big falling out when Flame broke up Flame's Heat and started doing the religious stuff?"

"I guess they did," Berenger agreed.

"And Bristol and the rest of the band wanted to use the name Hay Fever but Flame wouldn't let him. So they started calling themselves Blister Pack."

"There are some writing credits in dispute, too," Patterson said. "Bristol filed a lawsuit against Flame two years ago, did you hear about that?"

"Yeah, I think I did, now that you mention it. So you think Bristol had a grudge big enough to warrant murder?"

Gina said, "You know Dave, don't you? He has a temper worse than Flame's. And a drinking problem, if you ask me. I think he's into the nose candy as well." She tapped her nostrils and sniffed.

Berenger acknowledged that. Bristol had always been an unpredictable and volatile soul. He was usually in trouble with the law—for drugs more than once and for vandalism of public property at least three or four times.

"Is that all?" he asked.

"Well, what about his second wife?" Gina suggested.

"Carol Merryman?" Rudy interjected with disbelief.

"Sure, why not?" Gina countered. "She's VP of Flame's company. I'm sure she stands to inherit a shitload of money. Her son, Joshua, probably does, too."

"When did they divorce?" Rudy asked.

Patterson answered, "Nineteen eighty-seven. But they remained friends. She was already a partner in the business. It was part of the settlement that she be made a vice president."

"You think she'll inherit Flame's estate?" Berenger asked.

"Either she will or Joshua will. Or they both will."

"He sure isn't going to leave anything to me or Adrian, that's for damn sure," Gina muttered.

There was an awkward moment of silence. Berenger shrugged. "Is that everything?" he asked.

Patterson cleared his throat. "There is, uhm, one other thing."

Gina frowned and nodded, preferring to let the lawyer explain it.

"What's that?" Berenger asked.

"Adrian was selling drugs," Patterson said, "for the Jimmys."

"Oh shit," Berenger said. "What was he doing associating with the Jimmys?"

"Dealing drugs!" Patterson answered. "He hasn't admitted as such, though. The police found a bunch of evidence in Adrian's apartment that indicated he was selling for the Jimmys. That's a big strike against him."

"Sorry, but as I live in California, I don't know a lot about them," Gina said. "Just what's been reported in the news."

Berenger shook his head. "The Jimmys are only the most ruthless and violent gang operating in the New York area," he explained. "Unless you want to count the Cuzzins. They're probably just as bad."

"They're rock bands, too," Rudy added.

"I guess you can call them that. The Jimmys play death-metal punk to the extreme—really angry stuff. They incite riots and always cause a lot of destruction whenever they play somewhere. As a gang, they allegedly supply drugs to a wealthy clientele—Manhattan's rich and famous. Not a lot is known about their organization other than it might have originated in the Caribbean and immigrated to America sometime in the nineties. Legend has it that they send a package full of broken guitar strings to the people they plan to knock off. A very nasty bunch."

"There's an ongoing war between them and the Cuzzins," Rudy said.

"At least I like the Cuzzins' music better," Berenger added. "It's mostly fifties-era rock 'n' roll. Needless to say, both gangs have gone a long way toward giving rock 'n' roll a bad name in this town."

This information caused Gina's eyes to cast downward. "I see," she said. "Why haven't they been arrested?"

"By the time the cops arrive at one of their concerts—which always occur unannounced—they're already speeding away, leaving a mess in their wake. They like to start fires, things like that. It's what you might call 'guerrilla punk'."

"Unfortunately, the kids in New York love them," Rudy said. "The gangs have become underground heroes. The word gets out, usually over the Internet, that the Jimmys or the Cuzzins are going to play somewhere and magically the high schoolers and college-aged kids show up. Both camps sell homemade CDs through various dubious distribution centers that do *very* well. In fact, you can probably buy them at any of the indie shops in the East Village."

"Wow, that's totally bizarre," Gina said. "I had no idea."

Berenger looked at Rudy and asked, "You've already discussed terms and stuff?"

Rudy nodded. "The case is ours if you want it."

Berenger looked at Gina.

"Please, Spike? We need you," she said.

He gazed into the green eyes that had once exhibited a great passion for him. He didn't want to go back there but he couldn't help it. Gina Tipton was a beautiful, intelligent woman. He still liked her. And he believed her.

"Okay."

"Great," Patterson said. "I'll arrange a meeting with Detective McTiernan tomorrow morning and then we'll try to get into Rikers by lunchtime. Is that okay with you?"

"Sure."

"Tomorrow afternoon is the reading of the will and we'll be attending that," Patterson said.

"Flame's will? Really?"

Gina nodded. "Carol didn't want me there but I insisted. I have certain rights, too, you know."

"Can you get me in to that?" Berenger asked. "It would be very helpful."

Patterson replied, "I'll see what I can do."

Everyone stood and shook hands. Gina held on to his a little longer.

"You know, I had one of my premonitions that I'd see you today," she said.

"Well, if I remember correctly, you were usually right on those things," Berenger said.

"So I'll see you soon?" she asked. Her eyes sparkled with promise.

"Sure," he said.

4

Roll With the Changes

(performed by REO Speedwagon)

Berenger gave the team three hours to get up to speed on the case and then they gathered in the Rockin' Security conference room. Suzanne happened to get to the sound system first, so Tori Amos was singing her way through the *Little Earthquakes* album on the overhead speakers, replacing Danny Lewis's earlier pick, *Licensed to Ill* by the Beastie Boys. Berenger liked Tori Amos and thought that her first album was still the best one. At any rate her music was more conducive to a planning meeting.

"Good afternoon," Berenger said.

"Hi," replied Melanie Starkey, the office assistant. She never went by Melanie—she preferred Mel—but most of the time everyone called her "Ringo" because of her last name. Anyone interested in the Beatles knew that Ringo Starr was a stage name for Richard Starkey. Mel didn't seem to mind the nickname. She happened to wear several rings, too.

Berenger poured a cup of coffee from the freshly brewed pot on the hot plate. Besides being a damned good office assistant, Mel made a superb pot of coffee. And she looked great today, as usual. She was a twenty-eight-year-old feisty redheaded babe. Berenger didn't

RAYMOND BENSON

know if she was Scottish or Irish by heritage—she was most likely a mutt. It didn't matter, really, because she spoke with a thick New Jersey accent.

Danny Lewis was a smart-aleck kid from Harlem who was perhaps the brainiest hacker he had ever known. He was nineteen, half Caucasian, half African American, and had no loyalties to either race. He called himself a "mix," hence the nickname "Remix." Lewis could probably write his own ticket into any major corporation as a systems manager but most employers would likely resist hiring someone so young for such an important position. The dreadlocks and nose piercing didn't do much to inspire confidence in a white-collar human resources executive either. Berenger had recognized Lewis's talents when the teenager came in one day to repair a Roland 64-voice synthesizer module. Danny had taken it apart, fixed it, and had it back together within twenty minutes. The "kid" was a genius.

Tommy Briggs was Berenger's contemporary. At age forty-nine, he had made the most cracks the other night about Berenger turning fifty. Briggs used to be a field agent for the FBI and had held the job for nearly twenty years until he decided to give it up one day and work for Rockin' Security. Briggs maintained a good relationship with the bureau and had pals on the inside. He could usually get any information he wanted from the organization. Outside of Berenger's musician friends, like Charlie Potts, Briggs was the closest thing to a best friend that Berenger had.

Last and certainly not least was Suzanne Prescott, Berenger's second-in-command and personal sidekick. At least he liked to think of her that way. Originally from California, Suzanne was thirty-eight, had short dark hair and brown eyes, and was just the type of

30

woman that Berenger found attractive. Berenger couldn't imagine how she might have looked back in the late eighties when she was a Goth devotee, sporting the classic black clothes, dark makeup and pale white skin. After doing a bit of maturing she had gone to the Far East for a few years and come back a student of Eastern philosophy and martial arts. After the love of her life overdosed in the mid-nineties, Berenger and Suzanne had a brief love affair. He had always felt it was merely a rebound for Suzanne—no one could replace drummer Elvin Blake—but it was nice while it lasted. Several months later he had asked her to work for him. It was one of the wisest moves he'd ever made. These days Suzanne was certainly a beauty with brains.

"We waiting for Rudy?" Briggs asked.

"Appears so," Berenger replied.

Remix piped up. "Did you hear about the gang fight last night?"

"Nope."

"The Jimmys and the Cuzzins got into it down at Astor Place. The Cuzzins were playing and were into their second song when the Jimmys showed up. They actually beat the police there. It got pretty nasty."

"Anyone hurt?" Berenger asked.

"I heard two Cuzzins were messed up pretty bad and are in the hospital."

Rudy hurried in at last, poured a cup of Mel's coffee and sipped it as he sat down. "Did you wait on me? You shouldn't have," he said.

"It's all right, Rudy," Berenger said. "We've only been here an hour."

"Funny. Hey, why didn't you tell me you and Gina Tipton were an item?"

Suzanne raised her eyebrows. "What? Is that true, Spike?" The others in the room were equally surprised.

"All right, all right," Berenger said. "Yeah, we dated for a few months. It was a long time ago."

"Is she as weird as people say?" Tommy Briggs asked.

"What's that supposed to mean?"

"I heard she can read fortunes and shit like that."

"No, not really," Berenger replied. "That's all a myth. She has some kind of heightened intuition, that's all."

"Man, don't they call her 'Gina the Gypsy'?" Remix interjected.

"Yes, they did call her that. A long time ago."

Suzanne smiled at Berenger. "Gee, Spike, you really did get around in the old days, huh?"

"Hush. Let's get started. Remix, suppose you begin and give us the quick and dirty lowdown on Flame."

Danny Lewis sat upright in his chair, a big change from his usual near-horizontal position, cleared his throat, and spoke as he looked at notes.

"Okay, folks, here's the skinny on Flame, aka Peter Flame, aka Peter Donald Duncan," he announced.

"Peter Donald Duncan!" Suzanne gasped.

"Yep, that's the name he was given when he was born on November 24, 1952," Remix explained. "Which is why his sons are named Adrian *Duncan* and Joshua *Duncan*. May I continue?"

"Go ahead, Remix," Berenger said and then spoke to the others. "Let's keep comments and questions until the end of the presentation, shall we?"

"Anyways, as we *all* know, Flame grew up in New York City and played with a number of amateur bands before he hit the big time with a little outfit called Hay Fever."

Tommy Briggs let out a whispered, "Yeaaaa!"

"Hay Fever consisted of Flame—he changed his name and dropped the 'Peter' when he was a teenager—Flame on guitar and vocals, Dave Bristol on drums and vocals, and Greg Patterson on bass and vocals. The power trio's self-titled first record was released in 1971 on a do-it-yourself label called Liquid Metal Records and was produced by none other than the big, bald-headed Al Patton. Within six months, the band had two hit singles from the album and it had gone gold. The follow-up LP, *Sneeze*, came out at the end of the year and was another big one. By 1975, the band had made five albums and presented their adoring public with seven number one hit singles. But things were not very rosy in Denmark. Flame and Dave Bristol, as we *all* know, were the best of friends and the worst of enemies. Due to that age-old excuse, 'artistic differences,' Hay Fever broke up. Millions of people cried themselves to sleep that night. The suicide rate jumped 150 percent. The stock market plummeted to an all-time low. Women and children—"

"Okay, okay, Remix, we get the picture," Berenger said.

"Sorry. Anyway, the fans weren't too happy. Flame went on to try a solo career, simply as . . . Flame. By now, Liquid Metal Records was a goddamned *industry* and Al Patton was one of the demigods of the music business. Thanks to Flame and Hay Fever. Now as we *all* know, Flame's solo career was very successful from a financial standpoint, but not necessarily from a critical one. It was hit and miss. His first solo album, released in 1977, was called, simply, *Flame*. That was probably his biggest solo album, wouldn't you say, Spike?"

"Yeah, I guess."

"That had 'Keep On Rollin' to Me' on it and a few other hits. And that's when the John Lennon and David Bowie rumors started flyin'.'"

Rudy spoke up. "John Lennon? What rumors?"

Berenger hushed his partner and nodded at Remix to continue.

"Yeah, in 1974, Flame was hangin' with John Lennon and David Bowie in L.A. That was during Lennon's 'lost weekend' era, when he was separated from Yoko and was spendin' his time with Harry Nilsson and May Pang. You know, *Walls and Bridges*. Bowie, he was in the middle of his *Diamond Dogs* period, trying to cope with super stardom and a nasty coke habit. There was talk that the three of them were going to form a supergroup, along with Nilsson and Dave Bristol. Nothing ever came of it, though. Man, wouldn't that have been somethin'?"

"I'll say," Suzanne replied. "Flame and Lennon together? And Bowie?"

"They'd have knocked Wings out of the ballpark, that's for sure," Briggs surmised.

"Now that you mention it, Flame was a lot like Bowie during those years, wouldn't you say?" Suzanne said. "I mean, he had that androgynous thing going, too."

"Yeah, some Bowie and a little Rod Stewart thrown in," Remix added. "Anyway, Flame's career plodded along through the rest of the seventies and it wasn't until—"

"Better go over his first marriage, Remix," Berenger said.

"Oh, I was savin' all the personal stuff 'til after I got through the creative stuff."

"Let's keep it chronological."

Remix wrinkled his brow and whispered, "You're so *anal,* boss!" He continued at full voice. "Okay, so he got married to Gina Tipton in 1971, just as the first Hay Fever album was takin' off. Gina was only seventeen at the time and I guess she started out as Flame's groupie. Their son, Adrian, was born on May 4, 1973. A year and a half later, in 1975, Flame and Gina divorced. And it was *nasty.* Lawyers up the wazoo, money flyin' this way and that, threats and counterthreats, you name it. Bottom line is Flame and Gina don't get along too well these days. Gina never remarried and brought up Adrian by herself. She was often linked to a slew of other rock stars though, *and to certain private investigators whom we will not mention.*"

This elicited snickers and catcalls from the group. Berenger smirked and motioned for Remix to move it along.

"In 1982, Flame married Carol Merryman after being linked to a number of Hollywood actresses, Playboy Playmates, and supermodels. Some guys have all the luck, I guess. This marriage lasted until 1987 and the divorce was much more amicable than the first one. Carol remains a vice president of Flame's company and has a hand in his business affairs. They had one son, Joshua, born March 14, 1983. Now—back to the guy's career. After only four solo albums between 1977 and 1982, Flame formed the band that would surely secure his place in rock 'n' roll history if he didn't already have one. And that, as we *all* know, was Flame's Heat."

Briggs whispered, "Yeaaaa!" again.

"Flame's Heat consisted of Flame and Dave Bristol again, along with Brick Bentley on bass and Moe Jenkins on keyboards. Combinin' the best of jazz-rock with the commercial sensibilities of mainstream pop, the first self-titled Flame's Heat album went gold when it was released in 1983, again on Al Patton's Liquid Metal Records."

"Remix, you sound like you're reading off the press releases," Suzanne muttered.

"Quiet, girl!" the boy snapped.

"Excuse me, but do you mean that Dave Bristol and Flame didn't have much to do with each other during the solo years?" Briggs asked.

"That's right. They didn't get along during those days. But they patched things up in time to form Flame's Heat," Remix said. "So anyways, throughout the rest of the eighties, Flame's Heat challenged such acts as U2, R.E.M., and Michael Jackson for favored status on the charts. They were often described as Steely Dan meets XTC—they could whip out cool riffs and catchy melodies, immaculately produced, but they could also rock. Hmpf. I guess I was too young to appreciate them back then."

Remix turned over his page of notes and continued.

"Let's see, in 1991, Flame was arrested for fightin' in public. That was in L.A., where that kind of thing happens all the time, don't it? It turned out he had a shitload of coke on him and he got busted. He got off easy, though. That's what money can do, I'm tellin' ya. He had to pay a big fine and go into rehab. No jail time. He spent three months at a clinic in upstate New York but he went AWOL. He got picked up and spent three days in jail before his heavy-hittin' lawyers got him out. This time he went to another rehab joint and stayed nine months. He got out in late 1993 and Flame's Heat went on a worldwide tour. There was a lot of exposure in the music press about how Flame looked good at the beginning but must have jumped off the wagon halfway through the Far East. By the end of the tour he was strung out again. He pretty much went into seclusion and the band released a couple of outtakes and B-sides albums in the interim. Finally, in 1998, Flame announced he was going back into rehab. We didn't hear anything else from him until a couple of years later, when he reappeared on the scene to say that after six killer albums, Flame's Heat was no more and he was devoting himself to making music for, ahem, Christ."

Remix looked upward and silently mouthed the word "Why?" He then went back to his notes.

"He had a new girlfriend, Ms. Brenda Twist, whom he met in rehab. She was another born-again fundamental-ist, a member of the so-called Messengers. Flame was forty-eight. She was twenty-four. Flame and Brenda be-came the John and Yoko of the new millennium and did everything they could to promote the Messengers and Flame's new music. Flame released his first religious album in 2002 and released a second one in 2006, nei-ther of which has enjoyed the sales and popularity of his earlier work. And man, I can think of a million people that would probably want to kill that guy!"

"I'll say," Briggs added.

"Anyways, that's the end of my report. You have heard 'The Life and Times of Peter Flame' by Remix." He imme-diately reclined in his seat, one leg draped over an arm of the chair.

"He *has* picked up an entirely different audience, though," Suzanne said. "Hasn't he?"

"Yeah," Berenger replied. "Don't underestimate the popularity of Christian rock. It may not make it on *Bill-board*'s Top Ten, but it does very well. And Flame's fans run the gamut of ages. Remember he started back in 1971. Hell, I was even a Flame fan back when he was with Hay Fever."

"Golly, I guess that makes you an old fart," Remix said, chuckling.

Berenger ignored him. "I think it's important that we find out exactly what happened to Flame at the turn of the century to make him turn to religion. I mean, we're talking about a guy who was into drugs and groupies and the whole rock 'n' roll lifestyle for *years*. Why did he make such a drastic change?"

Rudy shrugged. "Maybe he just saw the error of his ways?"

Briggs said, "You gotta remember that the operative words here are 'fundamentalist' and 'cult'. It's just my opinion but there's nothing wrong with Christian rock or being Christian or Muslim or Jewish or Hindu or whatever you want to be. It's the *fundamentalist* and *cult* parts of it that put it into questionable territory. From what I understand, the Messengers use Christianity as a starting place and then take it into outer space, like those wackos in California that believed they were all aliens and that a great big spaceship was going to come down and take them all to Heaven. They ended up killing themselves in a gigantic religious ritual."

"I totally agree," Berenger said. "It's always the cult sectors of religions that cause controversy."

"And often violence," Briggs added.

"Do we know if Flame ever had a medical emergency related to drugs?" Suzanne asked. "Did something happen that scared him?"

"Good question," Berenger noted. "Not that we know of, but they could have kept it quiet. I'll look into that. In fact, I'm going to tackle the families and the former bands. I know Gina already and can look at her side of things. I've met Carol, too, and hopefully she'll cooperate with me. Dave Bristol and I go way back. Tomorrow I'm going with the lawyer to see Adrian at Rikers. I'm very interested in hearing his side of the story. There's some indication that the guy was involved with the Jimmys."

"Uh oh," Briggs said.

"Yeah," Berenger nodded. "Not good."

"Hey, have you heard their latest CD?" Remix asked.

"No," Berenger said, rolling his eyes. "But I'm sure you were the first on your block to have it."

"As a matter of fact, I was. Man, it kicks ass."

"They're thugs, Remix," Briggs said. "Throw it away."

"No way, man. Just because you don't like their politics don't mean you can't like their music."

"Politics my ass. The Jimmys are not about politics, they're about crime!"

"Okay, okay," Berenger said. "I think we all know that the Jimmys are not the best role models these days. We'll have to evaluate their involvement in the case when we learn more about it. Anyway, first I'm going to pay a visit to our friend Lieutenant McTiernan."

There was a collective groan from the group.

Berenger slipped into his low-voiced imitation of the man. "Yeah, he's in charge of the goddamned investigation." This elicited a laugh from the group and then he switched back to his normal voice. "So they've *got* to have the wrong guy in custody, wouldn't you say?"

"What if they're right, though?" Suzanne asked. "What if Adrian did kill his father? I mean, what's all this with the Jimmys?"

Berenger gestured with his hands. "I don't know yet. Look, if he's guilty, then there's not a lot we can do about it, is there? Suzanne, I want you to start looking into Brenda Twist. Find out more about her. Flame did a good job keeping her personal life out of the press. We don't know very much about her, so let's educate ourselves."

"I guess that means looking into the Messengers, too," she said.

"I guess you're right." He looked at Briggs. "Tommy, I want you to use your sources at the bureau and see what you can find out about all the interested parties in this case. Especially the Messengers."

Briggs tapped a legal pad full of scrawls that sat on the desk before him. "I've already done a little digging and I'll tell you what I know so far."

"All right."

"The Messengers are an elite ultraconservative religious cult that began here in Manhattan in 1992. The front man is a guy named Theodore Ramsey, but he goes by the name 'Reverend Theo.' He's from Jamaica but he married an American woman, Juliet Lacey, so that gave him the necessary right to stay in the country. As far as I can discern, the Messengers are just a bunch of harmless weirdos. There are no blood sacrifices involved or anything spooky like that, as far as I know. They don't say they're aliens or anything like that. They have their own church, over on Tenth Avenue and West Forty-fourth. No problems with the IRS, no problems with the city, nothing. But I'll dig deeper. I'll find out more about this Reverend Theo. He may have some skeletons in his closet, you never know."

"Seeing that he's from Jamaica, do you think he might have any ties to the Jimmys?" Berenger asked. "Didn't they start in the Caribbean?"

"Nothing I've found out so far indicates that, but you never know. I'll keep that in mind."

"Good," Berenger said. "Remix, you keep doing what you're doing, but if you get a chance, see if you can hack into the Messengers' e-mail."

Remix looked surprised. "That's not legal, is it, boss? I'll get right on it!"

"That's all for today, folks. I'll know more tomorrow after I talk to McTiernan and to Adrian. I'm also going to the reading of Flame's will tomorrow afternoon."

"That should be interesting," Briggs said. "You think someone'll bring punch and cookies?"

Berenger sighed and replied, "I just hope no one brings any weapons."

5

Morning Has Broken

(performed by Cat Stevens)

Berenger was up early the next day. Having a case that was as high profile as this one was invigorating. And it was a *case*, not some run-of-the-mill security job. He didn't particularly relish playing bodyguard for Elton John, which was the most exciting thing he'd done in the past few months. He'd accompanied the superstar across the Far East and Australia and was on call twenty-four/seven. Berenger liked Elton personally and was compensated well for the work, but he would rather have been ferreting out clues in a criminal investigation. It was what he was good at and what he was trained to do back in the army's CID. Southeast Asia seemed like a century ago, but everything he had learned in the Criminal Investigations Division could be applied to nearly any situation.

Now, here he was, working on what might be the biggest rock 'n' roll crime since Lennon's untimely demise. Flame's alleged murder was certainly being compared to that. The nonstop outpouring of sympathy and grief from fans all over the world had been overwhelming. It also made good press. Every day the second-tier papers in New York published some new angle on the case. Did Adrian Duncan really do it? Was Flame into drugs again? Was it a mob hit? Was it a government-sponsored conspiracy?

Fans and family alike were upset with the details of Flame's interment, yet another controversy that fueled the rumors. That morning's *New York Times*, of all places, revealed that three days before Duncan's arrest, Flame had been cremated and the ashes were given to none other than the Messengers, per Flame's own instructions. Carol Merryman was already in the process of fighting this decree tooth and nail but until it was resolved, Flame's urn was being kept under lock and key at the Messengers' church on the West Side. If anything was going to give the Messengers fifteen minutes of fame, that was it.

Berenger left his apartment at Sixty-eighth and Second Avenue—just down the block from the Rockin' Security office—and picked up a coffee with cream and sugar and a chocolate-frosted doughnut from a street vendor. He then flagged a taxi heading downtown. The lawyer, Patterson, was supposed to meet him at the Sixth Precinct at nine o'clock. Berenger gave himself a half hour to fight the traffic and get over to the West Village in plenty of time. The breakfast he could eat in the backseat of the cab.

The Sixth Precinct was located on West Tenth Street between Bleecker and Hudson, not far from where the crime occurred. Its jurisdiction covered most of West Greenwich Village and Berenger had been there on several occasions. He knew many plainclothes detectives as well as uniformed officers all over the city—some he got along with and others he didn't. The Sixth's Lieutenant Billy McTiernan was one he would just as soon keep at arm's length.

The sergeant at the front desk looked up and recognized the big man that walked inside.

"Spike Berenger, what brings you down to our beautiful neck of the woods?"

"Hello Mackie, how's it going?" Berenger greeted the uniformed officer.

"Can't complain too much. Hey, I'm glad you're here. I've been meaning to give you a call."

"What's on your mind, Mackie?"

"Can you get tickets to the Stones? They sold out in, what, sixty seconds?"

Berenger smiled. "Sorry, Mackie, I can't get no satisfaction. Their manager is pissed at me for something, I don't know what. I'm sure you can get a good deal outside the venue the night of the show, though."

"Oh yeah, for about three times the original price of the tickets!"

"So, just flash 'em your badge and tell 'em to give 'em up for face value."

The sergeant shrugged. "That's not a bad idea. So what can we do for Rockin' Security this morning?"

"Is McTiernan here?"

"Yeah, he came in just a few minutes ago. Is he expecting you?"

"No, but Adrian Duncan's lawyer is supposed to meet me here and I think McTiernan is expecting *him*."

"He's already here. I sent him back two minutes ago." The sergeant buzzed the door so that Berenger could walk through. "You know where it is?"

"I'll find him. See you later, Mackie."

Berenger moved past the administrative offices and into the detectives' bullpen, a room that resembled every police squad HQ on television and in the movies. A half dozen of New York's finest occupied just as many desks. The noise level was high because everyone had to speak loudly in order to be heard over the others. Uniformed officers moved in and out of the room, picking up and dropping off paperwork, while plainclothes detectives shouted into phones or called across the room to somebody. Berenger had considered joining the police force after he got out of the army. He was glad he didn't—he couldn't have taken such a claustrophobic atmosphere with no privacy whatsoever.

He spotted Derek Patterson sitting beside McTiernan's desk. Patterson waved at him and McTiernan scowled. If the Incredible Hulk had been white and sported a red crew cut, he'd have looked like Billy McTiernan. The guy was as bulky as a toad and had the sense of humor of one as well. He also didn't like rock 'n' roll, which Berenger considered to be a serious social disability.

Patterson stood and shook Berenger's hand. "Hi Spike," he said. "Do you know Lieutenant—?"

"Sure, Billy and I go way back," Berenger said. McTiernan stayed in his seat but held out his hand for Berenger to squeeze.

"How you doing, Berenger?" McTiernan asked in the low, gravelly voice that Berenger liked to make fun of. "I see you haven't got your fucking hair cut yet."

"And I see you must've just mowed yours, Lieutenant," Berenger replied.

McTiernan ran his hand over the flattop and grinned. "Hey, it feels good when the goddamned wife scratches the top of my head."

"And then you sit like a good boy?"

"Funny. I see you haven't changed, Berenger. You're still a goddamned hippie. Come on, let's go someplace where we can talk in private."

McTiernan heaved up his massive frame with a grunt and led the two men out of the bullpen and into one of

45

the bare interrogation rooms furnished with only a table and three chairs.

"So, I understand you're working for the fucking defense, is that right, Berenger?" McTiernan asked as he shut the door. He sat in the single chair on one side of the table while Berenger and Patterson took seats across from him.

"That's correct, Lieutenant."

Patterson spoke up. "As I said on the phone, we've come to talk to you about Mr. Duncan. It's going to take a while for the DA to supply me with the evidence that'll be used to prosecute my client. We were hoping that you'd give us an idea of what we're facing."

"I don't have to tell you guys jack shit, you know that, don't you?" McTiernan said.

"We'll find out eventually once the DA—"

"I know, I know. I just don't know if I want to help you. The guy's a major scumbag and he murdered his own father. And I could care less about the victim being some famous fucking rock star. I'm not into that crap."

"Yeah, I know," Berenger said. "Your favorite singer is Raffi."

"Who?"

"Never mind."

McTiernan glared at Berenger and then addressed Patterson. "Look, we've got an ironclad case against Adrian Duncan. I'll tell you what we've already told the press. Duncan's fingerprints were all over Flame's office and in the bedroom where the crime occurred. He was seen fleeing from the town house by two witnesses, before the discovery of the body."

"So?" Berenger suggested. "Adrian is Flame's son. He's probably been to Flame's place a zillion times and left fingerprints. Maybe he was in a hurry to get home. There's plenty of doubt there."

McTiernan looked at Berenger and said, "Yeah? Well we also have several witnesses that saw the suspect in a heated argument with the deceased earlier in the evening. Before Flame's concert. And even more witnesses observed the suspect in a very agitated state backstage after the concert."

"Could have been a typical father and son spat," Berenger said.

"And then there's the postmortem," McTiernan continued.

"I'm very interested in hearing about that," Patterson commented.

"Well, I'm not going to tell you fucking everything, but suffice it to say that it proves that Peter Flame didn't commit suicide. He was already dead before he was hung from the ceiling. Duncan strangled him prior to that, then strung him up and tried to make it look like Flame had killed himself. I'm not going to list all the goddamned pieces of evidence that confirm it. We know a staged crime scene when we see one. And this one was *definitely* staged."

Berenger had figured as much but he wasn't going to let on. "At first you were fooled, though, isn't that right? Didn't you believe Flame had committed suicide?"

McTiernan shrugged. "At first glance, sure. Anyone would. But we've got a lot of experience with shit like this. Lots of things struck me as just plain wrong about the crime scene. The next day when I was looking at the photographs it hit me. The postmortem confirmed it."

"You did a good job keeping it a secret," Patterson said.

"Yeah. We didn't want the killer to bolt so we conducted our investigation quietly and privately. We had our eyes on Adrian Duncan within twenty-four hours of the murder. Given the history between the father and son, it didn't take a leap of faith to conclude that he was the prime suspect."

"Weren't there other fingerprints at the town house?" Berenger asked.

"Sure! Lots of 'em. But Duncan's just happened to be in all the right places, or rather, in all the *wrong* places."

Berenger rubbed his beard and asked, "I understand you've got something linking Adrian to the Jimmys?"

McTiernan smiled. "I think I'll let the DA give you that. If you ask me, it just proves that Duncan was up to no good."

Patterson looked at Berenger. The lawyer didn't have to say anything for Berenger to know what the guy was thinking. This was going to be harder than they thought.

"But just 'cause I'm a nice guy," McTiernan said, "I'll share with you the capper. The piece of evidence that's going to make the case."

"What's that?" Berenger asked.

"Flame was clutching something in his hand when we found him. It turned out to be one of those color-coded, numbered backstage passes that they give out to people for the after-show meet and greet. You know, you peel off the back and stick 'em on your shirt or jacket."

"Yeah?"

"The tour manager keeps a record of what number pass is given to who." McTiernan raised his eyebrows. "The one in Flame's grip was the pass that had been assigned to Adrian Duncan."

6

Jailhouse Rock

(performed by Elvis Presley)

The next port of call for Berenger and Patterson was Rikers Island. Berenger had been there on numerous occasions and it never failed to depress him. By far the largest penal institution in the United States, Rikers usually hosted 15,000 prisoners on any given day. The island, officially a part of the Bronx but accessible only from Queens, was half the size of Central Park and was the location of ten separate jails, each one of varying security.

As Patterson's Lexus left Queens and crossed the Rikers Island Bridge, with LaGuardia Airport's runways looming uncomfortably close on the right, Berenger was once again amazed by how much like a small town the corrections facilities had become. Schools, chapels and mosques, ball fields, grocery stores, medical clinics, barbershops, a bus depot, a laundry, a bakery, a power plant, and other amenities now stood among the cell blocks, some of which had been constructed as far back as the 1930s. "The Rock," as it was unofficially known, also went by the moniker "Land of Darkness." Berenger thought the latter term was more appropriate. Rikers was a place where that elusive thing called Hope had no haven.

The car passed the sign that proclaimed that Rikers Island was HOME OF NEW YORK'S BOLDEST and Berenger wondered what that was supposed to mean. Boldest criminals? Boldest guards? Boldest wardens? They drove along a narrow two-lane road lined by the cell blocks—aging brick structures as well as high-tech modern ones—and twelve-foot-high fences crowned by razor-sharp barbed wire. Eventually they came to the commissioner's office, a yellow trailer that was the first stop in coordinating visits.

"I take it Duncan's in NIC?" Berenger asked.

"That's right, it's where they keep all the prisoners requiring protective custody," Patterson replied. NIC was the North Infirmary Command, which consisted of two buildings. One of these was the original Rikers Island Hospital, built in 1932. Housing approximately five hundred inmates, NIC was also the dormitory for inmates with AIDS. Berenger knew it was a better spot to be than one of the general population buildings, such as C-95, where mostly young toughs resided. NIC was where they put the "Maytags"—what they called the inmates considered too soft to be in the dangerous general areas. "They're washing socks," was how the protective-custody prisoners were described in other cell blocks on the island.

After Patterson parked the Lexus, they went inside and immediately felt the oppressive silence. For some reason, NIC was always quiet, whereas the other cell blocks reverberated noisily like high school gymnasiums. Perhaps it was because more of the inmates in NIC were in solitary confinement, protective custody, or were too sick to make a sound.

The two men filled out the paperwork, declared they had no weapons, and were admitted into a room manned by three guards. A couple of prisoners sat at separate tables, speaking to their respective lawyers. Another was having a tearful reunion with his mother.

Berenger and Patterson sat at the only empty table and waited five minutes before the steel door at the end of the room squealed and opened. An officer led Adrian Duncan, dressed in standard-issue prison overalls, to the table. Berenger noted that he appeared tired and defeated.

"How are you, Adrian?" Patterson asked.

"Okay," Duncan replied. He looked at Berenger and wrinkled his brow.

"Adrian, this is Spike Berenger," Patterson said. "He's a private investigator that we've hired to help us with your case."

Berenger leaned over the table to shake Duncan's hand.

"I know you, don't I?" Duncan asked.

"We met many years ago," Berenger answered. "In the eighties."

"Yeah, I remember. Weren't you a manager for a band or something?"

"Back then, yeah."

"How are they treating you?" Patterson asked.

Duncan shrugged. "Okay, I guess. I'm pretty much alone all the time. I'm going stir-crazy, to tell you the truth. There's one guard that's a real prick, but he's that way to everybody." He looked out the barred window onto a field, where teams of bulky African American and Hispanic inmates played ball. "At least I don't have to go out there with them."

"We've made the motion for a speedy trial," Patterson said. "I'm sorry about the bail thing, it's just the way the DA wants to play it. Besides, you do realize you're safer here than anywhere else?"

Duncan barely nodded his head. "There are even some Flame fans in *here* that would like to get their hands on me." He slumped in his chair and sighed.

"Mr. Berenger would like to ask you some questions. All right?"

Duncan rolled his eyes and said, "Sure. I don't know what good it'll do."

Berenger had always possessed fairly good intuition when it came to interrogating suspects but he had to be face-to-face with them.

"Adrian, I'd like you to look at me," he said.

Duncan glanced up. "Yeah?"

"Tell me the truth. Did you kill your father?"

Duncan frowned. "Fuck no." He looked at Patterson and said, "What the hell is this? You bring this guy in here to ask me that? You're my lawyer, you're supposed to believe I'm innocent."

Berenger answered, "Adrian, I had to ask you before I begin, it's just the way I work. Chill out. I'm here to help you."

Duncan waved at him, indicating that he was ready to continue.

"Why do you think the police suspected you?" Berenger asked.

"Don't you know?"

"I want to hear what *you* think."

Duncan looked away and mumbled something.

"Excuse me?" Berenger asked. He was sure that the young man had cursed at him.

"Nothing," Duncan said. "Look, what's the use? They've got their evidence and they're gonna crucify me because it's convenient for them. I mean, I understand why they picked me. I was the *obvious* suspect, you know? Everyone knew my father and I hated each other."

"Adrian, your mother asked me to help," Berenger said. "I know this is a shitty place to be and I know you feel persecuted. But really, if you talk to me you'll go a long way toward helping yourself get the hell out of here. It's up to you. If you want to stay here and rot, be my guest."

Duncan was quiet for a moment as all this sunk in. Finally, he looked at Berenger and asked, "What do you want to know?"

"Tell me about the relationship between you and your father. Whatever comes to mind."

The prisoner reflected on this and said, "When I think of my father, all I remember are the fights. We were fighting since I crawled out of the crib. He hated me. He didn't like me because he didn't like my mother anymore. I don't think he ever *once* told me he loved me, or anything like that. Ever. Even when I was a kid. He never supported anything I ever did. He never came to the school for parent/teacher talks, he never saw me perform in the band, he didn't want me to become a musician . . . The man is a first-class bastard. Er, he was."

There wasn't much Berenger could say to that. "Tell me about the night of the murder. I know you've told the cops, you told Mr. Patterson here, now please tell me. I need to hear it from you."

"My mother was in town from L.A. My dad was playing his final show of the current tour at the Beacon Theater and his manager sent me a couple of tickets."

"Al Patton?"

"Yeah, him. He's a real piece of work, that guy. What an asshole. Anyway, I think he always had the hots for my mom, and he knew she was in town or something. So he sent over a couple of tickets and backstage passes.

I didn't want to go but Mom thought we should act like we cared. So we went. What a mistake that was."

"What happened at the theater?"

"Well, we got there early and went backstage. Dad had finished sound check and was in his dressing room with that weird girlfriend of his, Brenda. She made some excuse to leave us all alone for a big family reunion, you know, so it was just Mom, Dad, and me. So he talks to Mom about what she's doing in L.A. and all, and he seems pretty friendly. But he doesn't even look at me. When I try to talk to him he just changes the subject, like I'm some kind of bug. Finally Mom picked up on what was going on and she told him to please talk to me. She stepped out of the room so Dad and I were alone.

"I asked him for the second or third time if he would do me a favor, a father-to-son thing, you know? There's this album he recorded in the seventies that he never released. I thought if he'd give me the rights to it, I could remix it, you know, as a kind of techno-dance thing. I could produce it and release it myself. It would be just the thing to get me started as a record producer. Hell, it would probably set up my mom and me for the rest of our lives. But no, his response was the same as it always was. Back in, what, 1987, I think, I asked him to help me get a record deal for my own band. He wouldn't do it. He kept saying if I was going to play music, I had to do it on my own. And I knew that. Hell, I was really young then, but I knew I had to *make* it on my own, on the strength of my own material. But he could have at the very *least* helped me a little. He could have made a phone call or two. He could have put in a good word here or there. Hell, he's so goddamn rich that he could have paid for the studio time and never batted an eye. You know, as a *gift*. But he didn't do it. I ended up spending my entire life's savings to make that record. Do you remember it? It came out in 1989."

"I do," Berenger said. He could see that Duncan was in denial about the album. It had not been a good one. It suffered the same fate as the products made by many other famous rock stars' children—they were always unfavorably compared to the parents' work.

"Anyway, we practically got into a fistfight there in the dressing room. He started yelling at me to get off my ass, stop being a lazy bum, that kind of shit. As if he had any idea what I do every day."

"Then what happened?"

"So I left the dressing room. I found my mom and wanted to leave, but she insisted that we stay for the show. So we did. And I really, *really* hate the crap he's doing now—damn, I keep thinking the bastard's still alive—I mean what he was doing before he . . . you know."

"You mean the religious music?"

"Yeah. What garbage."

"So you stayed for the show and then what?"

"Mom and I went to the meet and greet. I refused to talk to him. He was surrounded by those weird Messenger freaks. Finally, when even my mom couldn't get near him, we left."

Berenger nodded and then asked, "Okay, now what about later? Witnesses saw you outside of his town house."

"Yeah, I went over there," Duncan admitted. "I was drunk. After Mom went back to her hotel, I went to a bar and got smashed. I was really mad at my father, man, and I wanted to do something about it. At the same time, I thought if maybe I let out some of my anger I could, I don't know, maybe *apologize* for whatever it was he hated about me. And then, out of nowhere, he calls me on my cell phone."

"Flame did?"

"Yeah. He said he was at his town house and he sounded drunker than I was. He wanted to apologize to *me*, can you believe that? He wanted me to come downtown to talk to him, right then. So I took the subway downtown and walked over to his place on Charles Street."

"What time was that?"

"I don't know. Pretty late. Maybe one thirty or two?"

"What did you do when you got there?"

"I let myself in the office door."

"How did you do that?"

"I have a key. I had one made a long time ago. I don't think my dad knew about it. He hasn't changed the locks in, like, forever. I never went there but that night I did. So I go inside and I remember being a little disoriented. He had remodeled the place or something and I really wasn't sure if I was in the right place or not. Of course, I was pretty drunk. Anyway, I went into the main office and saw that it was a mess. There was a bottle of booze spilled everywhere and a bunch of papers and stuff on the floor. I remember stepping on a piece of broken glass."

"Did you pick up the bottle of booze?"

"I don't remember. I might have. Yeah, I think I did. I probably took a drink."

"Then what?"

"It's hard to remember. I'm pretty sure that's when I noticed all his gold records on the wall. For some reason I just lost my cool. I started picking up things from the desk and throwing them at the gold records. The frames shattered and everything. One fell down, I think. It made

a lot of noise. I was just waiting for him to come downstairs and find me tearing up the place. I swear if he had,
I probably *would* have killed him. He never did though."

Duncan fell silent for a moment. Berenger allowed
him to pick it up at his own speed.

"Then, I guess when I finished smashing the gold records, I heard the music," Duncan said.

"The music?"

"It was coming from upstairs, in the living quarters.
There's a door at the back of the office that opens to the
stairway leading to the rest of the house. And I heard this
music coming through it, faintly, like he was playing a
CD in one of the rooms upstairs. So I opened the door.
I called up the stairs. I said something like, 'Come down
here, you bastard!' No one answered me. So I started
climbing the stairs. I let the music lead me. When I got
halfway up I realized that something was wrong with the
music. It was skipping, you know, like a record with a
scratch? In fact, that's what it was . . . he had put on an
old 45 of one of his hits. And it was scratched."

Duncan turned away, a look of panic in his eyes. "It
was awful. I got up to the third floor and went into the
bedroom. And there he was. Hanging from the ceiling.
I think I lost it and puked. I stumbled through the bedroom and went into the bathroom."

"The master bathroom?"

"Yeah. I threw up there. I took some time to wash my
face and stuff. Now I realize I left my goddamn fingerprints everywhere. I went back into the bedroom and
looked at him again and I guess I just panicked. I really
thought he'd killed himself and I might be the reason for
it. I ran. I fucking ran down the stairs, through the office,
and out to the street. I ran all the way to the subway and
I took the train home."

"Do you remember seeing anyone else on the street? Someone that saw you?"

Duncan shook his head. "No. Wait, a cab almost ran over me. I couldn't see inside of it. I just kept running. That's all I remember, I swear."

Berenger nodded. "Okay, Adrian. Now I'd like you tell me what was going on between you and the Jimmys."

Duncan glowered at Berenger and then turned his head to Patterson. The lawyer shrugged and said, "I told him you wouldn't tell me about them. What was I supposed to do?"

"What did the cops find in your apartment, Adrian? What's going on? You gotta tell us," Berenger said.

Duncan tapped his foot in annoyance and finally said, "I've been working for them, all right? I had access to some . . . people . . . they wanted for clients."

"To sell drugs to?"

Duncan nodded.

"Rock stars?"

He nodded again. "Actually it started out with me producing their next CD. They thought it'd be a good idea for 'Flame's son' to produce them. I was in negotiations with the band through a liaison and then one thing led to another. I started selling coke and H for them instead."

"So what did the cops find in your apartment?"

"I imagine it was all the stuff on my computer. Records. Names. Addresses. E-mail correspondence with Snort. Luckily there wasn't any stash there at the time."

"Snort?"

"Yeah, Snort's my contact with the Jimmys. I don't know his real name."

Berenger thought of suggesting that Duncan turn State's evidence in exchange for some kind of deal. He was certain that the DA would be happy to receive some useful information about the Jimmys. Berenger decided to wait and bring it up with Patterson later.

"One more thing, Adrian," he said. "Do you happen to recall what you did with the backstage pass from the concert?"

Duncan looked up, confused. "The backstage pass?"

"You know, the sticky pass you put on your shirt for the meet and greet?"

Duncan shook his head. "I don't know. I took it off. I *ripped* it off. It may have been at the theater. I can't remember. I'm pretty sure I threw it away. Why?"

"The police claim it was in your father's hand when they found him."

Duncan's eyes went wide. "That's impossible! That's crazy!" he yelled.

One of the guards reacted to Duncan's agitated state and moved toward him quickly.

"It's all right, Officer," Berenger said, holding up his hand. "He's just upset."

But Duncan continued to rant and rave. "There's *no way* that could happen! This is *bullshit!* It's all *bullshit!* You, and the goddamn lawyer, and this fucking *jail!* You can all go to hell!"

Another guard joined the first one and they grabbed Duncan by the arms. He began to curse and resist, so they pulled him away from the table and slammed him against the wall. Berenger and Patterson stood and the lawyer shouted at them to handle his client properly. One of the guards announced that "visiting hours were over," and led Duncan away.

Patterson was shaken by what had just happened but Berenger had seen it before. The Rock did that to people. Duncan had been there twenty-four hours and already he was losing it.

As the two men drove off the island in silence, Berenger couldn't help but think that Adrian Duncan was a mean, spoiled thirty-five-year-old brat who was unappreciative of his mother's efforts to clear his name.

He also wasn't terribly convinced of Duncan's innocence.

As they crossed the bridge into Manhattan, Berenger pulled out his cell phone and dialed Tommy Briggs. When his colleague answered, Berenger said, "Tommy, it looks like Adrian Duncan was indeed involved with the Jimmys. See what you can dig up about a guy who goes by the name of Snort."

Briggs chuckled. "Okay, I'll do that. That's all?"

"Yeah. Thanks."

"Okay. Hey, Ringo wants to talk to you."

"Put her on."

When Mel got on the line she said, "Spike there's a package here for you. It was sitting outside the front door when I went out for lunch."

"Who's it from?"

"Doesn't say."

"Open it."

He could hear the tearing of paper and scuffling sounds. Then Mel went, "Ewww!"

"What?"

"Spike, it's . . . it's a bunch of *wire!*"

"Wire?"

"No, wait, these are *guitar strings*—they're all broken and sticky like they've got some kind of goo on 'em."

Uh oh. Berenger knew what that meant.

"Look, Ringo, give the box to Tommy. Okay?"

"Okay. Yuck."

Berenger hung up and stared out the window as they passed traffic on the FDR.

"Anything wrong?" Patterson asked.

"Not really," Berenger said. "I just received a little message from the Jimmys. It appears I'm suddenly on their death list."

7

Family Affair

(performed by Sly and the Family Stone)

The gathering took place at 3:30 in the afternoon in a large conference room located within the law offices of Castro, Miles, Pratt, and Sloan (Berenger thought they could have been a folk rock band in the seventies). As expected, it was a large turnout. Ross Miles, the attorney for Flame's estate, sat at the head of the table. Carol Merryman, her son, Joshua, and her lawyer occupied the seats closest to the head of the table, on the left. Brenda Twist, Flame's most recent girlfriend, sat next to the lawyer. On the other side of the table, the legendary record mogul Al Patton held the position closest to Miles, facing Carol. Apparently he didn't need a lawyer. Berenger was amused at how Patton's shiny bald head reflected a mirror image of the overhead fluorescent lights. Gina Tipton and Derek Patterson occupied the seats next to Patton. Berenger took the chair beside Patterson.

There had nearly been an altercation in the lobby when Brenda Twist showed up with Reverend Theo in tow. She was dressed in her Sunday best—even though it was Thursday—and carried a Bible along with a small black purse. Both Carol Merryman and Gina Tipton were appalled that Flame's girlfriend was present.

"What the hell are you doing here?" Carol asked Brenda to her face.

"I have a right to be here, Carol," Brenda replied sweetly but with a subtle firmness that indicated she would stand her ground. "So does the reverend."

"The hell you do. This is for family only." Carol looked at Gina for support, probably the only time the two women were on the same side of an issue.

"I lived with Flame for the last seven years," Brenda said with a smile. "I'm just as important to him as you."

"Why, you little b—"

"Ladies, please," Reverend Theo interrupted. Berenger noticed that the reverend retained his huge, wide smile throughout the conversation. It was as if he had trademarked his grin. "I will gracefully bow out," the man continued. "I was merely accompanying Ms. Twist. I do believe she has permission from Mr. Miles to be present today. Please accept my condolences once again for your loss. Brenda, I'll wait for you out here." He smiled even more broadly, bowed slightly, and backed away. He took a seat in the waiting room and picked up the latest *People* magazine.

Carol stormed into the conference room and Joshua meekly followed her. Gina rolled her eyes at Berenger as the rest of the group filed in.

Now they sat facing Miles, waiting to hear what was inside the will of one of the world's greatest rock stars. The estate's financial worth had not yet been determined. In all likelihood it would take months to sort it out. Everyone at the table knew this but Berenger swore he could see dollar signs in everyone's eyes. He figured that Flame's estate was valued at a minimum of a billion.

Flame had been with Ross Miles for years and the attorney was a tough man to deal with. He was somewhere in his sixties, came from Brooklyn, and looked as if he could go the distance with Mike Tyson. Berenger knew him as a sharp and ruthless lawyer. Miles handled several other big-name celebrities and he had a reputation of wielding a big stick when it came to looking after his clients' best interests.

"So, we're all here," Miles said. "I don't think we need to beat around the bush so let's get right to it." He opened a sealed document and placed it on the table in front of him. "Flame and I made this will three years ago. He amended it seven months ago and it was witnessed by myself and Jimmy Castro."

He read the legalese that was standard for all wills in New York State. Berenger noticed Carol Merryman nervously chewing her lower lip in anticipation of the good stuff. She was the only one at the table who had a notepad and pen, ready to jot down in detail how the pie was to be distributed. Al Patton was cool and calm. Gina acted as if this meeting was an entire waste of time. Brenda Twist was trying her best to appear relaxed but her eyes darted apprehensively around the room and she clutched her Bible as if her life depended on it.

Finally, Miles got to the nitty-gritty. "Ownership and rights in Flame Productions Inc. shall be granted to Joshua Duncan. This includes all copyrights and licenses as well as physical property. A transition period of one year shall transpire with Carol Merryman presiding over the company until which time Joshua will take the reins."

There were no gasps but Joshua Duncan's eyes grew wide and his mouth dropped. Carol made a slight face of disapproval. She had been expecting something like that but didn't realize she would have no control of the company after a year's time. That meant she would be in charge of all the hard stuff—the probate, settling accounts, taking care of legal commitments that Flame had made, and putting the business in order. Just when it was about to become fun, she'd have to hand it over to her son.

Berenger wondered if Joshua Duncan had the chutzpah to run Flame's business. The young man had always struck him as an introverted shrimp that followed his famous parents around the world like a puppy. Sometimes life didn't make much sense.

Miles continued. "Eight million dollars in cash will be granted to Carol Merryman."

This time there were a couple of quiet intakes of breath. Berenger was pretty sure they came from Carol and Gina. Carol scribbled the news on her notepad with vigor.

"Three million dollars in cash shall go to Brenda Twist."

Carol made no attempt to disguise her dismay and nearly choked. *"What?"*

Gina made a sour face and slumped a little in her chair.

Brenda looked to the ceiling and whispered, "Oh, sweet Jesus." She pressed the Bible to her chest and went into a silent prayer.

"And finally," Miles said, pausing for dramatic effect. Gina slightly turned her head to look at the attorney, just in case Flame had seen fit to leave something for his first family. "Twenty-five million dollars in cash shall go to the organization known as the Messengers."

"Praise God!" Brenda said quietly.

Gina muttered, "Well, hell."

Carol gasped and proclaimed, "You've got to be fucking kidding!" She looked around the room searching for sympathetic faces. Joshua sat staring at his hands, which lay palms down on top of the table. Al Patton merely nodded as if none of this was any surprise. Gina folded her arms in front of her and refused to look at anyone else. Brenda continued to pray even more intensely. The attorneys in the room shook their heads, betraying their true feelings with bemused looks on their faces.

"There's one more thing," Miles said, gaining everyone's attention once again. "There is a clause indicating that if anyone contests the contents of the will, then no one will receive a thing and all aforementioned cash, rights, and property shall be bequeathed solely to the Messengers."

"That son of a bitch," Carol said.

Gina looked at Berenger and sighed. She and Adrian had been completely shut out.

"Well that went over like a lead zeppelin," Gina said to Berenger out in the waiting room.

"I don't know what to say, Gina," Berenger said. "I know you're disappointed."

"Ah, well, what did I expect? I really didn't think Adrian and I would get anything. I'm mostly surprised by the gift to those religious fanatics." She looked over at Brenda and Reverend Theo, who were embracing and crying tears of joy.

She turned back to him and asked about Adrian.

"He's fine," Berenger replied. "He's upset, of course, and it's a real drag for him to be in jail, but he's being treated all right. It's a good thing he's in protective custody."

"I wish they'd let me see him more often. They really restrict visiting hours."

"Yeah, I know."

Carol entered the waiting room from the conference area. Her face was flushed and it was obvious she had been taking Ross Miles to task. Berenger was pretty sure that Miles put her in her place. Joshua stuck close to her, slightly in back, and refused to look anyone in the eye.

"Excuse me a second," Berenger said to Gina. He approached Carol and said, "Hello, Carol."

"Well, well, Spike Berenger," she said, stopping and looking him up and down. "I heard you were working for Flame's murderer."

"Come on, Carol, we've known each other a long time," Berenger said. "For one thing, Adrian's innocent until proven guilty in a court of law, you know that."

She made a sound of disgust. "Oh, he's guilty, all right." Her eyes met Gina's and she continued, "It's in his breeding."

Gina blinked, turned and left the office.

"Gee whiz, Carol," Berenger said. "That was harsh, don't you think?"

"This whole day has been *harsh,* Spike. Did you hear what went on in there? My husband gave twenty-five— no, *twenty-eight*—million dollars to those crazy religious fanatics over there!" She gestured with her head toward Brenda and Theo, who were too elated with each other to hear what was said.

"He's your *ex*-husband, Mom," Joshua said quietly.

"Whatever." Carol folded her arms and looked at Berenger. "So, I suspect you'll want to talk to me about the case?"

"As a matter of fact—"

"You know, I don't have to do that," she said. "I talked to my lawyer this morning when I heard you'd been retained by the defense. He said I'm under no obligation to talk to private investigators."

"That's right, Carol, you don't have to talk to me if you don't want to. But seeing as how we've known each other a long time—"

"Save the speech, Spike. I'll talk to you. It's against my better judgment but I'll do it."

Berenger nodded at her son. "I'd like to make an appointment to talk with Joshua as well."

Joshua shrugged. "I don't mind." Carol looked at him and he added, "If Mom doesn't."

Berenger tried to smile without giving away his true feelings. For a young man well over twenty-one years old, Joshua Duncan certainly wasn't in control of his own life.

"Fine," he said. "I'll be in touch. It's good to see you again, Carol."

"Yeah, I wish it had been under more pleasant circumstances. Come on, Joshua, let's get out of here." She took her son by the arm and strode out the door.

Berenger lingered to shake hands with Derek Patterson and say he would be in touch, and then he took the elevator to the building lobby. He walked out onto Sixth Avenue and noticed the large black limousine parked at the curb in front of the building. Al Patton stood on the sidewalk, his hulking physique leaning down and speaking to the driver. Berenger waited a moment so he could talk to Patton and heard the door open behind him. Reverend Theo and Brenda Twist came outside. Berenger was surprised to see Brenda open the back door of the limo and get in. Patton ended his conversation with the limo driver and greeted Theo. While the two men shook hands and exchanged pleasantries, Berenger got a look at the driver, another bald fellow that resembled Bruce Willis on a bad day. The reverend said good-bye to Patton, nodded at Berenger in a "How are you, today?"

friendly gesture, and then got into the limo beside Brenda. As the car pulled out into the busy avenue and sped away, Berenger noticed that the vanity license plate read: FLAME.

Patton moved toward Berenger and said, "How are you, Spike?"

"Fine, Al." The two men shook hands. They had known each other for years but maintained a cool, professional relationship with each other. Berenger gestured at the departing limo. "Is that Flame's limousine?"

"Uh huh," Patton said. "Flame's driver works for the Messengers now that Flame is dead."

"And they're using Flame's personal car? For Messenger business?"

"Actually, Flame would have wanted them to," Patton said. "He often lent Mr. Black's services and the limo to Reverend Theo. That's how Ron got the new position."

"What's the driver's name?"

"Black. Ron Black. He's been with Flame for, what, five or six years. I think he was with the Messengers before that. It's how he got hooked up with Flame."

"I see. What did you think of the proceedings upstairs?"

Patton shrugged. "It's pretty much what I expected. I knew Flame wouldn't leave *me* anything. Why should he? I must say I'm pretty surprised by the gift to the Messengers."

"I think everyone was thrown by that."

"Yeah. I don't know, Spike. Flame was pretty mixed up these last few years. He was throwing his career away, what can I tell you? Look, I have to run. I'm late for another appointment."

"Sure, Al. Listen, I'd like to talk to you about all this. You know I'm working for Adrian?"

"Yeah, I heard. Sure, Spike, give me a call at the office. I'll talk to you." Patton held out his arm and flagged an approaching taxi.

"Great. See you later, Al."

He watched as Patton got in the cab and sped away. Berenger began to walk uptown when his cell phone rang.

"Berenger," he answered.

"Mr. Berenger?" A woman's voice.

"Yes?"

"This is Betty Samuels at Franklin Village."

Berenger felt a shot of adrenaline. Was it bad news? Betty Samuels was the director of the assisted living facility in Hempstead, Long Island, where his mother currently resided. "Yeah?"

"Don't be alarmed, everything's fine with your mother. But we need to talk again about what we discussed before. About your mother moving."

"What happened?"

"Well, she had another episode. She waited until the receptionist wasn't looking and she walked right out the front door. No one realized she had left until a half hour later, when it was time for dinner. We looked all over the building and finally John—you know John, one of the attendants?"

"Yes."

"He went outside to look for her. He found her two blocks away, wandering aimlessly. She was lost and confused."

"Oh dear."

"It's okay now. John brought her back and one of the nurses gave her a sedative. But I'm sure you can appreciate the seriousness of the situation. We simply can't be responsible for her if she's going to continue to wander off."

"I understand."

"When can you come out and talk about this? I think it's time we move her into the Neighborhood."

Berenger winced. The Neighborhood was the special locked wing reserved for patients suffering from dementia and Alzheimer's.

"You think it's come to that?" he asked.

"I'm afraid so."

Berenger looked at his watch. "Okay, I—uhm, I'll drive out there this evening. Is that all right?"

"Sure. I'll be here until nine o'clock tonight."

"I'll try to be there between seven and eight."

Berenger put away the phone and continued walking uptown, where he could catch a crosstown bus to his apartment.

News like that called for a stiff glass of vodka and ice.

71

8

Jesus is Just Alright

(performed by The Doobie Brothers)

Suzanne Prescott emerged from the Times Square IRT subway station at the Forty-fourth Street exit and walked west. The nine-to-five work force had been let out for rush hour and the area was packed with people. Perhaps the most populated tourist attractions in the city, Times Square and the theater district were a mass of humanity twenty-four/seven. Once upon a time Suzanne had hated coming to the area because it had been such a cesspool of sleaze. In the nineties, though, New York's mayor cleaned it up and now it was so family-oriented that Walt Disney would have been proud. The sex shops, "live nude girls" peep shows, and drug trade was for the most part relegated to points outside of Manhattan, leaving Times Square a haven for visitors.

That didn't mean the area was no longer dangerous. Con artists and opportunists of every kind, hookers, and thieves could still strike the naive and unsuspecting traveler. Street-smart New Yorkers, though, rarely encountered such vermin, and Suzanne was definitely savvy when it came to navigating around the city. One of the most valuable things that Master Chen taught her during her five-year stay in the Far East was a highly developed sense of awareness. She liked to call it her "spider sense," named after her favorite comic book superhero's ability. While Suzanne's intuition certainly didn't equal that of Spider-Man's, she seemed to have a knack for detecting danger before it reared its ugly head.

It's too bad her insight never worked when it came to her love life, but that was another story and she didn't like to dwell on it.

Suzanne made her way toward Eighth Avenue and on to Ninth, noting that the crowds diminished as she went westward. Hell's Kitchen, as the area was commonly called, was a lower-class neighborhood that happened to border the elite theatre district. Suzanne thought the moniker was a misnomer, for the people she had encountered in Hell's Kitchen had been among the friendliest in all of New York. There was probably a fair share of drug addicts, pushers, gangs, and bad guys in the neighborhood, but Suzanne had never encountered them. As a matter of fact, there was a pizza joint at Ninth Avenue and Forty-fourth Street she liked to frequent and she was tempted to do so now. But she had a job to do so she kept walking toward Tenth, where the Messengers' church and offices were located.

It was once a traditional church but the building was now painted an earthy green, a color that stuck out in the otherwise drab neighborhood. A glass display case protected a marquis scripted by plastic white letters that could be rearranged according to the organization's plans for the week. Today it read: THE MESSENGERS—A CHURCH FOR THE ENLIGHTENED SOUL—TONIGHT'S MESSAGE: ARE YOU AN APOSTLE?—7:30 P.M.—REVEREND THEO, DIRECTOR.

Suzanne ascended the stoop's four steps and opened the large wooden door. The interior smelled musty and old, like most of the buildings in the area, but it was clean and well lit. A rack full of Messengers literature was prominently situated in front of the office, which was separated from the lobby by a closed door. Suzanne saw an African American woman through a sliding-glass window, working at a computer. The woman looked up, smiled, and rose. She slid open the window and said, "Good afternoon. How may I help you?"

"Oh, I'm just here to look around. I saw your building and I was just curious," Suzanne replied.

"Well then, we welcome you," the woman said. "I'll come right out." She closed the window and unlocked the office door. She appeared and stood beside the rack of literature. Suzanne guessed the woman was in her forties. She was slightly overweight, wore glasses, and was dressed in the type of loose black dress that Suzanne imagined elderly church ladies in the South might wear. In fact, the woman's speech had a Southern drawl to it.

"I'm Juliet Ramsey," the woman said. She held out her hand and Suzanne shook it. Reverend Theo's wife, Suzanne recalled.

"My name is Suzanne. Pleased to meet you."

"Likewise." The woman picked out two or three pamphlets from the rack and handed them to Suzanne. "Here are a few pieces of our literature. They'll tell you a little bit about us and what our mission is."

"What denomination are you?" Suzanne asked. "I mean, you *are* a Christian church, right?"

"Oh, Lord, yes, we're a Christian church. But we're our own denomination. There's no one like us on the planet. I think you'll find us a unique congregation. We are blessed with a reverend who's in daily communication with Jesus and all the other Holy Ghosts."

"*Ghosts,* as in plural?"

"Oh, yes, there are several. Our reverend talks to them daily."

Suzanne couldn't help raising her eyebrows. "Is that Reverend Theo?"

"Yes. Have you heard of our reverend?"

"I saw his name on the sign outside."

"Oh, of course. Our good reverend comes from Jamaica. He and I founded the Messengers—oh, it's going on fifteen years ago or so. Our congregation is one hundred and thirty strong and climbing."

"A hundred and thirty?" Suzanne asked. "That's not very many, is it?"

Mrs. Ramsey continued to smile warmly. "We're continually growing. The difference between our congregation and those of others is that our members remain with us once they've joined. If you go down the street to another church, you'll find that the membership fluctuates. We're one big loyal family and we like it that way."

"How on earth do you manage to finance yourselves? Surely the dues from the membership can't possibly support the organization."

"We don't call them dues, child. They're offerings. Not only that, offerings are purely voluntary. We don't require our members to contribute anything. But they all do. We raise money through other activities, though. Fundraising is an integral part of religion these days, I'm afraid!" She laughed a little.

The front door opened and an imposing black man entered, followed by an attractive Caucasian woman whom Suzanne recognized as Brenda Twist.

"Hello dear," the reverend said to his wife. He smiled at Suzanne and said, "Hello."

"Hi," Suzanne replied.

"I was just telling this young lady about the Messengers," Mrs. Ramsey said. "Suzanne, this is Reverend Theo."

The reverend shook her hand and said, "I'm pleased to meet you. What brings you to our happy home today?"

"Oh, I was just walking by, saw the building, and was curious," Suzanne said. "I'm kind of a church junkie. I like the architecture. I set a goal several years ago to visit every church in Manhattan. I don't think I've made it through half of them yet!"

"I would think you haven't," the reverend said. He grinned from ear to ear and Suzanne noted that the man exuded an intoxicating charm. "You should come to our service tonight. The only way to really find out what we're all about is to experience us."

"Thank you, I might do that," Suzanne said.

The reverend turned to Brenda Twist and said, "Brenda, perhaps you'd like to give this young lady a tour? I need to make some phone calls in the office."

"I'd be delighted," Brenda said. She smiled sweetly at Suzanne.

Reverend Theo addressed Suzanne again and said, "It was a pleasure to meet you. I do hope I'll see you again." He gave a slight bow and went into the office.

His wife said, "I'll leave you in Brenda's good hands, child. Have a nice day."

"Thank you," Suzanne said. Mrs. Ramsey followed her husband and shut the door.

Brenda held out her hand and said, "I'm Brenda Twist."

Suzanne shook it and said, "Suzanne Prescott."

"Let's go inside the sanctuary, shall we?"

As they walked through the double doors, Suzanne asked, "And what, may I ask, is your function at the church? Are you an employee?"

"Yes, I've been with the Messengers for about eight years. I guess you could say I'm the reverend's executive

assistant, if such a title is applicable in a religious institution." Suzanne noted that Brenda was dressed demurely
as if she had just come from or was on her way to Sunday school—a black skirt that covered her knees, flat
shoes, a white blouse, and a scarf around her neck—
and she was carrying a Bible. Suzanne wondered if she
had been at the reading of the will that afternoon. She
may have met Spike.

The sanctuary was small, simply because it was in a
narrow brownstone on the West Side of Manhattan. Two
sections of six pews occupied the floor. The altar at the
front appeared to be fairly typical, except that the
iconography surrounding it was strikingly gruesome.
Nailed to the crucifix behind the altar was an extremely
bloody effigy of Christ—something Suzanne thought
was more at home in medieval passion plays. The expression of pain and suffering on Jesus' face was unnat-
urally lifelike and the blood seemed to be freshly wet.
Also unusual for most Christian churches, the two
thieves that had been crucified along with Christ were
also present, mounted on opposing sides of the central
cross. They, too, were depicted in a graphically brutal
fashion.

Suzanne looked around the entire sanctuary and
noted that the walls were also decorated with particularly unnerving sculptures and paintings. These por-
trayed the saints and apostles that met violent deaths.
One of them—she thought he was Peter—was nailed to
the cross upside down.

"Ewww," she muttered involuntarily.

"Powerful images, aren't they?" Brenda asked.

"Uh, yeah."

"We believe in touching one's emotions with the
Lord's word. Most people don't realize how great our

Lord's suffering really was. Or the sacrifices made by his apostles. The Messengers believe in enlightenment. That's our primary goal. To enlighten those who don't believe, or to strengthen the faith of those that already do. Enlightenment is the key to Heaven."

Suzanne felt a shiver run up her spine. The place was truly creepy and Brenda Twist reminded her of one of the pod people from *Invasion of the Body Snatchers*.

"Interesting," was all that Suzanne could say as she did her best to smile cheerfully. Then she noticed a glass case atop a pylon near the altar. It contained a metal urn. Suzanne moved closer to the case until she could read the plaque mounted on the front—HERE SIT THE ASHES OF FLAME, TRUE AND DEVOTED MEMBER OF THE MESSEN-GERS.

Suzanne was too shocked to say anything. Why in the world would they display Flame's ashes in their *sanctuary?*

She turned away, attempted to smile at Brenda, and said, "Okay, what else?"

"This way, please." Brenda led her back to the lobby and through a door marked TO CHAPEL. "We also have a space for private meditation and reflection," Brenda said. "Personally, I find the chapel to be extremely com-forting when I'm stressed out. It's my favorite room in the building."

They moved through a short hallway that opened onto a landing. A dark, narrow staircase led to the base-ment. Brenda touched a light switch on the wall, illumi-nating the stairwell, and descended the steps. Suzanne had a fleeting thought that she was about to enter the depths of Hell.

The "comforting" chapel was a room the size of a meat locker and was nearly as cold. It, too, was covered in violent and frightening iconography that would have given Suzanne nightmares had she chosen to remain there for any period of time. Screaming out from the walls of the chapel were paintings of Christ being flogged by Roman centurions, up-close-and-personal images of the nailing, and numerous head shots suggesting just how painful that crown of thorns really was. Even the ceiling was painted with images of angels that appeared to be horrified at what was taking place on earth below them. Oddly, there were also paintings representing Eastern religions on the wall. A Hindu god—was it Krishna?—appeared to be crying as he looked upon the broken body of Christ. There was no way that Suzanne could feel any sort of serenity here.

This was Brenda Twist's favorite spot in the building?

"Wow, this is really something," she said to Brenda. "Now let's see something else."

Brenda stood a moment, staring at one of the bloody Christs, and sighed. "All right," she finally said. She led the way upstairs, back to the lobby. From there they continued to ascend another staircase to the second floor of the building.

"This is where we run our day care," Brenda said, opening a door to a playroom containing small desks and chairs, cushions for naps, boxes of toys, and other accoutrements of a nursery. Suzanne was shocked to see crayon drawings of the crucifixion adorning the walls.

"When are the children here?" Suzanne asked.

"Earlier. From around seven o'clock in the morning until about five thirty. You just missed everyone. There are roughly twenty children that come here on weekdays. Their parents have to work, you know."

"Of course."

As they descended the stairs toward the lobby, Brenda said, "You really should come to one of our services. They're held every evening, and twice on Saturdays and Sundays."

"That's a lot of services."

"Not all of our members can come to every service, so we hold them often."

"I see." Suzanne decided it was now or never. "So, was Flame really a member of your congregation? I read that somewhere."

A visible change came over Brenda. The sweet smile and angelic aura suddenly disappeared and was replaced by a frown. The brown eyes, earlier so sparkling and pretty, turned cold.

"So," she said. "That's why you're here."

"I beg your pardon?"

"You're just a Flame fan, aren't you? That's why you came here. You wanted to satisfy your morbid curiosity. I saw you looking at his urn."

"Uhm, that's not true."

"I know it is. I can see it in your face. You know who I am, too. Don't you? The Lord knows you're lying."

Suzanne was taken aback. "Look, I just came in here to look around."

Brenda abruptly strode toward the front door and opened it. She held it and addressed Suzanne. "If you care to come to one of our services, then I might believe you. Otherwise I must ask you to leave. We've had a lot of problems with fans coming here, wanting a piece of Flame. Or me."

"Sorry," Suzanne said, sweeping past her. "I'm not what you think."

As she stepped over the threshold, a large bald-headed man was coming up the steps in front of the building. A black limo that wasn't there earlier was parked in a reserved space in front of the church.

"Good-bye," Brenda said behind her. "The Lord knows all and will judge you."

Suzanne looked back at her guide and couldn't think of anything to say except, "Thanks!"

The bald man moved past Suzanne and glanced at her, but he said nothing. Brenda held the door open for him and then shut it once he was inside.

Suzanne felt yet another chill—the second one that day. An incredibly weird vibe emanated from that guy. Who was he? She had a vague feeling that he was familiar to her, but it could have just been the willies she had been experiencing ever since stepping into that freaky place.

One thing was for sure—the Messengers were a scary bunch of grade-A wackos.

9

Mother

(performed by John Lennon)

After he had taken a look at the mess of guitar strings that had been delivered to Rockin' Security, Berenger threw the package in a drawer and tried to forget about it. He had more pressing things on his mind at the moment, so he ate a quick meal from the deli on Second Avenue, got his 2005 Nissan Altima 2.5 SL sedan out of his building's garage, and headed for the Queens Midtown Tunnel. He paid a fortune for a parking space in the garage but it was a necessary expense. The car was his CD player on wheels and he was loath to park it on the street. He rarely used the Altima when his work centered in Manhattan. Public transportation and taxis were the way to go within the city. But when he had to travel beyond Manhattan island, Berenger preferred to travel in style. The SL came standard with a four-cylinder engine mated to an automatic transmission, and it coddled occupants with heated leather seats, an eight-way power driver's seat, a trip computer and a six-disc CD changer with stereo controls mounted on the leather-wrapped steering wheel. It was a luxury vehicle but not so much that it would attract attention in the event he had to shadow someone or sit and stake out a building. Berenger had originally considered purchasing a Corvette but decided it was too much of an eye-catcher.

He had put on Gentle Giant's classic prog rock CD, *Free Hand*, and tried to groove to the syncopated complexity of "Just the Same" when he realized it didn't fit his mood. That was an album for feeling good and ever since he had received the call from Franklin Village, he had not been jumping with joy. He changed the CD to something to match his gloom—Neil Young and Crazy Horse's *Sleeps With Angels*. There was something about Young's plaintive voice and the raw grunge guitars of the Horse that fit neatly with melancholy.

Berenger's seventy-nine-year-old mother, Ann, had moved to Long Island after she found her second husband in 1973. The period when she and Berenger's real father were married, back in Austin, Texas, now seemed like a fairy tale. The memories of his parents were good but things changed drastically after their divorce. It happened when he was still in high school. The announcement came as a shock to him, for he naively thought his parents were happy. One day Berenger had come home from tenth grade to find his father crying in the kitchen. His wife had left him for another man. Berenger remembered that he didn't believe his father and refused to accept it, even after two weeks. When he finally spoke to his mother he was still in denial. She didn't waste any time moving to New York with her new beau, Abraham Berkowitz, a tailor she had met at the department store where she worked. Berenger stayed in Austin with his father so he could graduate in 1975 without having to change high schools. His younger brother Carl wasn't so fortunate. He moved to Long Island with their mother and new stepfather with the idea that he would begin high school at the new location.

It took several years for Berenger to realize that his decision to join the army after graduating was a direct result of his mother's sudden departure. He had been full of anger during those years and the army provided him an outlet. Three years in Southeast Asia did little to ease his anger, though.

Even though the war was officially over, there was still enough covert military activity for the U.S. in Vietnam and surrounding areas to keep Berenger occupied. Berenger was based in the Philippines and worked as a special agent in the Criminal Investigations Division, which may have served to dampen his feelings of resentment toward his mother but it also gave him a radically new outlook on life. When he finally returned to the States, he had more or less forgiven her. By the mideighties, he had come to love and admire his stepfather and tried to visit his mom in New York as often as he could.

Daniel Berenger never remarried. He had died of heart failure in 1990 but Berenger knew that the old man's heart had actually failed in 1973, when Ann left him. Ann's husband Abraham died of cancer in 1999 and that's when things started to fall apart with Berenger's mother. She had already begun to show signs of dementia and Abraham had expressed his concern to Berenger on several occasions. After his stepfather's death, Berenger made the difficult decision to move his mother into an assisted living facility. His brother, Carl, now an attorney in Los Angeles, supported the move and flew east to help with the transition.

Nothing produced guilt more than doing something like that to one's parent.

Berenger attempted to convince himself that he wasn't sentencing his mother to a prison. After all, she would receive full-time care and be around other people her age. She would have activities and things to keep her mind occupied. And most importantly, she'd be safe—from herself. Still, it saddened Berenger every time he went to visit. Franklin Village was a beautiful and well-run outfit, and it was certainly better than a nursing home, but he still found it depressing. It was a constant reminder that everyone eventually grew old and had to deal with the final days of life.

Traffic was lighter than he had expected so Berenger reached Hempstead in record time after leaving Queens. He pulled into the Franklin Village parking lot and took a moment to prepare himself. This wasn't going to be easy.

He went inside the building, signed in, and went to the administrator's office, where Betty Samuels was waiting for him.

"Hello, Mr. Berenger, how are you?" she said, greeting him.

"Fine, thanks. How's my mom?"

"She's doing swell. I thought perhaps we'd talk before you went to see her."

"Okay."

He sat in one of the chairs in front of the woman's desk as she spoke. "Your mother was examined today by one of the nurses. She didn't pass many of the simple memory tests we can administer here. I suggest you make an appointment with her physician to do some more thorough testing. But we talked about this the last time you were here. She's definitely showing more pronounced signs of Alzheimer's, I'm sorry to say."

"I know," Berenger replied. "It's been getting worse since she got here. Last time I was here she wasn't sure if I was my brother or me. It must have something to do with the lack of companionship. You know, her husband dying and all."

"Yes, I'm sure that contributes to it. At any rate, we've picked out a room in the Neighborhood that's identical to the one she's in now. You've been through the Neighborhood, haven't you?"

Berenger nodded. The dementia unit was indeed a mirror image of the regular wards except that the residents were unable to leave the wing. They were kept separate from the rest of the population and even had their own dining room. Unfortunately this accentuated the notion that the occupants were "patients." Some of them felt like inmates.

Mrs. Samuels continued. "I did mention last time that because your mother has been a resident for more than two years, you'll receive a discount on the monthly payments. Normally the Neighborhood rooms run 20 percent higher than those in the open wards; in your case it's 10 percent."

Berenger shrugged and said, "Thanks." It didn't matter. A prison was a prison even if the attendants were kind ladies in white uniforms instead of mean, burly male guards. He couldn't imagine having to live the last days of his life in such an environment, but there was no telling how things would turn out. The bottom line was his mother was ill and there was nothing else he could do about it. He had to keep telling himself that he was doing the right thing.

"So if it's all right with you, we'd like to move her tomorrow."

"Tomorrow?"

"I think it's best," Mrs. Samuels said.

Berenger stroked his beard. "Gee. I didn't expect it to happen so soon."

"We just can't be responsible if she pulls another stunt like she did today. Our staff is diligent but they can't have eyes on everyone all the time. You understand."

He shrugged and nodded. "Okay. Do I need to help with the move?"

"Oh, no. We have people to do that. All you have to do is come back tomorrow evening and see her in her new place. I'm telling you, very few of our Neighborhood residents actually realize they've been moved."

"Well, my mom's not *that* far gone yet."

Mrs. Samuels pursed her lips.

"Is she?"

"Why don't we go look in on her?" Mrs. Samuels suggested.

They stood and walked out of the office and into the commons, a large open area where the residents sat with visitors, played cards at tables, or read. There were other recreational rooms with televisions, a gym, a beauty salon, a library, and a snack bar. Berenger liked the place because it felt more like a hotel than an assisted living facility. He supposed that perception would change once his mother moved into the Neighborhood.

Ann Berkowitz was in one of the two television rooms off to the side of the commons, watching *Friends*. Three other women sat near her—they were laughing and enjoying the program but she was not. Every time he saw her now, she appeared smaller for some reason. Was she shrinking? She was much tinier than Berenger remembered her being when he was growing up. Now she looked so fragile and elderly. It nearly broke his heart.

When he entered the room she looked up. He could swear that there was a moment's pause before the glint of recognition appeared in her eyes.

"Hi Mom, how you doing?" he asked.

"There wasn't any butter," she said.

"What's that?"

"There wasn't any butter. I told them a hundred times they need butter on the table."

He looked at Mrs. Samuels for an explanation. She didn't have a clue either.

"Come on, Mom, let's go for a little walk." He helped her up and she walked with him out of the room.

"I'll leave you two alone for a bit," Mrs. Samuels said. "I'll be in my office if you need me."

"Thanks," he said. He allowed his mother to put her arm through his.

"Such a gentleman," she said, smiling. It was good to see her smile. "Just like Abe. You met Abe, didn't you?" She meant her late husband.

"Of course, Mom. Abe was a great guy."

"Of course you met him, how could I be so silly. Yeah, he was a great guy. My parents liked him a lot, too."

Berenger wrinkled his brow. Her parents were long dead by the time she'd met Abraham Berkowitz. He didn't say anything until they reached the commons and sat on one of the big sofas in front of an unlit fireplace.

"Listen, Mom, tomorrow they're gonna move you into a new room," he said.

"Huh? Why?"

"Well, it's a better room. We thought you'd like a nicer room."

"I don't want a nicer room. Not unless I can have my apartment back."

"What apartment, Mom?"

"The one I shared with Cindy."

"Cindy?" At first he couldn't remember anyone named Cindy. Then it hit him. "You mean *Cindy?* Your college roommate?" His mom's best friend from school was named Cindy Watkins. She had been around when Berenger was a kid. Cindy was dead now, too.

"Cindy and I have a nice apartment. Can I go back there?"

"Mom, you lived with Cindy when you were going to college at Florida State. That was a long time ago."

"Oh. I miss Cindy. Have you seen her lately?"

"No, Mom, I haven't." Mrs. Samuels was right. It was getting worse. "Look, Mom, don't worry. You're gonna love the new room. You may not even know the difference. They're gonna take you someplace fun tomorrow, like to the mall or something, and then when you come back in the afternoon all your things will be moved."

She wasn't listening. Instead she was fumbling through her little purse that she always carried with her. There wasn't much in there. Residents didn't need to keep billfolds, money, keys, or other items younger people took for granted. She finally found a tube of lipstick and showed it to Berenger.

"Here it is," she said. "I've been looking for this."

"Whatcha need lipstick for now, Mom?" he asked.

She looked confused. "Lip—?" She eyed it and put it back in her purse. "Oh. I thought it was . . ." She shook her head slightly and then shrugged it off. "So how's work?" she asked.

"Work's fine, Mom. Hey, I talked to Carl the other day. He said to send you his love."

"Carl's a good boy," she replied. She patted Berenger on the cheek. "So are you, honey. You're just like a son to me."

Aww geez, he thought.

Berenger made a glass of Jack Daniel's on the rocks and sat in the easy chair that dominated the living room of his Upper East Side apartment. He picked up the television remote and almost switched on the set but decided against it. He was too depressed to watch the crap on TV.

It had been a trying evening. He hated seeing his mother in her condition. At least she still maintained a pleasant composure. He knew some Alzheimer's patients became terribly angry and belligerent with the world around them. In many ways they were aware of what was happening to them and couldn't deal with it—hence, they lashed out at their loved ones and anyone else that invaded their space. It was truly a cruel disease.

Berenger allowed himself to wander through memories of Ann Berkowitz when she still lived at home. Of course, she had been Ann Berenger then. She had been a babe and enjoyed flirting with other men. His poor father didn't have a chance. She had always set her sights above and beyond Daniel Berenger and nothing was going to stop her from attaining the level of satisfaction with life and love she desired. It was only recently that Berenger began to admire this trait in her because he recognized it in himself.

He reached over the arm of the chair and picked up his CF Martin D-15 acoustic guitar from its stand. It wasn't particularly high-end—all his good stuff was at the office studio—but it was a wonderful instrument to mess around with at home. He set it in his lap and wrapped the fingers of his left hand around the rosewood fingerboard and strummed a loud E-minor chord. From there he went to an A-major and back to E-minor. Berenger began to riff on the two chords, creating a melancholy melody that complemented his mood. After a minute or two, he went into an old song he had written for his band, the Fixers. It was their one single, a tune called "Moonbeams on Mars." As far as he knew, it was never played on any radio station, even in Austin, where the band enjoyed a small following.

Berenger formed the Fixers with his friend Charlie Potts after he had come home from Southeast Asia in 1978. He had learned his current trade in the army but he wouldn't explore it further for another fifteen years. The stint with CID had toughened him and given him discipline—but his heart had always been in music. His high school band had been a lot of fun but as with most teenage garage bands, there was no money to be had. Lugging around equipment in a borrowed van was more hassle than it was worth. With the money he had saved from his army salary, Berenger invested in a decent rig, called up Charlie, and before long they were jamming in Daniel Berenger's garage, just like they had done in high school. When they added two more guys to fill out the sound, Berenger realized that they had something worthwhile going.

The Fixers was a prog rock/art rock group that fit in well with the underground club scene in Austin. Luckily, Austin was always a haven for eclectic music. Just about any musical genre could thrive in Austin as long as it was *good.* The Fixers were talented indeed. A local manager heard them and signed them for a one-record deal. They recorded it in a week, released the album and a single in 1979, and buried the unsold copies in a landfill in 1980. Apparently, prog and art rock just didn't have the impact it once had earlier in the decade. The latter seventies were dominated by disco in one camp or by punk and new wave in the other. The failure hit Berenger hard and he drowned himself in liquor and drugs throughout most of the rest of that year. In early '81 he took the job as tour manager for Grendel and his life turned around.

Berenger continued to strum the guitar, every now and then stopping to take a sip of the whiskey. With his throat wet he started to sing some of his old tunes as he played, wallowing in the nostalgia.

The eighties had taken him deeper into the rock music industry. He became a manager and producer for a handful of Texas bands until he decided to move to Los Angeles and try his luck there. For five years he managed a couple of top-grade acts and produced a few notable albums. Finally, in 1988, he produced his friend Charlie Potts's solo album, which made it into the top ten. The collective experiences gave Berenger footholds into every aspect of the business. He had gotten to know all the great rock stars and some not-so-great ones, had partied and broken bread with the best of them, and made a name for himself.

Those were the good years. He had even married and had children, but Berenger couldn't help thinking that had been just a side project. Linda Steinman had certainly rocked his world and for three years it had been a blast. But like his mother, Berenger had wanderlust and couldn't stay at home.

He had experienced a difficult time staying faithful as well.

Then, in 1991, he met Rudy Bishop. Already an entrepreneur with a successful concert security business, Bishop asked Berenger to help him with a delicate situation. Bishop was working security for Maggie Tantra, one of the hottest heavy-metal performers at the time. She was on the verge of becoming a superstar with a number one album that was popular in the alternative scene. The problem was Maggie's ex-husband. The guy, also a musician, was jealous of Maggie's success and had issued a death threat against her. When Maggie's band was scheduled to play in the husband's hometown of Seattle, Berenger was hired as a bodyguard. During the show the husband leaped onto the stage and came at Maggie with a hatchet. Berenger tackled the bastard, wrestled him down, and disarmed him in front of 10,000 screaming fans. Luckily, they all thought it was part of the show.

After that, Bishop made Berenger an offer and Rockin' Security was born.

His cell phone rang and Berenger stopped playing the guitar. He dug it out of his pocket and saw from the caller ID that it was none other than Charlie Potts.

"Hey bud, I was just thinking about you," Berenger said after he connected and held the phone to his ear.

"Aw, really? Is that why my ears are burning?" his friend asked. "What's up?"

"Nothing. I was just playing some of our old songs while I got drunk. What's with you?"

"Just wondering when we're gonna jam again. It's been a while."

"Yeah, I know. Later this week, maybe. I'll have to call you. I'm kind of on a big case right now."

"No big deal. Hey, guess who I ran into today."

"Who?"

"Dave Bristol."

What a coincidence. "Really? What'd he have to say?"

"Oh, the usual. He and the band are having the usual troubles. He was sure bad-mouthing Flame."

"Yeah? What'd he say?" Berenger asked.

"Some shit like Flame got what was coming to him. Pretty tasteless if you ask me."

"Hmmm. Well, you know Bristol and Flame. They were natural enemies that happened to make incredible music together. They didn't have to like each other."

"I guess not."

"Anyway, he's playing at Mortimer's tomorrow night. You wanna go?"

"Blister Pack is playing?"

"Yeah."

It might be a good opportunity to talk to the band about Flame. "I just might. Can I let you know tomorrow?"

"Sure."

"I may bring Suzanne. Listen, Charlie, I've gotta go. Right now I just want to finish my Jack Daniel's, take a shower, and crash. S'ok?"

"Sure, man. Don't let the bedbugs bite."

"Whatever."

Berenger hung up and considered what Dave Bristol had said.

Flame got what was coming to him.

Maybe he did. Maybe he did.

The phone rang again. Berenger quickly picked up the receiver and was bombarded by loud, distorted punk music coming through the earpiece. He winced and held the phone away from his head. Then someone on the other end added "vocals." Screaming into the phone in punk rock fashion, the caller shouted in rhythm—

"You're gonna DIE tomorrow night, mister mister mister, you're gonna DIE DIE DIE, you're gonna DIE tomorrow night, mister mister mister, you're gonna DIE DIE DIE!"

And the phone went dead.

10

Trouble Every Day

*(performed by Frank Zappa
and the Mothers of Invention)*

Rockin' Security's morning began with a team meeting. Berenger dragged himself in with an annoying hangover. It had been a bad night for him but the booze had helped him get through it. The disturbing phone call—most likely the handiwork of the Jimmys—had put him in a foul mood and he had to continue playing his guitar for a while longer before crashing. He seemed to remember the clock reading 3:00 A.M. before he finally went to bed. Seven hours wasn't quite enough to sleep off the drunk but he'd handled much worse. After a good hot shower and a glass of tomato juice, he thought he could fool his body into thinking he was sharp enough to tackle the day. However, when he walked into the conference room and heard the heavy beat of Rage Against the Machine's self-titled first album pounding through the speakers, Berenger felt wrecking balls demolishing what was left of his brain. He went over to the sound system and shut off the music.

"Hey, man!" Remix said. "I was diggin' that!"

"Nine o'clock is too early for rap-metal, Remix," Berenger said. He ran his finger down the stack of CDs they kept in the room, pulled out Paul Simon's *Graceland*, and slapped the disc in the machine.

Remix groaned when the opening track began.

"Sorry, Remix," Berenger said. "That's one of the privileges of being the boss. I can pick whatever the hell I want to play during team meetings."

"I like this album," Suzanne said. "Good choice, Spike."

"It sucks, man," Remix added.

"Yeah, it only won, like, seven hundred Grammys," Briggs commented.

"Grammys? You put stock in those damn things?" Remix asked. "Grammys don't mean shit. I gave up on Grammys the year Jethro Tull beat Metallica for best heavy metal album!"

"Actually, Remix," Berenger said as he poured a cup of Mel's coffee, "the category that year was hard rock *slash* heavy metal, that is, hard rock *or* heavy metal. Jethro Tull's *Crest of a Knave* certainly qualified as a hard rock album and it's a damn good one, too. Frankly, I think the Grammys did right that year. Metallica got what was coming to them later on."

"Well, whoop-di-doo," Remix replied. "Ain't you the statistical know-it-all."

"But to tell you the truth, Remix," Berenger added, "I don't put much stock into the Grammys either." He sat at the table and surveyed his crew. They all looked at him as if they were waiting for some sort of revelation.

"What?" he asked.

Suzanne cleared her throat. "So, uhm, what about those guitar strings, Spike?"

Berenger shrugged and looked at Briggs. "You take a look at 'em?"

Briggs nodded. "Yeah. It's from the Jimmys, all right. Any idea why you're on their hit list?"

"Not a clue. Unless it's got something to do with the case. Adrian was working for them as a dealer but I don't see the relevance. Did you find out anything about Snort?"

"Nothing," Briggs replied. "It's an alias that doesn't have a record."

"Hmm. Well, let's move on. Suzanne, tell me about the Messengers' place."

She shook her head. "Whew, what a bunch of strange people. Their so-called church is full of really gross religious paintings of Christ being crucified and all that—stuff that would make even Mel Gibson blanch. I found it pretty sick. And the staff is just too sweet for words. Oh, and Flame's *ashes* are there, which I find totally weird. I brought back some of their literature, which on first glance appears perfectly respectable. However, if you read between the lines you can see they have some pretty strange ideas about religion."

"Such as?"

"That we're all the same 'person' connected to Jesus once we've accepted Him, but anyone who hasn't accepted Him isn't a person at all. Heaven is a much more elite country club than is widely believed and space is very limited. You have to be really, really, *really* good to get a reservation and it's implied that the more rent you pay up front, the better chance there is of you getting a room."

Suzanne glanced at her notes. "Let's see, what else . . . Oh, they don't have a lot of members, just a little over a hundred. They do have a bunch of services each week and I find that strange."

"You feel like attending one?"

She snorted. "Do I *feel* like attending one? Gosh, you couldn't *pay* me to attend one . . . but seeing as how you *are* paying me I guess I will if you want me to. They certainly made the pitch for me to come and join in on one."

Berenger rubbed his beard. "I may want you to go to a service but don't rush in yet. Let's play it by ear. Did you see Reverend Theo?"

"Yes, I did. I met him and his wife, briefly. Mostly, though, I was in contact with none other than Brenda Twist."

"And how was that?"

"Strange. It was like being led around by a Girl Scout with a halo. Unfortunately I made the mistake of mentioning something about Flame's connection with the Messengers. She immediately froze up and told me to get the hell out, although not in those precise words."

"I understand she's pretty private about Flame," Berenger said. "Not a publicity seeker."

"I got that impression, too. She doesn't like to talk about Flame from what I could gather."

"You think she's capable of murder?"

"Gut feeling? No. I mean, she obviously can be a bitch if she wants to, but I don't think she's capable of strangling her boyfriend and then stringing him up to make it look like a suicide. She may be crazy, but she's not a psycho."

"You think she got the idea you're an investigator?"

"No, I don't think so."

"Fine. Let's hang loose on them for the time being. There are other angles regarding the Messengers I want to investigate before we rush in and start asking questions they don't want to hear." Berenger looked at Briggs. "You got anything new, Tommy?"

Briggs cleared his throat and opened his notebook. "As a matter of fact, I do. I talked to Plaskett at the bureau and he helped me with some immigration information on our Reverend Theo. It appears he's not the saint everyone thinks he is."

"Do tell."

"Theodore Ramsey is an ex-con. He served seven years in a Jamaican prison for drug trafficking and assault. This was during the eighties. Before that, in 1973, he was charged with murder but was acquitted. The deceased was a drug dealer. Apparently Theo didn't find religion until after his release from prison in 1987. Most of his life, though, he was just a common yardie, a Jamaican thug. I think he's trouble."

"Speaking of trouble, didn't Immigration give him a problem when he wanted to enter the U.S.?" Berenger asked.

Briggs shrugged. "Yeah, but he got around it by marrying an American. He was also an ordained minister. He and his wife formed a small church in Ocho Rios in late 1987, after he got out of jail. She vouched for his integrity when they moved to New York in 1990. As I said last time, the Messengers' church was established here in 1992. As far as we know, Reverend Theo has been a model citizen since then."

"What about the wife?"

"Juliet Ramsey was born Juliet Hawkins in Valdosta, Georgia. We don't have a lot on her, she's squeaky clean. Worked as a schoolteacher most of her life, then spent most of the eighties in Jamaica."

"When did she and the reverend get married?"

"They married while Theo was still in prison! It's not clear when they met, but the records show they were married in 1985, while Theo was incarcerated."

Mel spoke up. "I'll never understand why women marry guys who are in prison. That's nuttier than an Almond Joy."

"What's the possibility of Theo being hooked up with the Jimmys?" Berenger asked.

"I'm still working on that angle," Briggs replied. "I don't know yet."

"I have a question," Suzanne said.

"What?" Briggs asked.

"When I was at their church yesterday, I saw Reverend Theo's driver. A big bald guy, very scary looking. Do you know who he is?"

"I do," Berenger said. "That's Ron Black. He was actually Flame's personal driver—and bodyguard—until Flame died. I'd like to know a little more about him, too. He was a part of the Messengers' organization before he started working for Flame, and now he's back working for the Messengers again. They're using Flame's limo, too. Al Patton told me about it. Says it's all aboveboard per Flame's wishes. Did you talk to Black, Suzanne?"

"No. I was leaving and he passed me coming in. I just got a weird vibe from him and there was something familiar about the guy. I don't know, it's probably nothing."

"We'll see if we can find out more about him," Berenger said. He looked at Remix and asked, "You having any luck hacking into the Messengers' server?"

"Shouldn't be a problem," Remix replied. "I'll have it soon."

"Fine. I guess that's it for now. I'm off to interview Joshua Duncan and from there I'm going to talk to Kenny Franklin. Everyone, try to keep busy today but be on hand in case I need you for something. Okay?"

"Okay, boss," Remix said.

They got up from the table and Remix went to the CD player. He shut off Paul Simon and rolled his eyes at Berenger. As the team filed out, Berenger touched Suzanne's arm. "Hold on a sec, Suzanne." When they were alone, he said, "Blister Pack is playing at Mortimer's tonight. I figure it might be a good opportunity to catch Dave Bristol after the show. You wanna go?"

Suzanne's eyes brightened. "Sure. Sounds fun."

"Unfortunately, before that I have to go out to Long Island and check on my mom. They're moving her into a different room in the Alzheimer's unit today. You wouldn't . . . you wouldn't want to come with me, would you? We could have a bite to eat in-between and then go to the show."

"Sure, Spike," Suzanne said. "I like your mom." She gave him a little pat on the shoulder. "Call me on my cell to let me know what time and all that."

"Will do."

After she left, Berenger stood in the empty conference room and became aware that his headache hadn't subsided. He went over to the coffee counter, opened a drawer, found the ibuprofen, and popped a couple tablets into his mouth.

The day was just beginning and he was already ready for a nap.

11

Son of Your Father

(performed by Elton John)

Berenger took a taxi across town and up to Columbia University's Morningside Campus, which was located on Broadway between 114th Street and 120th Street. The campus was situated in a lovely part of Manhattan, just a couple of blocks east of Riverside Park. Although it was technically on the edge of Harlem, the Upper West Side had maintained the reputation of being one of the more desired areas of the city in which to live. Berenger always found it to be a pleasant place and he enjoyed visiting the streets around the campus. It didn't hurt that attractive young women usually populated the area.

Joshua Duncan didn't want to meet on campus, though. He had suggested a rendezvous at the Hungarian Pastry Shop, a popular spot for students and Upper West Side intelligentsia. It wasn't far from Columbia, just a few blocks south on Amsterdam Avenue, right across the street from the magnificent Cathedral Church of St. John the Divine. Berenger loved the shop but tried to avoid it. He had a weakness for croissants and pastries and they tended to pack on the weight more than anything else he put in his mouth. Nevertheless, he steeled his resolve and showed up in front of the eatery at

10:30, the appointed time. Joshua Duncan was already there, sitting at one of the small wooden tables on the sidewalk.

"Hello, Joshua," Berenger said, stepping up to the young man and extending his hand. Joshua half-rose from his seat and shook hands.

"Hi, Mr. Berenger."

"Sit, sit. I'm gonna get me a coffee and something I shouldn't. I'll be back in a second." Berenger went inside the shop, bought a large coffee and a cinnamon bun—he was tempted to buy a blueberry tart as well but admirably resisted—and joined the young man at the table. Joshua was dressed in casual school clothes— baggy pants, T-shirt, tennis shoes—and had a backpack with him. He had finished his own coffee and had been reading the *Times*.

"You got classes today?" Berenger asked.

"Yeah."

"You're in Columbia Law School, right?"

"Uh huh."

The young man appeared to be a little nervous. He fidgeted in his seat and couldn't keep his leg from bouncing.

"How are you holding up, Joshua?" Berenger asked.

"I'm all right, I guess."

"I'm really sorry about your dad. I knew him a long time."

"Yeah, I know. Thanks."

"I really appreciate you taking the time to talk to me. I understand how you might feel, me working for the defense and all."

"That's okay. Adrian's my half brother." Joshua shrugged.

"Are you and Adrian close?" Berenger asked.

Joshua smirked. "Are you kidding? We have nothing to do with each other. I see him once in a blue moon and we *might* exchange a 'hello' or 'how are you' but that's about it. If we do have a conversation at all it's usually about how much he hates our father."

"Do you have much of a relationship with his mother?"

"Gina? Nah. My mom can't stand her. I guess I'm supposed to follow suit." He chuckled a bit. "It's all pretty silly, if you ask me."

"Why do you think there's such bad blood between them? I mean, Flame had divorced Gina long before he and your mom got together."

"That's a good question," Joshua said. "I really don't know. You'll have to ask my mom that one. Gina's always been pretty nice to me. Maybe mom was embarrassed for her all those years that Gina had the party-girl reputation. And that kooky 'Gina the Gypsy' stuff. Gina always got more publicity than my mom ever did."

Berenger nodded but said, "Well, your mom was a bit of a party girl at one time, too."

"I know. Don't ask me to explain those women." He smiled sheepishly.

"Why do you think Flame stayed on good terms with your mom and not with Gina?"

"Again, I don't know the answer to that one. I think it's because Gina really gave my dad a hard time when they divorced. She tried to take him to the cleaners and he didn't like it. They were pretty nasty to each other, from what I understand."

Berenger remembered the tabloids. It was indeed a messy divorce and it played out much like John and Cynthia Lennon's did in the late sixties.

"As for my mom," Joshua continued, "I guess they simply stayed friends. They respected each other's spaces.

I thought my dad would get really angry at Mom over the IRS business but he didn't. He supported—"

"Hold on," Berenger interrupted. "What IRS business?"

Joshua's expression suddenly went to one of self-reproach. "Oh, uhm, maybe I shouldn't have said anything. Shit. I guess it's not common knowledge."

"What is it, Joshua? Can you tell me?"

He shrugged as if it didn't matter. "Mom's being investigated by the IRS for possible tax evasion." He laughed sardonically. "Don't tell her I told you."

"I won't."

Tax evasion? *Damn,* Berenger thought. Carol Merryman flaunted her wealth. Could it be possible that she might be *embezzling* from Flame Productions? He decided to change the subject.

"So why do you think your dad and Adrian were such enemies?" he asked as tactfully as he could.

Joshua made a face as if to say, "don't you know?" "I don't like to talk about my brother this way but everyone knows he's an asshole. It's like he has this entitlement thing going. He thinks just 'cause he's Flame's son he can have a free ride through life. I could have had that attitude, too, but I don't. I mean, I'm going to college and all that. I want to make my own money and have my own life, not ride on a celebrity's coattails."

"And your father didn't like Adrian's attitude?"

"No way. He didn't like moochers. Dad really liked his money, if you know what I mean. He wasn't a very charitable guy, I'm sorry to say."

"But you got along with him okay?"

"Sure. Yeah, we were friends. But you know, as close as we were, I never saw him. We lived in the same city but I *never* saw him. I mean, he wasn't on tour *that* much. I wish . . . I wish we could have spent more time together, that's all. I'll miss him a lot." Joshua looked away and stared at the cathedral across the street.

"Were you surprised to inherit his estate?"

Joshua turned back and said, "Hell, yes. I thought it would go to Mom." He chuckled slightly. "She did, too."

"Did that cause any problems?"

"Not really. Mom's a good sport. She's still in charge for a year so she'll get something out of it. I don't know, maybe I'll let her have it anyway."

"Why would you do that?"

The young man turned up his hands. "What the hell do I know about rock 'n' roll? I have nothing to do with the music business. I know nothing about it and never wanted to. I want to be a lawyer, not run the great Peter Flame's estate. To tell you the truth, I have no desire whatsoever to be in charge of Flame Productions."

"You could always hire other people to manage it. Then all you have to do is sit back and rake in the dough."

"I know. That's probably what I'll do. But even so, there's still a lot to do. I'd have to make a lot of decisions about what kinds of archival recordings to release and stuff like that. There's tons of unreleased material in the vault. Live concerts, bunches of studio outtakes, whole albums that never saw the light of day . . ."

"That's a potential gold mine."

"You're telling me. And you wouldn't believe all the vultures circling around it, too. I'm getting 'advice' from just about everyone associated with my dad."

"Like who?"

"Well, everyone. Al Patton, my mom, Dave Bristol . . . you name 'em. Anyone who has a vested interest in my father's music from a business standpoint stands to gain from him dying. It's going to be up to me and my mom to control the floodgates."

Berenger finished his pastry and downed the coffee. "Who would want to kill your father?" he asked.

"What do you mean?"

"Do you have any ideas of who'd want to kill him?"

"Adrian did it, Mr. Berenger."

"You're so sure about that?"

"Well . . . yeah. I mean, the cops arrested him and all. There's evidence against him. He must be guilty. They wouldn't have arrested him if there wasn't a case."

"A man is innocent until proven guilty in a court of law, Joshua."

"I know, I know. I'm studying law, remember?"

"Then you should know that police can make mistakes. District attorneys can make mistakes. Adrian's in a fight for his reputation and for his life. You have to understand that we're going to do everything we can to show the court that the prosecution *doesn't* have a case. This thing will never go to trial, Joshua."

"But he *did* it, Mr. Berenger. I know he did."

"How do you know that?"

"Because I know Adrian. He's always said he'd like to kill my dad someday. That's one of the few things he ever said to me. And he said it more than once. Adrian's a mean, spoiled jerk. It's like he hates the world and everyone in it. I'm convinced he certainly has it *in* him to commit murder. And he *hated* my father. Adrian had the motive and the means to do it. Mr. Berenger, I believe the police got the right guy."

12

Band on the Run

(performed by Wings)

Berenger skipped lunch and headed downtown to see Kenny Franklin and the members of Flame's current touring band. Franklin had told him they would be in a midtown recording studio all day long. Berenger decided to take public transportation. He walked to the IRT subway line and figured he'd ride the train to Times Square, get off there, and walk over to Sixth Avenue, formally known as Avenue of the Americas although no one in New York called it that.

Before boarding the train, Berenger phoned Remix and asked him to hack into the IRS server (which he had done on numerous occasions) and get the scoop regarding Joshua's claim that Carol Merryman was being investigated for tax evasion. Remix added it to his "to do" list. Berenger then got on the train and reflected on his meeting with Joshua Duncan. It had gone about as well as he expected. What struck him the most about Joshua was that the young man seemed to be terribly unhappy. This was a kid who had everything—money, opportunities, a bright future—and yet Joshua Duncan exuded an attitude of defeat. Perhaps it was just the lad's introverted personality to which Berenger reacted, but there was shyness and then there was *shyness*. Berenger believed

Joshua to be clinically depressed. Of course, the boy had just lost his father so that might have something to do with it.

Berenger arrived at the studio a little after noon. It was located in a commercial district on Sixth Avenue at Thirty-ninth Street. He went inside and up the flight of stairs to the second floor, into the makeshift lobby, and through the door marked PRIVATE. This led into a corridor that separated the studio and control room from the main office, kitchen/break room, and washrooms. It wasn't a state of the art studio by any means but it had all the necessary accoutrements.

Kenny Franklin sat at the mixing board, puffing on a cigarette and concentrating on a guitar riff that Dewey Wayne was attempting to perform. The other members of the band—Zig Rubel, Corky Clark, and Chas Miller— sat in the studio with Wayne, watching intently and stay- ing silent.

"Hi, Spike," Franklin said, not turning his head. "Come on in, we'll be able to take a break in a minute."

"No rush, Kenny."

Berenger stood and listened. Wayne was playing a Gretsch Electromatic Hollow Body guitar and it sounded good. The piece had a Spanish flamenco feel and Berenger was curious how the rest of the song fit with it.

"Dewey can play," Berenger commented.

"Sure he can," Franklin answered. "He only got to play bass in Flame's band 'cause Flame was the guitarist. Dewey's doing double duty on guitar and bass on these recordings."

"So they're carrying on without Flame?"

"Yeah. Dewey and Zig asked me to come in and act as engineer today. They're trying to put together a new act and wanted to know what I thought."

"Do they have a name?"

"Not yet. But they've got some good material. Stuff Flame would never let them play. We laid down a track this morning that was kick-ass. We're working on number two now. They're hoping to put together a demo with four or five songs and then flog it to managers around town. Al Patton said he'd give it a listen but I don't put too much hope there. He says that to everyone and then never does it."

Wayne finished the riff and asked, "How was that, Kenny?"

Franklin turned on the mike and spoke to the band from the control room. "That was good. I think we should take a lunch break, though. I can tell you're tired, Dewey. Let's have some grub and I bet you'll do a better take after some rest."

"Okay."

The guys came out of the studio and met Franklin and Berenger in the break room. It was equipped with a microwave oven, refrigerator, vending machines, a couple of couches, and two small tables and chairs.

"Hi, Spike," Wayne said. "Whatcha doing here?"

"Hi, Dewey. Sounded good in there."

"Thanks."

"I'm here to ask you guys some questions about Flame, if you don't mind. Kenny agreed to talk to me earlier and I figured I'd kill several birds with one stone, if you know what I mean."

Wayne shrugged. "Sure, I don't mind." He turned to the other band members. "You guys know Spike Berenger?"

Berenger had never officially met the other members but they all knew who he was. After a series of handshakes and "nice to meet you's" the men sat around the room. Two of them retrieved sack lunches

110

from the fridge and another bought a Coke from the vending machine.

"You gonna eat, Kenny?" Miller asked.

"I thought I'd go out and hit McDonald's or something after we talk to Spike."

"I'll go with you."

"This won't take long, will it, Spike?"

Berenger shook his head. "Shouldn't think so. I just have a handful of questions."

"Spike here is working for the defense, just so you know," Franklin explained.

Berenger felt a sudden coolness in the room. He felt obligated to say, "Just 'cause I'm working for Adrian Duncan doesn't mean I don't sympathize with you guys. Flame was a friend of mine, too."

At first no one said anything but then Zig Rubel snorted and replied, "I wouldn't say we were really *friends* with Flame. Would we?"

The others shook their heads.

"What do you mean?" Berenger asked.

"He treated us like second-class citizens for the most part," Rubel continued. "Like he could always go out and get another backup band if he wanted. He was always holding that over our heads."

"Is that true?" Berenger asked Franklin.

The tour manager nodded. "Yeah, Flame was a hard guy to work for. He was a perfectionist when it came to his band."

Chas Miller spoke up. "But it was okay if *he* made mistakes on stage."

The others murmured agreement. Rubel continued, "Look, I probably speak for everyone here. We're sorry about what happened to him, we really are. The guy was a legend and we all had a lot of respect for him.

But . . . well, hell, I don't know. He was getting sloppy, wouldn't you say?"

Dewey Wayne agreed. "Yeah. You were at our last show, weren't you, Spike?"

"No, I'm sorry, I wasn't."

"Oh. Well, Flame was really off that night. He messed up a lot."

Corky Clark chimed in. "No one noticed but us, though. The fans didn't care."

"No, the fans cared more about *what* we were playing rather than how we were playing it," Rubel said.

Berenger used that as a lead-in to his next question. "Are you saying you didn't agree with Flame's current musical direction?"

Rubel shook his head. "I'm not sayin' nothin' like that. We've been playing with Flame for five years and we're happy to have the work. I'm just sayin' the *audience* might have preferred he didn't play the religious stuff."

Berenger addressed all of them. "Is that how all of you feel?"

They shrugged and murmured affirmatively. Chas Miller added, "We were hired guns. We had no vested interest in the band other than a regular paycheck. But now since Flame's gone, we thought—hey, we have something good going here. We click together. Instead of just going our separate ways, why not give it a shot and continue? We're a band and we decided to run with it."

"I take it none of you are members of the Messengers?" Berenger asked.

That elicited more snorts and chuckles. Corky Clark said, "Hey, I'm a Christian but I'm not sure what to call *those* people."

Rubel spoke again. "Actually Flame wanted us to join. That was another thing he hung over our heads. He told me flat out that I needed to join the Messengers during the break between tours or I might not be coming back to the band."

"Really?" Franklin asked.

"He pretty much hinted the same thing to me," Dewey Wayne answered. "He didn't give me an ultimatum like that, though. It was more of a 'I sure wish you guys would join the Messengers and I'd feel a lot better about keeping you in the band if you did.' It was a subtle threat, I guess. I actually went to one of their services to check it out."

"What did you think?" Berenger asked.

"I thought it was bullshit. I mean, I'm not a very religious person to begin with but I believe in God and stuff. I had no idea what they were talking about. They wanted me to sign up and go on a retreat in Jamaica with the group before I could 'fully appreciate' what the Messengers had to say. I didn't want to spend another hour with those freaks, much less go away for a week with them."

"Is that usual?" Berenger inquired. "Going away on a retreat?"

"Yeah, apparently all the new members go to their founding church in Jamaica."

"And Flame went, too?"

Franklin answered him. "Yeah, he went way back at the beginning. Right after he got out of rehab in 2000."

Berenger found that interesting. He'd have to find out more about the Messengers' so-called "retreat."

"All right," he said. "I want each of you to think about this before answering. Is there anything you know that might indicate someone else's guilt in Flame's murder?"

The men looked at each other, shrugged, and shook their heads. Rubel said, "I wasn't surprised when I heard they'd arrested Adrian."

"Me neither."

"Same here."

"Tell me about that night at the last show," Berenger said. "Everything you can remember."

Franklin spoke first, vividly recalling that last concert at the Beacon Theater.

He was overseeing the many tasks associated with pre-show setup. When Franklin saw Dave Bristol come through the stage door accompanied by the other two Flame's Heat members, Brick Bentley and Moe Jenkins, he knew that trouble was brewing. Still, Franklin greeted Bristol as an old friend, just as he should. The two men embraced and slapped each other on the back.

"Dave-o, my man," Franklin had said. "I didn't expect to see you!"

"We've been recording," Bristol explained. "Al said we could drop by. Maybe Flame would let us join him on stage for a number or two."

Franklin frowned. He hated when Al Patton did shit like that. Unfortunately, there was not a whole lot anyone could do to stop one of the most powerful music moguls in the world from doing what he wanted. Like everyone else, Patton was terribly unhappy that Flame disbanded Flame's Heat and geared his music in a different direction.

"I don't know, Dave," Franklin had said. "You know how Flame feels about it."

"Well, can we at least talk to him? Where is he?"

"He's in the dressing room, meditating, or whatever he does in there before a show. Brenda's in there with him, too."

Bristol rolled his eyes. No one had to express the general opinion of Flame's latest girlfriend, the one they blamed for turning Flame into a cult fundamentalist.

"Any of those other Messenger freaks around?" Bristol asked.

"Of course," Franklin said. "They're like groupies. And Flame is their new messiah." He gestured with his head further backstage. "You'll find a couple of 'em outside the dressing room, standing guard."

"Shit," Bristol said. "Well, we'll give it a try." He turned to Bentley and Jenkins and said, "Come on, let's go interrupt the Last Supper."

Franklin continued helping Louis rig the monitor board so the band could hear each other with the in-ear devices. Technology for touring bands had improved immensely in the last ten years. Franklin had been at it since the midseventies, just as Flame had disbanded Hay Fever and gone solo. Franklin stayed on as tour and production manager through the rest of the decade and into the beginning of the Flame's Heat period. Those had been the years, when Flame's Heat was one of the biggest bands in the world. But ever since Flame went religious on everyone, Franklin had considered moving on to work for someone else or perhaps even retiring. At fifty-seven he figured that he was probably too old to be doing this stuff but he truly loved it.

"As soon as you get that working," he told Louis, "you better start the guitar checks." As monitor and guitar tech, Louis was an invaluable member of the stage crew. Flame wanted no one but Louis to touch his precious Hugh Manson custom-made guitar from the Manson brothers' shop in Exeter, UK. Flame's rig had been fairly constant for the last several years but it was a bitch to set up. Pumped through an Ibanez Tube Screamer, which produced less auxiliary noise than most sustainer/compressors, and out of Soldano Decatone amplifiers, Flame's signature sound was one of the things that made him a guitar god. That, and his un-canny songwriting ability.

Ten minutes later, Franklin heard shouts from Flame's dressing room area. Apparently Bristol's request wasn't received very well. When the three musicians walked back past him with their tails between their legs, Bristol simply shook his head at Franklin.

"Sorry, Dave," Franklin muttered. "You still gonna stay for the show?"

Bristol shrugged. "I played with the guy for what, over twenty years, and I still can't get enough. Sure, we'll stay."

"Come to the meet and greet," Franklin said. "You got passes?"

"Yeah."

Berenger listened to Franklin's story with interest.

"So did Dave come to the after-show?"

"No. I didn't see him. But I was pretty busy with strike, so I'm not sure who all was there," Franklin answered.

"Anything else occur before or during the show that might be significant?"

"Flame had an argument with Adrian before Dave and his crew showed up. I could hear shouting but I didn't think it was anything more than what *usually* happens between those two. Adrian and Gina had arrived backstage and went to visit Flame in his dressing room. Flame and Adrian were like oil and water, you know that. Flame didn't care much for Gina either. Oh, and Carol Merryman had breezed in with Joshua as well and the two ex-wives had collided outside the dressing room. The two half-brothers spoke to each other but the women turned up their noses. Seeing the spoils of two failed marriages one right after another couldn't have been a joyous moment for Flame either. Maybe that's why he was off that night."

"Anything else?"

"Well . . . I also heard that Flame and Al Patton had a blowup during the meet and greet. I didn't witness it but I had a feeling something might happen. You see, Patton showed up backstage during the concert."

Flame was nearing the end of "Forever Hot." In a few moments the band would run offstage and wait the obligatory four minutes while the audience screamed for an encore. Franklin noticed that Flame mumbled the lyrics on the third verse, almost as if he had forgotten them. How was that possible? Flame had sung that song at every concert since 1986, when it was a number one hit.

Something was wrong.

"Is he okay?" the voice behind him shouted into his ear, startling Franklin. He turned and saw none other than the hulking presence of Al Patton. His shiny bald head reflected the various colors of the stage lights.

"Hi, Al, how are you?" Franklin managed to shout above the din in the auditorium. "Did you just get here?"

"I'm fine!" Patton yelled back into Franklin's ear. "Flame is off tonight."

"Yeah, I know."

"What's up?"

"Hell if I know!"

"Did Blister Pack show up?" Patton asked.

"Yeah. They're in the audience. Flame and Dave had a big fight before the show."

"Writing credits again?"

"I don't know. I think Dave wanted to go on stage for a number or two. You know, like a reunion. He said you suggested it."

Patton frowned. "Damn, I wish they had. That would have been exciting."

"Flame wouldn't go for it."

"How did the new material go over tonight?"

Franklin shrugged. "Same as always. All they want to hear is the old stuff."

Patton nodded. It was the answer he was expecting. "His next album is gonna tank like the last one," he said.

The song finally ended. The stage manager called the cue for the stage lights to black out and Peter Duncan— aka Peter Flame—ran offstage, followed by Dewey, Corky, Zig, and Chas, the guys that made up his current touring band. He saw Franklin and Patton in the wings and gave Patton a big, sweaty hug.

"Hey Al! Glad you came by!" Flame shouted.

"Sounded great!" Patton managed to yell over the noise.

"What?"

"Sounded great!"

"Oh, thanks!" Flame grabbed a towel from the roadie that stood nearby. The pop star used it to wipe the sweat from his face and neck, and then he grabbed the bottle of mineral water from the roadie's hand. He swigged it down, bent forward with his hands on his knees, and breathed deeply. Performing a rock concert was terribly hard work, especially when one got to be fifty-five years old. Flame was in excellent shape though. Called the "World's Sexiest Man" just after his release from rehab— around the time of his conversion—he had aged well. He knew he could still attract groupies by the dozens, although he had given up that lifestyle when he met Brenda Twist.

The four minutes went by quickly. The stage lights burst back to full as Flame waltzed back to the adoring praise of the sell-out crowd.

"They still love him, though," Franklin said into Patton's ear. "All he has to do is sing one or two of the old songs and he's got 'em back in the palm of his hand."

"Yeah, I know," Patton replied. "I just wish he'd drop that fundamentalist religious shit and get back to what he used to do. You know as well as I do he's not selling like he once did. He's either gonna have to give up the sermons and go back to doing Flame's Heat or Hay Fever material—or even his solo stuff—or he'll find himself without a record contract."

Franklin nodded. Patton had threatened that sort of thing before. Even back when Flame was solo, before the Flame's Heat days. It seemed that Flame did his best work within the context of a band.

"I'll see you later, Kenny," Patton shouted into Franklin's ear as Flame and the band launched into another religious number from his latest album. The audience's response remained at a high level as they tolerated it, knowing full well that Flame would give them one more classic Flame's Heat or Hay Fever tune to close out the concert.

The various answers Berenger received from the band were consistent. Rubel and Wayne shared the dressing room next to Flame's and they had heard the argument between Adrian and his father. They couldn't discern the actual words said, only that they were heated and malicious. Wayne confirmed that Flame also had a not-very-friendly conversation with the Blister Pack boys—Bristol, Bentley, and Jenkins—prior to the fight with Adrian. The entire band agreed that Flame was in a foul mood when the concert began that night.

None of the band members thought that Flame had been using any drugs.

After the concert, they attended the meet and greet with family and friends, as did everyone else. The band members noted the presence of Reverend Theo and the other Messengers, Flame's former wives and their respective sons, Al Patton, and Flame's girlfriend, Brenda Twist. Dewey Wayne thought Brenda had Flame "wrapped around her finger" and couldn't see the attraction. Rubel admitted he thought Brenda to be very pretty but "vacuous."

Each band member left the meet and greet before Flame did. None of them noticed when Adrian departed. Franklin confirmed this because they all came and said good-bye to him on stage.

"I did poke my head into the meet and greet and saw Adrian and Gina briefly," Franklin said. "Adrian was pretty agitated."

The meet and greet was more crowded than usual. As it was the last gig of the American tour, the hallway and rooms backstage were packed with people. Each of the band members had family and friends that had been given passes but most of the crowd was there to see Flame.

Franklin noticed that Flame appeared tired. It was probably a relief to finish the tour and have some time off. Al Patton was there with him and some of the personal assistants were keeping an eye on things. Of course, Brenda and her gang of born-agains were hovering around the star. Franklin moved to return to the stage and supervise the strike, which also gave him a sense of closure. It had been a long three months of mixed venues—mostly theaters that held about five thousand—unlike what it was in the old days when Flame was playing sports arenas.

Gina Tipton and Adrian Duncan were in the hall. Adrian looked angry—his face was flushed and his mother appeared to be trying to calm him down. She looked up and said, "Hi Kenny."

"Gina. Adrian," Franklin said. "Everything all right?"

"Sod off," Adrian said.

"Adrian!" his mother said. She looked at Franklin and explained, "He's a little upset with his father."

Franklin nodded understandingly. "What else is new?" He thought it best to move on, so he did. As he went through the stage door he noticed Adrian pull off the after-show pass that had been stuck on his shirt, wrinkle it up, and throw it on the floor.

Berenger raised his eyebrows. "Are you sure about that? You saw him tear off that pass and throw it on the floor?"

"Yep."

Berenger made a note of that. "Okay," he said. "Kenny, tell me about afterward, when you saw Adrian at Flame's town house."

Franklin recounted how he had found himself in the unenviable position of taking the money to Flame's office in the Village. It was nearly two in the morning. When the cab got him to Flame's street it was probably 2:10 or 2:15.

"He was running from the town house," Franklin said. "At least it looked that way. Where else would he be running from down there at that time of night? He ran right in front of the cab and the driver had to slam on the brakes. I recognized Adrian and even called to him out the window. But he kept on running. I thought it was strange but I forgot about it until I got inside Flame's building. When I . . . when I found Flame, Adrian was the first one I thought of. I told the cops that, too. I hated to do it, but that's the story."

"How did Adrian look? Was he sober?"

"I couldn't tell. To me he just looked scared. Like he'd seen a ghost. The headlights from the cab were shining on him when I saw his face, so he was bathed in this big bright light. I couldn't say whether or not he was sober."

Berenger rubbed his chin. This was a lot of information to absorb.

"Kenny, going back to Dave Bristol for a minute," he said, "how bad do you think the blood was between him and Flame? Bad enough to nurture violence?"

Franklin thought about that and answered, "Yeah. I'd say it was."

13

Boys Don't Cry

(performed by The Cure)

Berenger picked up Suzanne at her apartment building in the East Village, not far from St. Marks Place, where she rented a funky old one bedroom. She had lucked into it when she was heavily into the Goth scene during the late 1980s and then sublet it to her sister when she left New York to travel through the Far East. The timing was perfect—her sister married and moved to Canada with her husband just as Suzanne returned to New York a changed woman. Leaving her alternative lifestyle behind her, Suzanne became a yoga and martial arts practitioner and eventually an instructor for several years in the nineties. Berenger knew that she loved the East Village and still felt at home among the punk and heavy metal crowd that congregated along St. Marks Place. Remnants of the Goth scene remained there, too. She once told him that the boys and girls dressed in black provided her with fond nostalgia for her rebellious era. At one time her short hair was coal black and she had worn pale makeup and black eyeliner and lipstick. There was even a dog collar, a few piercings, and an ankh that hung in her cleavage. Now her hair was back to its natural dark brown, she wore CoverGirl makeup, and she dressed in casual but hip thirty-something fashions.

Since they were going to a music club after the trip to Long Island, that evening Suzanne was dressed in a short black skirt, white camisole, and a blue jean jacket. Her legs were bare. She carried a small classy handbag from Kate Spade. As for Berenger, he had worn sporty khakis, a dark vest, and a white silk shirt.

"You look great," Berenger said as she got in the Altima. "Man, oh man!"

"Oh, hush. You don't look too shabby either," Suzanne replied. "It's nice to see you without blue jeans for a change."

"Baby, you can see me without my blue jeans whenever you'd like."

"Oh, stop. Step on the gas, mister, and let's go."

Berenger slipped XTC's *English Settlement* into the dashboard CD player because he knew Suzanne liked them and then he headed for the Queens Midtown Tunnel. She immediately began to look through the small case of compact discs Berenger kept in the car.

"These are different from what you had here before," she commented.

"Yeah, I change 'em every two or three weeks. I'm a man who likes variety."

"Did you ever see XTC live?"

"Nope. Andy Partridge stopped doing the live shows about the time I started getting into XTC. That was, what, 1982?"

"Yeah. I saw 'em a couple of times in L.A. before I moved here. Once they were on the same bill with Talking Heads. That was a great show."

"I'll bet."

"Gosh, I was, what, eleven years old? My sister and I went to see them and it was fabulous."

"Hey, how are your parents doing?"

"They're fine. They still love Southern California. They keep asking me if I'm ever gonna move back there. I tell 'em 'no.' "

"I guess they weren't too happy when you left home before you were eighteen, huh?"

"You can say that again. As soon as I finished high school, I was gone. Candy had already come east so I stayed with her in that ratty apartment she had in Brooklyn. Since I was staying with my sister my parents didn't mind too much. Little did they know I went out and got that apartment in the East Village a month later. I guess my parents thought maybe Candy'd be a good influence on me."

"Oh, right, I remember. You were a juvenile delinquent when you were a teenager," Berenger said, smiling.

"Yeah, I was a really bad girl, can you believe it? I was always getting in trouble. I damn near didn't finish high school. I wanted to drop out but the court wouldn't let me. That was part of the terms of the plea bargain—I had to finish high school and straighten up my act."

Berenger shook his head. It was hard to imagine the smart, completely together woman beside him sitting in a jail cell—which is what happened to her when she was fifteen years old. A boyfriend had talked her into stealing a car and going for a joy ride with him. Drugs were involved and the pair was caught.

"Whatever happened to, what was his name . . . ?"

"Jerry?"

"Yeah."

"Hell if I know. Mom and Dad wouldn't let me see him anymore after we got busted. I wouldn't be surprised if he's in prison somewhere. I was a bad girl at the time but he was a whole lot badder."

"Well, Suzanne, I must say I think you turned out all right. Look at you now. You're one of the nicest bad girls I know."

She slapped him on the arm. "Oh, stop."

On the way into Long Island, Berenger filled her in on his mother's condition and what to expect.

"I'm sure it's hard for you," she said. "I'm thankful my folks are still okay."

"When's the last time you saw them?"

"I went to L.A. a couple of years ago, remember? But it's been too long. I need to go see them more often. They're not getting any younger."

"How's your sister doing?"

"Candy's fine. I'll need to head up to Toronto sometime soon too and see my new nephew."

"How many does that make?"

"Two nephews and a niece. My sister's the 'Fertile Goddess of the Yukon' or something like that."

"Do I detect a little bitterness in your voice?"

"What do you mean?" She looked at him sideways.

"Are you sorry you're not married and having babies?"

"Are you out of your mind? I'm not ready for that. No way. The beauty of being an aunt is that I can hold the babies for a little while and then give 'em back. That's good enough for me."

"Aw, Suzanne, you'd make a great mom," Berenger said.

"Too late for that now, Spike. My biological clock stopped ticking a couple of years ago."

"I don't believe that. You're, what, thirty-five?"

"Thirty-*eight*."

"You could still get pregnant."

"Why, are you volunteering or something?" She jabbed him in the side.

126

He shrugged. "I seem to remember us fitting together pretty good."

"Yeah, but that was over ten years ago."

"So? We haven't changed that much."

"What is this, Spike, are you flirting with me? I thought this was a business date."

"It is. I'm just saying you could still go for motherhood if you really wanted it. Women a lot older than you have had healthy kids."

"Okay, okay, now let's change the subject."

They spoke about numerous topics, including other employees at Rockin' Security, the absurdity of the country's foreign policy, the merits of the newest CDs they had purchased recently, and what current films were worth seeing. By the time they reached Franklin Village in Hempstead, they were on to whether or not Madonna would be as lasting a sex symbol as Marilyn Monroe.

Berenger led Suzanne inside the building, signed in, and followed the corridors to the Neighborhood, where his mother now resided. Betty Samuels caught up with them, saying, "Mr. Berenger, I'm glad you made it before I left for the day."

"Hello Mrs. Samuels. You remember my colleague Suzanne Prescott?"

The two women shook hands.

"How's my mom?" he asked.

"She's fine but I must warn you she's a little agitated about the move. We brought her to the new room this afternoon after a leisurely walk through the mall. She enjoyed shopping, even though she didn't buy anything nor showed any desire to do so, and we had a nice snack at one of the bakeries there. She kept talking about you, I'm happy to say, although she believes you're still in college."

Berenger chuckled. "I wish."

"She also mentioned a dog named Birdie. At least I think it was a dog."

"Right. Birdie was the Irish setter she owned, gosh, when I was a kid."

"Well, she kept asking about Birdie, wondering if she was all right."

"Oh dear. Birdie's been dead for thirty years."

"I figured as much. At any rate, your mother did notice she was in a new room, even though it looks exactly the same as her old one."

"Well, she's pretty bright. I can't believe the disease has progressed so rapidly that she wouldn't realize she'd been moved."

"Yes, that's probably true. Anyway, it's a lovely room. The only difference is she won't have the run of the building now. She'll get used to it."

"I'm sure she will."

Mrs. Samuels showed him how to punch in the special code on the keypad to get into the Neighborhood— a precaution to keep the residents inside. They found Ann Berkowitz in the television room, where she and three other residents were watching *Chicago* on video.

"Hi, Mom," Berenger said. "How are you this evening?"

She looked up and said, "Spike! You finally came!"

"Sure, I told you I'd come this evening."

"You have to get me out of here. Something's different. Nothing's the same."

"They moved you into a new room, Mom. Don't you like it?"

"No. None of my things are in there."

"What do you mean? All your stuff is in there. They moved everything you have into the new room. Hey, you remember Suzanne? She came to see you, too."

"Hi, Mrs. Berkowitz," Suzanne said. She leaned down and gave the woman a kiss on the cheek.

"Of course I remember my daughter-in-law," the woman said. "How are you, dear? How are the children?"

"Mom, Suzanne's not your daughter-in-law. Suzanne's a colleague of mine. She works where I work."

"Oh? Does that mean you'll be getting married soon?"

"No, Mom. Suzanne's a friend."

"Dear me, what am I thinking? I'm being silly. You're already married," Mrs. Berkowitz said.

"Nope, Mom, wrong again. I used to be married but that was a long time ago. Linda was my wife but we got a divorce."

Mrs. Berkowitz shook her head. "I don't know what's wrong with me. I can't remember things like I used to." She looked at Suzanne and proclaimed, "I graduated in the top ten of my class!"

"That's very impressive, Mrs. Berkowitz," Suzanne said and smiled at Berenger.

"So are you going to get married again?" Mrs. Berkowitz asked her son. "It would be nice to have some grandkids."

"You do have grandkids, Mom. Michael and Pam. Remember? They'll be coming to see you soon, I'm sure. And don't forget Judy, Bill, and Davey—Carl's kids. They live in California. They're your grandkids, too."

"Oh, yes, Carl. I haven't seen Carl in the longest time. I'm going to have to tell Abe to take me to see Carl."

Berenger and Suzanne exchanged looks. *Uh oh.*

"Where is Abe?" Mrs. Berkowitz asked. "Isn't he supposed to pick me up soon?"

"Mom, Abe died, remember?"

"But I just talked to him on the phone. He's supposed to pick me up. We're going to the theater."

129

Berenger decided to try something. "Mom, do you remember *my* dad? Daniel?"

Mrs. Berkowitz scrunched her face. "Daniel. The name sounds familiar. You say he was your father?"

"Yeah. You were married to him before you were married to Abe."

"I was?"

"Uh huh. That's how come you're my mom!"

She laughed at that. "Oh, you'd still be my son no matter who your father is. How is Daniel?"

Sheesh, Berenger thought. "Well, Daniel died, too."

"My, my, we're dropping like flies. At least I still have Abe."

It was hopeless. They tried to steer her onto other topics and eventually got her to show them the new room. Mrs. Samuels was right—it looked exactly like the old one. Berenger made sure his mom had plenty of toilet paper in the bathroom and checked to see that her laundry had been done. Then they sat in the room for a half hour and looked at old photo albums. Mrs. Berkowitz kept going back to pictures of her Irish setter.

"Birdie was a good dog," she said. "I hope she's happy."

"I'm sure she is, Mom."

After a while, Mrs. Berkowitz showed signs of being tired. One of the staff nurses came in to help her get ready for bed, so Berenger and Suzanne said good night.

"I'll be back to see you soon, Mom," he said. He gave her a hug and a kiss and quickly walked out of the Neighborhood. Suzanne quickly said good-bye and rushed to catch up with him.

Outside, Berenger wiped a tear from his face.

"Spike, are you all right?" Suzanne asked.

"Yeah. Sorry. It's just hard to believe she could have deteriorated so quickly."

"I know. It's a horrible disease."

Suzanne gave him a hug and he squeezed her like a bear. When he finally released her, Berenger said, "Come on. It's time to rock 'n' roll."

They walked to the Altima and drove back to the city in silence.

14

Angry Eyes

(performed by Loggins and Messina)

Mortimer's was a relatively new club in West Greenwich Village, a rock 'n' roll venue established to compete with the older, more well-known jazz clubs like the Blue Note and Village Vanguard. The acts ran the gamut from unknowns and local groups to big-name talent. Mortimer's opening night featured none other than Eric Clapton. The place had rapidly become a hot spot and tickets were difficult to come by even when no one famous was playing there.

But Berenger had connections. The owner, Matthew Eisenberg, was a temperamental but savvy promoter who poured his life savings into creating the club, and it paid off. When Berenger managed bands in the eighties, he had worked with Eisenberg on several occasions to book his groups in the New York area. Eisenberg nearly lost his shirt when he tried to put on a festival a la Woodstock. Berenger had helped bail him out with a loan and providing some acts at the last minute when a headliner cancelled. Eisenberg was forever in Berenger's debt.

"Spike! Suzanne!" the entrepreneur shouted when he saw them. Eisenberg was bald, thin, and wore glasses with dark, thick frames. Despite the nerdy appearance, Berenger knew the man to be sharp and unscrupulous in his business dealings. He was well respected in the industry.

Eisenberg gave Berenger a hug and a slap on the back and then pecked Suzanne on the cheek. "You should have let me know you were coming! The place is packed."

"Can you get us a couple of seats at a table, Matt?" Berenger asked.

"I'll see what I can do. Follow me."

He led them through the crowded lobby, quickly got their hands stamped, and found a small round table near the back. "It's not close but it'll have to do. Is it all right?" he asked.

"It's great, Matt, thanks."

"No problem. First drink's on the house. What can I tell the waitress to bring you?"

"I'll have a White Russian," Berenger said. He looked at Suzanne.

"Just a glass of red wine," she answered.

"Oh, and Matt, if you can get word to Dave Bristol that I'm here and I'd like to speak with him and the band after the show, I'd appreciate it."

"Sure thing. Good to see you, Spike." Eisenberg rushed off, found one of the waitresses and gave her the order.

"Is there anyone in this business you don't know?" Suzanne asked.

Berenger scratched his head and said, "Hmm. I've never met Britney Spears, damn it."

She laughed. "She's too young for you."

"She sure doesn't act like it."

The drinks came quickly and Berenger felt his spirits lifting after the rather melancholy drive back to the city from Long Island. His mother's condition normally didn't affect him so strongly but for some reason it was particularly painful that night. Perhaps it was the fact that she couldn't remember his father. Never mind, he told himself. Enjoy the evening.

A local band by the name of Chicago Green opened the show. A four-man jam-band outfit, the members appeared to be just out of high school. Berenger was impressed with their musicianship, though. He thought that they were already good enough to attract some attention. Suzanne found the bass player particularly cute.

After a twenty-minute break, Blister Pack took the stage. Eisenberg introduced the band, announcing it as their debut performance. Dave Bristol, one of the tallest rock stars Berenger had ever known, waved at the crowd and received a standing ovation with catcalls and whistles. Brick Bentley and Moe Jenkins blew kisses and assumed their positions on stage. Without Flame, the trio focused on Jenkins's heavy array of keyboards, Bentley's bass, and Bristol's powerful drumming and vocals. The result was a power-pop jazz-rock fusion extravaganza similar to Flame's Heat but without Flame's distinctive vocals and guitar. Berenger noted that the material was mostly instrumental, which was a good thing because Bristol's voice wasn't made to carry a band.

Half of the ninety-minute set consisted of new stuff that Berenger had never heard. He thought it was damned good, and the way Suzanne was rocking in her seat she apparently enjoyed it as well. The rest of the set was filled out with a couple of early Hay Fever hits and a good deal of Flame's Heat material. Berenger felt the Flame's Heat songs didn't work as well without Flame's guitar and voice. However, the audience was very enthusiastic. It was as if they were witnessing the remaining two Beatles, reunited for a spin-off project. Half of the magic was missing, but what was there was certainly alchemy of sorts.

The encore was Hay Fever's title track from the album *Sneeze* and it brought down the house. No one remained sitting as a swarm of people packed the space in front of the stage. Suzanne stood on her chair and Berenger wrapped his arms around her bare legs to support her. Her skin felt smooth and enticing; he had to force himself to concentrate on the music. For a moment he missed the intimacy he had once enjoyed with her. It would most likely never happen again but it was a nice fantasy.

When the house lights came on, Berenger helped Suzanne down from the chair. She was giddy with excitement. "They were great, weren't they?" she gushed. "What did you think?"

"They're tight," Berenger said. "I would have liked it better if they'd stuck to new material. The old stuff doesn't work as well."

"Oh, don't be a snob. Think of it like new arrangements, or covers, or something. We going backstage?"

"Yeah."

Eisenberg worked his way through the crowd funneling out of the club and approached them. "Did you like it?" he asked.

"Sure did!" Suzanne said.

"Thanks for helping us out, Matt," Berenger said.

"No problem. Come on, Dave's expecting you backstage."

"They coming out to greet their fans?"

"Nah, Dave was never much for that sort of thing. He always left that to Flame, if you'll recall."

"Oh, right."

Eisenberg led them through the door guarded by a

burly bouncer and into the space that served as the wings, which consisted of a couple of dressing rooms and a storage area. Eisenberg knocked on one of the dressing room doors. A shirtless Dave Bristol opened it. He had just emerged from the shower and was dressed only in sweatpants. A good-looking, wiry man in his fifties, Bristol grinned widely when he saw Berenger.

"Hey, how ya doin', Spike?" The two men embraced each other.

"I'm good, Dave. You guys played great."

"Thanks, man." He looked at Suzanne and snapped his fingers. "Suzie, right?"

"Suzanne."

"I knew that. How are you, beautiful?"

"Fine. I really enjoyed the show."

"Good. Come in, come in." He held the door open for them and put on a T-shirt. "Grab a seat and I'll get the other guys." Apparently Bristol rated his own dressing room while Jenkins and Bentley had to share one. Bristol knocked on the other door and told his bandmates to join them.

Eisenberg left the quintet alone with a six-pack of cold Bud. Berenger had met Bentley and Jenkins on a few occasions but wasn't as close to them as he was to Bristol.

"I won't take up too much of your time," Berenger began. "I just have a few questions and want to get some impressions from you guys. As you know, I'm working for Adrian Duncan and his mom. I'm not here to say I think he's innocent or I'm doing my best to get him off. I'm here to gather information and facts to present to his lawyer. It's up to the lawyer to decide what to do and how to present a defense. So please, I'd appreciate your honesty and candor, okay?"

The three men nodded. Bristol took a long drink of beer and then said, "Just don't ask us if we're sorry that Flame got off 'd."

"All right, are you sorry that Flame got off 'd?" Berenger asked.

"I said don't ask us that."

"I'd like to know how you feel about it."

Bristol looked at Jenkins and Bentley. They shrugged as if to say, "Go ahead." Bristol faced Berenger and said, "We hate the guy, Spike. He was asking for it. I'm sorry to say that but it's the honest truth. Don't get me wrong. I loved Flame like a brother, we knew each other a long time, and we went through hell and high water together. But he did some things that will leave permanent scars."

"Besides breaking up Flame's Heat and becoming a fundamentalist cult member?"

Bristol nearly choked on a swallow and said, "Isn't that enough? We're talking about a very lucrative gig that Flame just walked away from. He threw *us* away like we were expendable pieces from some kind of game he was playing. We were discarded, man. Flame's Heat was huge and Flame turned his back on us to do *religious-cult* music! Is that *insane,* or what?"

Berenger shrugged. "I don't know. If he found religion you can't really fault him for that. You have to respect what an artist wants to do with his life."

"Yeah?" Bristol said. "Tell that to Cat Stevens's fans."

Jenkins and Bentley laughed. Berenger smiled and said, "You have a point, I admit. So, tell me. You guys were close to him when he converted. What happened? How do you explain it?"

Jenkins said, "He went crazy, man."

"Yeah, he went plain nuts," Bentley concurred.

"I'll tell you what happened," Bristol continued. "It was that girlfriend of his. Brenda Twat, or whatever her name is."

"Brenda Twist."

"Yeah, I know. She seduced him to the Dark Side, man."

"How did they meet?"

"They met in rehab. Remember Flame went into rehab in 1998?"

"Uh huh."

"Flame's Heat was really big at the time and for some reason Flame was doing every drug he could get his hands on." Bristol looked at the other two guys. "We weren't saints ourselves, but we weren't into the excess that Flame was into. It was like the guy *wanted* to kill himself. I was afraid he'd OD one night and we'd find him on his dressing room floor with a syringe in his arm."

"It was heroin?"

"Yeah, heroin, coke, you name it. He was into the speedball thing, mixing the two of 'em. He drank an awful lot, too. He was pretty bad off. Let's see, he was in and out of rehab two or three times in the early nineties. You guys remember?"

Jenkins answered, "I think it was twice, but he didn't stay long."

"Yeah, twice. Anyway, I was one of the folks who talked him into going in 1998. Me and his wife Carol. Ex-wife, that is. And Al Patton. Actually—hey!" He turned to his colleagues. "Did you guys see Al tonight?"

"No," they answered in unison.

"That bastard! He didn't show for our debut performance! What a prick!" Bristol threw the bottle of Bud against the wall, breaking it. It was an example of his famous temper. Berenger waited for him to cool down a second and then the man resumed talking as if nothing had happened. "Anyway, just about everyone Flame knew pleaded with him to get some help. Finally, there was one night he had to go to the emergency room. It was after one of our gigs in England—Liverpool. He really did OD and had to be rushed to the hospital. We were lucky to keep it out of the newspapers. I think Al Patton paid off some people to keep it quiet. It was touch and go but Flame got through it. We had to cancel some shows. Oh, and the police there charged him with possession of narcotics, too. It was a mess. I don't think they were gonna let Flame's Heat return to the UK. Not that it mattered, because we didn't play in public again after that. Flame went into rehab for good and came out a changed man."

"And Brenda was in the rehab place with him?"

"That's where they met. Apparently she was a recovering addict, too."

"How long was he there?"

Bentley said, "Five months, I think. I really don't know."

Bristol continued. "Well, he was in and out of rehab all through '98 and '99. It was after the new millennium, in 2000, when I was sure Flame was sober and truly out. So I went to see him, you know, to find out what we were gonna do. During those years we weren't recording in the midnineties, Al was happy to release a live album and a CD of B-sides and outtakes, but we needed to record something new. Flame told me the band was finished and he was doing something on his own. He gave me a Bible and told me to read it and join him in his new venture, which was singing for Jesus. I couldn't believe it. I asked him, 'What, are you nuts? Have you gone crazy, Flame?' And he said, 'Maybe I have, maybe I haven't. I just know that a new path has been laid out for me and I must follow it.' "

"Was that before or after he went to Jamaica?" Jenkins asked.

"That was after," Bristol replied.

"Tell me about that," Berenger suggested.

"Right after he got out of rehab for the last time he went to Jamaica with Brenda and the rest of those Messengers. He was there a week or two, I can't remember. They must have brainwashed him or something, because he gave them a shitload of money and returned to New York all Christlike and reflective. I had truly never seen Flame act so weird. He was like an automaton. Whatever Brenda said to do, he'd do it. They started living together and that was it. Bye-bye Flame's Heat. I tell you why her name is Brenda Twist—she *twisted* his mind. That's what happened."

Suzanne spoke up. "I've been to the Messengers' church. I find their philosophy a little extreme but I don't think they're particularly dangerous. Do you?"

"Yeah, I do. I think they're fucking evil. They have a hidden agenda, I know they do," Bristol said.

"Like what?" Berenger asked.

"Hell, I don't know. Taking your money. That's one thing they do. I can't tell you how much money Flame pumped into them. And what did he get out of it? You tell me."

"Peace of mind? Religious comfort?" Berenger proposed.

Bristol waved his hands in the air and rolled his eyes. "Whatever," he said.

"So I guess things deteriorated between the two of you then?"

"Yeah, you could say that. Actually, you know Flame and I never got along all that great as friends. We really clicked on stage and in the studio. Musically, he was the other half of my soul. I suppose we had to get away from each other every now and then. After Hay Fever split up I couldn't stand the guy. I wanted nothing to do with him. But then, a few years of water under the bridge, we got back together and did Flame's Heat. And for a few more years that was the best music I think I've ever done."

"Tell me about the legal problems you had with Flame."

Bristol's eyes flared angrily. "Had? I still *have* them. I'm suing his estate. The songs on the last three Flame's Heat albums are all credited to Flame. I wrote half of them and co-wrote another quarter. I should be getting composer royalties and I'm not."

Berenger looked at Jenkins and Bentley. "Do you agree with that?"

Obviously uncomfortable with the question in front of Bristol, they reluctantly agreed. "Flame was certainly stingy with the writing credits," was the most Jenkins would commit to.

"I think the kicker was when we wanted to call ourselves Hay Fever," Bristol said. "Moe and Brick and I wanted to stay together. We couldn't very well call ourselves Flame's Heat without Flame, so I thought, why not bring back Hay Fever? Hay Fever was huge in the seventies. It could be like a resurrected, reinvented Hay Fever. With me at the helm, and with Moe and Brick here, it could really work. The thing is, Flame owned the name Hay Fever. How he managed to finagle that legally, I don't know. I was under the impression that the name was owned by Flame, Greg Patterson, and me."

Berenger turned to Suzanne and said, "Greg Patterson was Hay Fever's bassist. He died of an overdose, when was it? Seventy-seven?"

"Seventy-six," Bristol said. "Greg went into a super depression when Flame disbanded Hay Fever. Anyway, it turned out Flame had somehow bent the contracts and Al Patton backed him up. We couldn't use the name Hay Fever, so we call ourselves Blister Pack."

"It's a good name," Suzanne said.

"I guess. I think we'd make more of a splash with 'The Return of Hay Fever.'"

"Are you going to play at Flame's memorial service?"

"Yeah, Carol asked us to do that. That was nice of her."

"Good. Now let's switch topics a little. Tell me about the last night you saw Flame."

Bristol said, "The three of us went to the Beacon and showed up just after sound check. Al Patton and I had spoken earlier in the week and he suggested we just show up and maybe Flame would let us perform with him, you know, as a one-off thing. I didn't think he'd do it and wasn't too enthusiastic, but we wanted to stay on Al's good side. He's working out our recording deal. So we go see Flame in his dressing room. Brenda's there and they're meditating or something. He wasn't happy to see us. I asked if we could join him onstage for a number or two and he got all pissed off and started yelling. Totally out of control and inappropriate."

"Yeah, it was weird," Jenkins said. "It was like we'd just asked him to shoot his dog or something."

"We heard later he had a big fight with Adrian before we showed up, so that may have had something to do with it," Bristol continued. "Still, he could have treated us with a little more respect. Anyway, we got into a huge shouting match. I said, 'Fuck this,' and we left. I can't believe we actually stayed for the show. I sure didn't want to but we did."

"Were you invited to the meet and greet?"

"We had passes but we didn't go. In fact, Flame had told us he didn't want to see us again, if you can believe that." Bristol turned to the other two. "Why *did* we stay for the show?"

Jenkins and Bentley shrugged. "I dunno," Jenkins said. "Curiosity?"

"Whatever. I thought the show sucked, by the way. Flame gave one of the worst performances I'd ever seen, and that's including all the times he was strung out during Flame's Heat. Anyway, we left the Beacon that night with really bad vibes."

"Did you see Adrian at the venue that night?"

"Yeah, we did. We were leaving the auditorium and we saw Adrian and Gina. Gina said hello and asked if we were coming backstage. I told her we weren't welcome. Adrian didn't say a word. He was his usual surly self."

"You know Gina thinks you're a good suspect in Flame's murder?"

Bristol rolled his eyes again. "The police interviewed me three fucking times. The third time I had to go down to the goddamned police station. It was awful. Look, I've been angry enough at Flame to wanna wring his neck, but I'm not a murderer. And I know you're gonna say my temper is legendary. I know. *Rolling Stone* did a lot to perpetuate that little myth. There was that article chronicling the time I got into a fight with Stephen Stills and wrecked a room at the Sheraton. I know."

"And you've been arrested a few times for, uhm, disorderly conduct."

"Rub it in, Spike, rub it in. Okay, I like a brawl every now and then. It still doesn't mean I'd kill the guy. I would have liked to punch his lights out a couple of times, but that's about it."

"Do you think Adrian did it?" Berenger asked.

"How should I know? Adrian really looked pissed off that night. Maybe he did."

"Sounds to me like Flame had the ability to piss you off really good, too."

"Shit," Bristol said. "Peter Flame could piss off a *lot* of people in one night."

As if on cue, what sounded like a sonic boom rocked the dressing room. At first Berenger thought a bomb had exploded in the club. He immediately recalled the package of guitar strings and the creepy threatening phone message he had received.

"What the hell was that?" Jenkins shouted. Amidst curses and exclamations, the band members jumped up and ran to the door. Berenger grabbed Suzanne's hand, prepared to lead her to safety if that was indeed what was required.

Then the noise of harsh electric guitars penetrated the walls. Something was going on outside the building. Eisenberg stuck his head in the door. "Better stay put. The Jimmys are here. They just decided to put on a show in front of the club. In five minutes the area's gonna be chaos!"

Suzanne squeezed Berenger's hand. "I want to *see!*"

Berenger agreed. He led her out of the dressing room, through the stage door and into a swarming mass of hyped-up, unpredictable young people filling the street.

15

Wild in the Streets

(performed by The Circle Jerks)

The noise was almost unbearable. The discordant, thrash-metal guitars pierced the air and the heavy, thumping bass shook the ground below them. Whoever was drumming had double-kick pedals and was beating the two bass drums with a ferocity that would put Mike Portnoy to shame. The crowd that had gathered consisted of older teenagers and twenty-somethings. Many of them were the stereotypical punk fans—shaved heads or spiked, colored hair, tattoos, piercings, dog collars—and they had formed a makeshift mosh pit that covered the width of the street. Berenger led Suzanne through the crowd so they could get a closer look at the band. He held her tightly, and thanks to his large frame he was able to push past the mayhem.

There were three musicians—a guitarist, bass player, and drummer. They wore the "Leatherface"-style masks and were dressed in tattered clothing. A decrepit white van had parked sideways in the middle of the street, no doubt the vehicle that had carried the two amplifiers and drums to the site. Several other Jimmys, also in masks and holding baseball bats, stood in front of the building where the power cords were plugged just in case someone got the bright idea to try and cut off the juice.

The guitarist approached the one microphone stand and screamed into the mike. The so-called lyrics—the ones that were discernable—implored the audience to break storefront windows and set the street on fire.

Berenger and Suzanne stood in the crowd and watched, simultaneously fascinated and repelled. *My God*, Berenger thought. These guys were criminals but *this was what rock 'n' roll was all about!* It was pulling the art form back to its basic, primitive roots—raw, energetic, and visceral. Not to mention dangerous. No wonder the city had outlawed these band gangs. The young people in the audience were already worked up to a fever pitch and were capable of doing anything. Berenger knew he should get Suzanne out of there but he was too entranced by the spectacle to move.

"This is *incredible!*" she shouted into his ear. All he could do was nod in agreement. Nevertheless, he kept his eyes moving around the area, anticipating anything unexpected, for here he was—standing in the midst of a bunch of Jimmys. The death threat weighed heavily on his mind. As Berenger scanned the scene he noticed none other than Dave Bristol standing by the white van, apparently conversing with one of the Jimmys' road crew, a man also wearing a mask. Bristol and the Jimmy leaned into each other, talking into the other's ears, and then Berenger noticed the Jimmy passing something to Bristol. Bristol slapped the man on the back and took off. Berenger wanted to follow him but there was no way he could break away from the tightly packed crowd in time.

The roadie then stepped in front of the bass player and began to ignite firecrackers with a cigarette lighter. He tossed them one at a time into the crowd, where they exploded with surprising force. Berenger assumed they were Black Cats—basically noisemakers but they had the potential to be harmful if one went off too closely to someone.

"Come on!" Berenger shouted. "Let's get out of here!"

"No, wait!" Suzanne was digging the excitement. He figured it must appeal to the 1980s Goth in her. Nevertheless, he pulled her toward the sidewalk where they would be out of the range of the firecrackers.

The band launched into a second song. Berenger figured they had about five minutes left before the police arrived. He expected to hear sirens at any moment but instead the sound of motorcycles with no mufflers nearly drowned out the heavily amplified guitar.

"Oh shit," he muttered.

The Cuzzins, clad in black leather jackets and black Zorro masks, arrived on supercharged bikes with spectacular fanfare. About twenty of them appeared on the other side of the white van and then they revved their engines and zoomed headlong into the stage area. One bike plowed into the guitarist, knocking him off his feet and flinging his guitar into the air. The resulting feedback and metal-crunching crash it made through the Peavey amp was akin to the sound of a wrecking ball. The bass player, suddenly aware of what was happening, stopped playing and swung his bass around to slam it into one of the Cuzzins, propelling him off his bike. The Jimmys' drummer picked up his snare and threw it at another Cuzzin, then drew a handgun from a holster he wore behind his back. He shot into the air, causing many in the crowd to scream. But the gunfire also inspired a greater number of people to cheer. The next thing Berenger knew, the glass window in front of Mortimer's shattered.

"Run!" he shouted to Suzanne. He grabbed her hand and pulled her down the street away from the melee, but they had to stop when he saw that a group of Jimmys had materialized behind the crowd. The gang had surrounded the perimeter of the audience and each member carried a baseball bat. Berenger and Suzanne were trapped with the rest of the crowd, which unfortunately now stood dead between the two rival groups. Before anyone could disperse, the Jimmys and the Cuzzins converged into the mass of humanity. With no regard for the innocent bystanders in the way, the gang members swung bats, clubs, and chains, aiming to maim or perhaps kill constituents of the opposite team.

"Spike, look out!" Suzanne shouted. Berenger turned in time to see a five-foot length of heavy chain swinging toward him. He instinctively ducked, pulling Suzanne down with him. The chain, wielded by a Jimmy and meant for a Cuzzin standing on the other side of the couple, missed its target and hit another audience member instead. The man cried in pain and fell to the ground as blood gushed from the wounds on his face.

On their hands and knees, the couple moved through the rampaging throng, but by being that close to the ground they were in more danger of being trampled. Better to stand and take their chances. Berenger helped Suzanne up and pushed his way through, but a Jimmy with a bat blocked the way to the sidewalk. He grinned at Berenger and apparently decided that any target was as good as a Cuzzin. He raised the bat high and Suzanne screamed. Berenger summoned what he remembered from his training as a CID special agent and immediately attacked his opponent with a *Mawashi-geri* "roundhouse" karate kick. He sidestepped the Jimmy, twisted his hips in a circular motion so that the ball of his foot swung inward at a right angle to the man's body. The blow hit the Jimmy squarely in the chest, knocking him backward. He dropped the bat before it could do any damage. Berenger followed through with his right fist, punching the man hard on the chin. The Jimmy fell to the ground, clearing the way for the couple to escape.

They ran to the sidewalk and hugged the wall as they moved down the street. By now they could hear police sirens growing louder. As Berenger and Suzanne turned the corner onto Seventh Avenue, three patrol cars soared past them and headed toward the brawl. The riot squad wouldn't be far behind.

"Damn, Spike, you sure know how to show a girl a good time," Suzanne said breathlessly. "I haven't had this much fun since I threw up at Coney Island."

He laughed. "You okay? You aren't hurt are you?"

"Nah. What about you?"

"My knuckles are a little sore from hitting that guy but that's just because I'm not used to it. I'm fine."

They were a bit stunned from the excitement but managed to walk quickly to the parking garage where he had left his Altima. It was a relatively new three-story structure that had been built to accommodate the overpopulated Village streets. The car was on the top level and Berenger had paid for the space when they first arrived.

He held the stairway door open for Suzanne and she went through. "We really could have been hurt badly, huh?" she said.

"Yeah. I should have got you out of there sooner."

"Don't worry about it."

As he followed her up the stairs, Berenger asked, "By the way, did you see Dave Bristol outside by the Jimmys' van?"

"No. Was he there?"

"Yeah. Looked like he was making some kind of transaction with one of their roadies."

"Must be where he gets his drugs. The Jimmys like to sell to rock stars, don't they?"

"Yeah."

They got to the third-floor landing and opened the door. All the parking spaces were full and the Altima was at the other end of the level. They walked toward the car as Suzanne said, "He seemed pretty together tonight, didn't you think?"

"He did. And he was nice, too. Sometimes Dave can be a curmudgeon and a half."

"So I've heard. I tell you, Spike, when those—"

BLAM!

The sound of gunfire interrupted her and Berenger felt the hot stream of the bullet sear the air in front of his face.

"Get down!" he shouted. The couple leaped forward and hit the pavement. Berenger immediately rolled toward her and covered her body. He then quickly turned his head and looked in the direction from where the shot was fired. A figure darted along the far wall, moving into the shadows beneath a section of burned-out ceiling lights. Was it a Jimmy?

"Over there, hurry!" he whispered, pointing to the cramped space between two vehicles to their left. Suzanne scrambled over, her eyes wide with fright. Berenger snaked across the floor behind her as another gunshot echoed through the garage. The bullet hit dangerously close to Berenger's side, chipping fragments off the pavement. The round ricocheted and smashed a headlight on a Range Rover next to where they were lying. Berenger pushed Suzanne beneath the SUV and then got to his knees.

"What are you doing?" she asked. "Get under here!"

"I have to see who that fucker is!"

"Don't!"

But Berenger ignored her. He desperately wished he had his weapon with him. He normally used a Smith & Wesson Model 638 "Bodyguard AirWeight" in a .38 Special with a snubbie barrel or a Kahr P9 semi-automatic, but Berenger rarely carried a handgun on the job. Nine times out of ten there was never a need to be armed. He did have a Class-G license that piggybacked his private investigator Class-C license and that allowed him to carry the gun in most states. Because Berenger knew the New York City mayor personally, he had a special permit to carry the weapon in Manhattan—which was usually taboo for most PIs. In fact, it normally took an act of God to get a firearm permit for New York City—but a special relationship with the mayor happened to be just as good. Berenger had to pay a small fortune for the permit but it was worth it.

Unfortunately, that didn't do an awful lot of good at the moment.

Berenger carefully peered over the Range Rover's hood and scanned the shadows on the other side of the level. Nothing.

"I know you're there!" he shouted. "Why don't you come out and show your face like a man? We'll settle this without your puny popgun!"

"Spike!"

"What?" He turned to Suzanne and was astonished to find her holding a Guardian 380 semiautomatic.

"Can you use this?" she asked.

"What the hell are you doing with *that?*" he blurted.

"Hey, it fits nicely in my Kate Spade handbag," she said. "I never go anywhere without it."

"Damn, Suzanne, do you have a permit to carry that thing?"

The sniper fired another round. The Range Rover's windshield shattered. Berenger ducked out of view.

"Well . . . yes and no," Suzanne answered. "Look, do you want it or not?"

Berenger took it, tested the gun's weight by transferring it from one hand to the other, and then gripped it firmly in his right. It was definitely a woman's handgun, lightweight and compact, less than five inches in overall length and less than four inches in height. It held seven .380-caliber rounds. Without another second's hesitation, he rose, stretched his arms over the SUV's hood, and aimed the Guardian in the direction of the shadows. He squeezed the trigger twice. The rounds hit the far concrete wall with dull, reverberating thuds.

"Two can play your game, pal!" he shouted.

Suddenly the figure bolted from the shadows and ran toward the stairwell door. Berenger took a bead on the running man but it was too late. The sniper burst through the door and was gone. Berenger wanted the guy's hide, so he angrily leaped from his cover and bolted across the floor to the stairwell. He flattened his back to the wall next to the door and took a breath. Using commando tactics, he grabbed the knob, thrust the door open, and assumed a squatting firing stance. The landing was empty.

"Where are you, you bastard?"

He moved inside and looked down the stairwell. Something was on the steps a flight below. Berenger slowly descended to the next landing and stooped to pick up what the shooter had left behind.

It was a Jimmy mask.

16

For What It's Worth

(performed by Buffalo Springfield)

Berenger's appointment with Carol Merryman was to take place at 11:00 in the morning, so when Berenger got up he didn't bother going into the office. He phoned in and discovered that Suzanne had also left word that she'd be in late.

It had been an interesting evening, to say the least. After the incident at the parking garage, Berenger decided not to involve the police. That would just complicate his investigation. He took the Jimmy mask with him and delivered Suzanne to her home. They sat in his car in front of her building for nearly a half hour talking about the case, the trouble she could get into by carrying a handgun in Manhattan without the proper permit, the street brawl, Berenger's mother, and Suzanne's love life. Regarding the latter, she had said it was nonexistent. Berenger reciprocated, telling her that he hadn't been on a real "date" in months. Suzanne must have sensed where the conversation was heading so she said she was tired and excused herself. Berenger let her go and watched her long legs move up the steps of her building. He drove home wondering what might have happened between them a decade ago if he hadn't broken off their relationship. Would it have lasted? He kept telling himself it most likely wouldn't have. Suzanne had been on the rebound. The love of her life, drummer Elvin Blake, had died of an overdose and Rockin' Security was hired to investigate the circumstances. Berenger would never forget walking into Blake's apartment and seeing Suzanne for the first time. She had been crying for hours, understandably distraught, and yet she was one of the most beautiful creatures he had ever seen. Two months later they were dating. It lasted approximately five months and Berenger felt the need to break it off. He still wondered why. A year passed, he and Suzanne remained friends, and eventually he asked her to work for him.

Before going to bed Berenger berated himself for playing the "what if" game. That was always a no-win situation.

A reasonable amount of sleep and the new morning cast a different light on things. He put the previous night out of his mind as he phoned Remix to ask if he'd found out anything about Carol Merryman's troubles with the IRS.

"Yeah, she's definitely being audited," Remix told him. "I couldn't find out a whole lot, but she's got income that isn't substantiated. Apparently she had something like $250,000 in her bank account last year that she was unable to account for."

"Do you think she might have been stealing from Flame Productions?" Berenger asked.

"That's certainly the easiest way she could have gotten it. But who knows?"

"Thanks, Remix."

At the appointed time, Berenger showed up at Carol's building. She lived in an exclusive apartment building on Madison Avenue and Eighty-second and could certainly afford to do so. Berenger understood her divorce settlement to be in the millions and she continued to make money working for Flame since the split up. Why would she feel the need to steal, if that was indeed what was going on?

Her door was open when he reached the fourteenth floor where she lived.

"Carol?" he called.

"Come in, Spike. I'll be right there!"

He went inside and marveled at the decor. The place was adorned with artwork and sculpture, a white grand piano, and ultrachic furniture that looked as if it came out of the Museum of Modern Art. The piano supposedly once belonged to Noel Coward or Cole Porter, he couldn't remember which.

"Nice place, Carol," he called.

"Make yourself at home." Her voice came from the bedroom. "Fix yourself a drink if you want one."

Berenger declined the invitation and instead went to the bookcase to examine the multitude of CDs and record albums. He couldn't help but notice the prominent display of Flame's entire works—not only U.S. releases but also copies of every official foreign release since the beginning of his career. It was an impressive collection.

Carol entered the room, dressed exquisitely in a striking black and gray business suit that must have come from some high-priced Fifth Avenue shop. She looked like a million bucks and could have appeared in any of the big fashion mags. She carried a garment bag that she draped over a chair.

"I'm sorry, but this will have to be short, Spike," she said, slightly breathlessly. "I have a lunch meeting with Al Patton that I couldn't move and then I have to rush over to the Music Box for some last minute arrangements."

That's right, Berenger remembered. Flame's star-studded memorial service was later in the evening, scheduled to take place at a rented Broadway theater.

"We could reschedule for another time," he said.

"No, no, let's get this over with." She stopped in front of a mirror near the front door, adjusted her skirt and examined her makeup, and then turned to face him.

"You look very nice, Carol," he said.

"Thank you, Spike. You know the press will be all over me today. I don't think I'll have time to come back and change so I'm bringing my gown with me. I hope I can stay together for the rest of the day." She gestured to a leather sofa. "Please sit down." She took a chair at a right angle from the sofa.

"I'd love to attend the service tonight, Carol," Berenger said. "I hope I'm not being too forward but—"

"Oh, Spike, just yesterday I realized you weren't on the invite list. I had a pair of tickets messengered to your office this morning."

"Carol, you didn't have—"

"It was an oversight. And please don't argue with me. You're on the guest list."

"That's very kind of you. Thank you very much."

"You're welcome. Now. How can I help you?" She looked up and smiled at him. Ever the glamour queen, Carol Merryman was well aware that she could break down the defenses of nearly any man she set her sights upon.

"Carol, we've known each other a long time, but since you and Flame were divorced I haven't run into you all that often. I'd like to know a little about the divorce itself—why it happened and so forth—and what your relationship with Flame has been like since then."

She took a breath and began. "Well, gee. We got married in 1982. The marriage was a close one until, oh, I'd say about 1983 or 1984, just after Flame's Heat started making it big. Then Flame's attention was focused on other things. We rarely saw each other after that. Flame was always on tour and he didn't seem to want me on tour with him. Joshua was an infant then and Flame didn't like having us around except under very controlled circumstances. So Joshua and I stayed at home while Flame traveled the world. Over and over. When he *was* home, he was either busy in the recording studio or he was getting stoned. The drugs started happening on a more frequent basis during those years. It didn't get really bad until after the divorce, but it was beginning to be a problem. Anyway, in 1987, we mutually decided to call it quits. For 'incompatibility reasons' was the official line. And that's the story."

"You had a very amicable divorce."

"Yeah, I guess we did. We had an understanding. You see, I knew Flame was cheating on me and stuff. He still believed he was twenty-five years old and was entitled to live the decadent life of a rock star. I caught him in bed with two teenaged girls one night and I suppose that was the last straw. He actually wanted me to join them but I walked out. So I told him I'd let him live the life he wanted as long as I could still be a part of it. And I wanted him to be a part of Joshua's life. I wanted him to be close to us, and if that meant giving him back his freedom, then I was willing to do it. So we worked out a deal. His lawyer and my lawyer did the work and everything came out okay. I got enough money to live on for the rest of my life and Joshua got a substantial trust, and I was satisfied with that. I also wanted to be involved in Flame's company—which was the one sticking point—but my lawyer was good. I got the title of vice president of Flame Productions. I suppose I'll continue to enjoy that title even after Joshua takes over next year."

"You got a good deal, all right. I guess he didn't mind you seeing other men and stuff?"

"He never said anything about it. I was seeing other men before our divorce was final, but it was nothing compared to what *he* was doing while we were still married."

"How come you never remarried?"

She laughed. "Who needs that, Spike? I've got everything I want. If I want some companionship for a brief period of time, it's not hard to find. I'm not looking for anything permanent anymore."

"So how much input did you actually have in what Flame was doing?" Berenger asked.

"Not much. None, really. I went to a board of directors meeting once in a blue moon and usually sat there listening to Flame argue with Al Patton. Now that Flame is gone, though, I'll be a bigger part of the decision-making process. There's a ton of stuff that has to be settled, so I'll probably be having some knockdown drag-outs with Al in the coming weeks. That's what we're meeting about this afternoon. It's a preliminary 'this is what we have to talk about' meeting. I wish he wasn't doing it today of all days, but there's not a lot you can say to Al Patton. He's who he is."

"How do you feel about Joshua being named to take over the company and owning everything?"

Carol was silent for a moment and then said, "At first I was hurt. Something inside me thought he'd give it to me. But now, rationally, I see that was impossible. There's no way he would do that. So I was very grateful he gave it to Joshua. Joshua's his son, after all."

"So is Adrian," Berenger said.

Carol made a face. "Adrian has *never* been a son to Flame. Flame never considered him to be a son."

"Why not?"

"Because Adrian hated him. Gosh, Spike, you know Adrian. He's a hateful, unpleasant person. I don't think I've *ever* seen him smile or laugh. It's as if he expects the world to be handed to him. He resented me and especially looked down his nose at Joshua. I'm really not surprised he's standing trial for killing his father. It's not a surprise at all."

Berenger thought it best to steer the conversation away from Adrian. "I had a nice talk with Joshua yesterday."

"Yes, he told me."

"He was very cooperative. One thing I wanted to ask you, though—are you aware that he's not really too excited about taking over Flame Productions?"

"Yes. He'll get over that, though. I think it's just an overwhelming proposition for him."

"But if he'd rather be a lawyer—"

"This will satisfy his early craving to be a musician like his father. He just doesn't realize it yet."

"Huh?" Berenger was confused. "What do you mean?"

"The music thing didn't work out for Joshua. He's always been angry about that."

"Hold on. I thought Joshua had no interest whatsoever in the music business."

"That's what he says now. When he was young—oh, junior high school and early high school age—he wanted to be a musician, too. Flame put a stop to that. Flame had a bad experience with Adrian over the music business and didn't want that to become a rift between them. So Flame nipped it in the bud. He forbade Joshua from any kind of musical aspirations. Joshua was angry about it at first but he quickly got over it. I think he realized what a cutthroat business it is. So he went into law."

Berenger was surprised. Joshua didn't mention this at all. Was it because it was simply no longer an issue, or was the young man deliberately keeping it from him? In fact, Joshua had told Berenger he "never wanted to know" anything about the music business. Was it a lie?

Carol kept talking. "So, for the next year, I'll continue to run the company and Joshua will learn the ropes. I hope by the time I hand over the reins he'll be fully indoctrinated and excited about it." She smiled and shook her head. "You know, Josh can do an *awesome* impression of Flame. He can sound just like him. He's got the voice inflections down perfectly. But I guess he won't be doing that anymore. You could never get him to do it in public anyway. He's always been so shy."

Berenger was still trying to understand the rift between Flame and his sons. "Why did Flame oppose his kids being in music? What's the big deal?"

"You know, I really don't have an answer to that," Carol said. "Gina pushed Adrian into it and Flame didn't like that. Maybe Flame had such a bad time with Adrian that it soured him forever."

"I take it you and Gina don't get along too well."

Carol made a sour face. "Gina Tipton's a calculating bitch. Sorry, Spike, I know you were sleeping with her at one time, but that's what I think."

Berenger said, "That was a long time ago, Carol. It was nothing."

"I don't really care, Spike," she said. "I think it's 'cause of her that Flame could never really commit fully to another woman."

"He seems to have done so with Brenda."

"Oh, *please*. Brenda Twist gives me the creeps. You knew Flame. Can you imagine him in a million years being with a girl like her? 'Miss Squeaky-Clean Bible-thumper'? It's a big fat mystery, if you ask me. I think those Messengers brainwashed Flame somehow. Whatever happened to him in rehab and shortly afterward changed him. He may have got off the drugs but I can't honestly say he was a better person."

She paused and shook her head. "Shit, what am I saying? Here it is the day of his memorial service and I'm putting him down. I loved Flame, Spike. I suppose I still do, for what it's worth. I still can't believe he was . . . murdered."

"Carol, are there any other possible suspects in your mind other than Adrian?"

"No. Adrian did it. It's so obvious."

"You don't think the Messengers might be involved? Or Dave Bristol and his buddies?"

"Dave and Flame always ruffled each other's feathers but I don't for one minute believe Dave could do something like that. As for the Messengers, well, I just don't understand them. I'll never comprehend why Flame turned religious. He never told me, even when I asked. He'd just quote some scripture and say he 'found the light' or some crap like that. I finally gave up asking. Flame always went his own way and that was just another chapter in his life. It's too bad we'll never see what the *next* chapter would have been."

Berenger rubbed his beard. "Can you tell me about that last night at the Beacon Theater? The meet and greet? What do you remember?"

"Hmmm, well let's see. Joshua and I went to the aftershow. I recall trying to get closer to Flame but I was frustrated by the horde of bloodsuckers around him. They call themselves Christians but they aren't *Christians* at all. The Messengers pervert the tenets of Christianity and they've become more like one of those bizarre cults, you know, like the ones that eventually committed mass suicide. Brenda always manages to get passes for a dozen of the Messengers whenever the band plays in town. I tell you, I hate that little bitch. Brenda is so unbelievably *straight,* crystal clean and all-American, a little Snow White. In the old days he always went for the bad girls. I suppose I was one of those once but people grow up, right? After Joshua was born and things fell apart with the marriage, what can I say, I cleaned up my act.

"Anyway, Joshua was busy chatting up one of the girls from the Messengers. He was looking down and smiling in that 'Gosh, ma'am,' way of his that women find cute. I may be his mother but I think Joshua is a real catch—it's too bad he's so shy and introverted. I did my best to get him to be more socially active, but all Joshua wants to do is finish his studies at Columbia and get a law degree.

"I tried to get closer to Flame and at least tell him I enjoyed the show. But Brenda was holding on to his arm, smiling like a saint. Reverend Theo was standing away from his flock, watching with that pleased expression on his face. That man has the widest grin of anyone I've ever known. He does have a lot of charisma, I'll say that for him. It's practically impossible not to like the guy, even though he exudes that creepy holy vibe that makes us nonreligious people uncomfortable. Flame was sold on the reverend, that much is certain. There's no telling how much money Flame donated to the Messengers.

"I finally decided to leave. I couldn't get in a word to Flame, and besides, why should I need to? I could contact him any time—I'm one of the privileged ones." At that she laughed sardonically. "So I walked over to

Joshua and interrupted his conversation with the young lady. I told him I was leaving and asked him if he wanted a ride uptown. He must have thought he was about to get lucky so he refused. He said he'd catch the subway. So I walked out. I do remember turning and glancing back at Flame. He had a glazed look in his eyes as all those born-again sycophants continued to pay homage to him. I felt disgusted and left the building."

"Do you know what time Joshua left?"

"No."

Berenger decided to take a chance and pop the question. "So this IRS audit you're going through has nothing to do with Flame or his company, does it?"

Carol's eyes widened. "How do you know about that?"

"I'm a PI, Carol. It's my job to know what's going on with anyone involved in a case. I don't mean to embarrass you."

"Well, I think that's where I draw the line and stop answering questions."

"That's certainly your prerogative, Carol."

She looked at her watch. "I really have to go," she said. "I'm sorry."

"Don't be sorry. Can I accompany you to Al's office?"

"Thanks, Spike, but I really need to go alone. I have to get my thoughts together in the taxi. Do you mind?"

"Not at all. I'll see you tonight?"

"Absolutely." Despite her façade of friendliness, Berenger could see that his last question had shaken her. Had his instincts been correct? Had Carol Merryman been stealing money from her ex-husband and been caught by the feds?

She stood, left the room for a moment, and returned with fresh lipstick on her mouth. Berenger went with her in the elevator and watched her hail a taxi. She coolly said good-bye to him once again and the cab drove away.

Berenger walked in the direction of the Rockin' Security office and thought about the case. The big question was—what made Flame become a cult member? The answer might hold a clue as to why the superstar was murdered. But even after speaking to Flame's family and associates, Berenger was no closer to uncovering any revelations. He would have to dig deeper into the Messengers and talk to Brenda Twist, if she'd talk to him.

Carol Merryman had just become a more interesting suspect. Even if she wasn't embezzling from Flame, she may have thought she stood to gain a great deal if he were to check out from the living. But she was a long shot.

Dave Bristol exhibited a lot of venom toward his former musical partner. Could bumping off Flame have helped Bristol with the pending lawsuits? Again, a long shot.

And why did the Jimmys want him dead? Why did they care? Berenger was trying to get Adrian—one of their dealers—*out* of jail.

But the most disturbing thing, Berenger came to realize, was that nothing he had seen or heard so far refuted the unanimous belief that Adrian Duncan was indeed Flame's killer.

17

The Wicked Messenger

(performed by Bob Dylan)

Berenger grabbed Suzanne at the Rockin' Security office
and said, "Come on, we're going to pay a visit to the Messengers."

"You want to blow my cover so soon?" she asked.

"What cover? You went in, asked questions, and never
said you were a private investigator, right?"

"Right."

"So you never had a cover. You just didn't say what
you really are."

She shrugged. "Okay, Spike, you're the boss."

They grabbed a taxi and went west and down to Forty-
fourth Street and Tenth Avenue. Suzanne noted that the
sign in front of the church now read: TONIGHT'S MESSAGE—
THE SACRIFICES YOU MAKE.

Upon entering the building, Suzanne gestured to the
office window and said, "The reverend's wife is in there."
Berenger saw Mrs. Ramsey at the typewriter and waved
at her. She stood and opened the sliding window.

"Hello, may I help you?" she asked. She then recognized Suzanne and said, "Hello there! Nice to see you
again."

"Hello, Mrs. Ramsey," Suzanne said.

"Good afternoon. I'd like to see Reverend Theo, please," Berenger said.

"May I ask what this is in reference to?"

Berenger gave her his card. "I'm investigating the death of Peter Flame. I have a few questions for the reverend."

Mrs. Ramsey's eyebrows went up when she saw the card. "But we've already spoken to the police. Several times."

"I'm not the police, ma'am. I'm a private investigator, hired by Adrian Duncan's defense team. Your husband doesn't have to talk to me but I would greatly appreciate a few minutes of his time."

The woman looked at Suzanne and frowned. "Does that mean . . . ? You . . . ?"

"Yes, Mrs. Ramsey, I'm a private investigator, too."

The woman made a sour face and muttered, "Brenda was right . . ." She stepped to the desk and picked up the phone. After a moment she said, "Reverend, there's a private . . . no, there are *two* private detectives here. They'd like to speak to you about Flame." She listened and nodded. "Very well." She hung up and addressed Berenger and Suzanne. "Go upstairs to the first office on the left. The reverend will give you a few minutes."

"Thank you very much," Berenger said.

Mrs. Ramsey closed the sliding-glass window a bit too roughly as they walked toward the stairs.

"I guess I won't be going to any services now," Suzanne whispered.

"Maybe you lucked out," Berenger replied.

When they reached the second floor, Reverend Theo was standing in his office doorway.

"Oh, hello there," he said. "I recognize you, sir. You were at the will reading."

"Spike Berenger, with Rockin' Security." Berenger held out his hand and the men greeted each other. "This is my partner, Suzanne Prescott."

"Ms. Prescott I've already met," the reverend said. "Come inside my office."

It was a small room. Berenger was unprepared for the intensely violent religious iconography that adorned the reverend's office. Along with several bloody paintings of Christ's torment, much of the room was filled with books pertaining to the world's religions. No electric lights illuminated the place; instead, the reverend had lit several candles. One of them, on the reverend's desk, sat next to what appeared to be a human skull. Berenger thought he was entering the study of a medieval wizard.

"Please sit down," the reverend said, gesturing to a small sofa beneath a particularly gruesome portrait of Mary holding the bloody body of her dead son.

"As I told your wife, reverend, you're under no obligation to talk to us," Berenger said. "But in the interest of fair play and justice, we'd like to speak with you about Flame."

"I understand," Reverend Theo said. He gave them his trademark bright smile. "I'll be happy to help any way I can." The musicality of his Jamaican accent filled the room as he wagged his finger at Suzanne. "You deceived us the other day, didn't you, my child?"

"I certainly didn't intend to," she said. "No one ever asked me if I was a private detective. If they had I would have told the truth."

"Hmmm," the reverend said, still smiling. He chuckled slightly and said, "I suppose I'll have to believe you. Now then, what would you like to know?"

Berenger said, "I'd be interested in learning how Flame came to be involved with the Messengers. How did he meet you? What brought him to you, or did you approach him?"

The reverend sat behind his desk and said, "It was Brenda Twist who brought him to us. When was it? I believe it was January 2000, just after the new millennium. As you probably know, Mr. Flame had spent much of the year in rehabilitation for drug addiction. He met Ms. Twist there, for she, too, had a problem with substance abuse for a while. She was already one of our sheep and had unfortunately suffered a relapse due to the death of her mother. She was able to find the strength of Jesus Christ and build herself back up to his graces once again. You'd have to speak to her, but I believe she simply got to know Flame in the clinic and convinced him that her path was right for him as well."

"If you'll pardon me, Reverend, but I've known Flame for over twenty years and I simply find it hard to believe that he would ever 'find religion' in this way," Berenger said. "We're talking about a hardcore rock 'n' roll superstar who always did things the way he wanted to do them."

The reverend nodded. "I know exactly what you mean. When Brenda first brought Flame to one of our services, he was extremely skeptical and standoffish, as most people are who don't want to believe. But he returned to the next service. And the next, and the next. It wasn't long before he was a convert and we welcomed him into the fold. A visible change came over him and one night in early 2000 he made a pledge of five thousand dollars to the Messengers and joined the group."

"Was he dating Ms. Twist by this time?"

"I believe he was. If I recall correctly, they were already living together at Mr. Flame's town house in the Village."

"Tell us about the retreat new members go on, the one in Jamaica."

The reverend smiled again. "It's a lovely event. We take new members to our founding church outside of Ocho Rios on the north shore of the island. It's beautiful there. You have the deep-blue Caribbean to look at, the sound of nature all around you, and the spirit of God at your side. Usually the retreat lasts a week, but sometimes we extend them if we need to."

"Why would you 'need' to?" Berenger asked.

"Sometimes God is busy elsewhere in the world and doesn't join us until after a few days have passed. We stay until Jesus has touched the heart of every new member."

"How do you know when He's done so?" Suzanne asked.

The reverend looked at her like a schoolteacher gazes upon a student who has just asked a stupid question. "We just know," he replied.

"And what goes on at these retreats?" Berenger asked.

"We study the Bible and we pray. We sing and we praise the Lord. We bring out the love of Jesus and we share it among ourselves."

Pretty ethereal stuff, Berenger thought. Time to move on.

"Reverend, I understand you've been in prison and were charged with murder at one time."

The silver smile immediately disappeared. The man looked away as he considered the question. When he looked back, Berenger could see the anger in the reverend's eyes.

"I was once a sinner. We are all sinners and I am no exception. I was fortunate to find the true path after my transgressions. When Jesus came and walked beside me one night, everything changed. I converted and never looked back at my evil past."

"So you created the Messengers."

"I didn't 'create' the Messengers. The Messengers have always existed. I simply brought the group to a physical plane of existence and provided a forum for us to communicate with God. You'd have to attend our services to fully understand."

Berenger was convinced the man was a nutcase. "Reverend, did you encourage Flame to leave so much money to the Messengers in his will?"

"Of course not, and I resent the implication."

"Reverend," Suzanne said. "Tell us about Mr. Black. The limo driver?"

"Ron Black? He's a valued member of our organization. He does much more than drive a limousine."

"I understand it's Flame's limo," Berenger said.

"Yes, it is. Flame allowed us to use it all the time while he was alive. I'm certain that he would approve us using it now. Mr. Black was Flame's driver since 2001, you know."

"Yes, we know."

"He had worked for the Messengers prior to his employment as Flame's driver. Sadly, after Mr. Flame's death, Ron had nowhere to go. We took him back. He's a capable man. We couldn't do without him."

"What happens if Carol Merryman or Joshua Duncan wants the limo returned?" Berenger asked.

The reverend shook his head. "They won't." The man looked at his watch and said, "I'm afraid I must attend to other matters now. I hope I've sufficiently answered your questions."

"We appreciate your time," Berenger said.

"You'd like to speak to Ms. Twist?"

"Yes, please."

"I'll send her in. Please stay seated." He got up and left the room.

"Doesn't this place really creep you out?" Suzanne whispered.

"That's an understatement."

"Look," she said, pointing to the bookshelf. There were over a dozen books on black magic, voodoo, and witchcraft.

Berenger shrugged. "He *is* from Jamaica." But he wondered . . . was this a holy man or a wicked one? And could there be a connection between the Messengers and the Jimmys?

After a moment, Brenda Twist stepped inside. Berenger stood but she said, "Sit down. I don't want to talk to you but I will since Reverend Theo asked me to." She looked at Suzanne and said, "And you, you're a terrible person. May Jesus spit on you."

Suzanne was shocked. "I'm sorry, Ms. Twist, but I never deceived you. And frankly, I don't think Jesus would 'spit' at anybody."

Brenda sat in the reverend's chair. "I don't believe you're qualified to know what Jesus would do or not do. What do you want to know?"

Berenger decided not to pull any punches. "I'd like to hear your take on how and why Flame, after twenty-five years of sex, drugs, and rock 'n' roll, would convert to an extremist religious cult."

Brenda's eyes went wide. "We are *not* a cult!"

"Okay, you're not a cult. How did Flame become so interested in it?"

"Flame and I became friends in a medical clinic."

"A rehab center."

She glared at Berenger. "Yes, that's right. If you must know, I was a heroin addict at one time. I'm not proud of

it. The devil had hold of me and it took the love of Jesus
to break us apart. The same thing happened to Flame.
We became . . . close . . . as we recovered. When we got
out of the clinic, I brought him here. These people are
my family. They became his family as well."

"You're saying he simply bought into the Messengers'
rhetoric and converted?"

"That's right. The retreat in Jamaica solidified it."

Suzanne asked, "I'd like to hear your version of what
happens on these retreats. How do you decide when a
new member is worthy to go?"

"A congregate must show serious intention of becoming a Messenger and contribute tangibly so we can do
God's work."

"You mean, congregates must give money to the organization."

"If you put it like that, yes. We see it as a sacrifice. An
offering."

"So they go on this retreat. What happens then?"

"We pray and study the Bible. We become one with
God and Jesus."

Same party line. He wasn't going to get anywhere like
this. Berenger chose to change the subject.

"I'd like to ask you about your whereabouts on the
night Flame was killed. How come you weren't with
him?"

She rolled her eyes. "I told the police this a million
times."

"If you don't mind, I'd like to hear it, too."

"Why, so you can place some doubt in the jury's mind
about Flame's killer? Adrian *murdered* his father and
there's nothing you can do to change that."

"Please, Ms. Twist. Just tell us about that night."

Brenda took a breath and said, "All right. After the concert I went backstage to the meet and greet."

She was holding on to Flame's left arm as he greeted the other Messengers and signed autographs. Then, Al Patton approached the couple and asked if he could have a word with Flame before the rock star retired to his dressing room with Brenda. She could hear everything they said.

"I heard that Bristol and the boys came to see you," Patton said.

"Yeah. I sent 'em away," Flame replied.

"Why?"

Flame gestured helplessly. "I just didn't want 'em around. They make me uncomfortable."

"It would have been a real kick for you guys to get onstage together again. One number wouldn't have hurt you."

"Yeah it would have. I don't want to play with those guys again."

"Why does there have to be such bad blood between you and Dave? You guys were the best of friends for a helluva long time. Not to mention the creative energy you two produced together."

Flame looked pained. "Drop it, Al. I don't want to talk about it. Tonight was stressful enough. Sheesh, my former band was here, my ex-wives were here, my sons were here . . ."

Patton nodded. "I saw them. What's with Adrian? He looked pissed off about something."

"Oh, we had another one of our usual fights before the show," Flame said. "Rotten brat. His mother raised him to be a lazy, good-for-nothing—"

"All right, all right," Patton interrupted. Best to change the subject. "The European tour is all but set," he said. "Kenny was able to book you into some decent-sized venues, more like the old days. You've got a month to unwind and relax and then I'd like you and your band to work up a little more of the older material. I think it's wise that we treat it like a nostalgia tour."

Flame looked at his manager as if the man were mad. "I didn't agree to anything like that, Al," he said.

Patton held up his hands defensively. "Wait, Peter, before you get all riled up—"

"No, *you* wait," Flame said. "You don't tell me what material I perform on my tours. I'm not playing old stuff anymore, you know that. I'm promoting my newer material and that's that."

Patton was a man with a short fuse. "You think you're going to maintain an audience with this religious garbage?" he spat, loud enough for some of the Messengers to overhear him. Brenda looked up in shock.

"Keep your voice down, damn it," Flame said.

"And another thing," Patton continued. "Why is your swag-man hawking Messenger merchandise? I went out to the concession and saw crucifixes and shit next to your CDs and T-shirts."

"I made a deal with Reverend Theo," Flame explained. "It's my decision what to sell at concerts, not yours, Al."

"Is that so?"

"Well, yeah."

"You know, Peter, your record contract is up with the next album. We can talk about what you sell and don't sell after you deliver it."

"Is that a threat, Al? You gonna drop the guy who put Liquid Metal Records on the map?"

Patton took a deep breath and looked around. Everyone was staring at him. He did his best to quiet down. "Okay, we'll talk about it later. Congratulations on finishing the tour. You feel all right? Everything okay?"

Flame affectionately put his hand on his manager's shoulder and said, "Yeah, I'm just tired. Look, Al, I love you. We'll work it all out. I just gotta do what I gotta do these days, okay?" He lightly slapped Patton's cheek. "I'll see you later."

Flame held out his hand to Brenda, who glided across the floor to him. He wrapped his arm around her and kissed her on the forehead. "Come on, baby, let's blow," he said.

Patton shrugged and said, "I'm gonna go find Kenny. Later, Peter."

As the record mogul walked away, Brenda asked, "How come he's the only one that's allowed to call you Peter?"

Flame shrugged. "I don't know. I didn't give him permission or nothin'. He just always has."

"Can I call you Peter?"

"Absolutely not!" He kissed her again. "Come on, I gotta get some stuff from the dressing room."

"Well, actually, I was going with Reverend Theo back to HQ to help him set up for tomorrow," she said.

"What? Honey, this is the last night of the tour. Don't you feel like partying a little?"

"I thought you were tired."

"I am, but I can still party a little."

"No, I promised the reverend that I'd help him prepare for tomorrow's service. We didn't get a chance to do it before the show. How about I meet you at home in a couple of hours? That'll give you time to unwind a bit."

175

She had him under her thumb. "All right," he said. He looked around. "Where's Ron?"

"Over here."

Ron Black, Flame's personal driver, stood at the back of the room. He waved a hand at his boss.

"Bring the car around to the stage door," Flame called to him. "I'll be there in five minutes. I want to avoid the fans tonight."

Black nodded and walked away. Flame kissed Brenda long and hard and then said, "Don't be long."

Brenda blushed and said, "I won't." She turned and ran toward Reverend Theo, his black face beaming with delight at the sight of his two "children" in love.

Berenger and Suzanne listened to the story as Brenda wound it up. "So I came back to the church with Reverend Theo. I was helping him with the sermon for the next morning. I often do that. I've been his sounding board for several years. We were stuck on some points and I promised him I'd help him work them out that night. We didn't want to save it until the morning, that would have been pushing it."

"Yet, it was Flame's last concert of the tour," Berenger said.

"That's right. But I came to the show. I was with him before and after. I went to the meet and greet. And I had planned to join him at home in a couple of hours. Flame said he'd go on and wait for me. When I arrived, the police were there and he was dead. That's all there is to it."

"I assume the police checked your alibi?" Suzanne asked.

"Of course they did," Brenda replied. "I'm sure you can check with them if you have to make sure for yourselves."

"So you came back here with the reverend to work on his sermon . . . after midnight?" she asked again.

"The Lord's work has no timetable," the young woman replied as if she were quoting scripture.

Berenger looked at Suzanne and said, "Okay, I suppose that's all for now. Thank you, Ms. Twist."

"You're welcome." She stood and came around the desk to show them out.

"Oh, one more thing," Berenger said. "You must be happy to receive such a generous bequest from Flame. Were you surprised?"

"It was a gift from God," Brenda replied. "I never expected it."

"Yet you attended the reading of the will. Surely you expected something?"

"Mr. Berenger, Flame was my companion. I had an interest in how he was dividing his estate. Is that too much to comprehend?"

"No, I suppose it isn't." He led Suzanne out and down the stairs. When they reached the bottom, Berenger glanced up and saw the young woman still standing at the top. Instead of the usual saintly and innocent aura she normally expressed, Brenda Twist stared at them with calculating coldness.

She was hiding *something*.

18

Legend in Your Own Time

(performed by Carly Simon)

The big event was at the Music Box, a 1,000-seat capacity theater located on West Forty-fifth Street between Broadway and Eighth Avenue. With a major network televising the show, Flame's Memorial Service and Concert was the hottest ticket in town even at $5,000 per seat. Proceeds, after expenses paid to the union stagehands and promotional firms, were to be donated to a number of charities that Carol Merryman had designated. The celebrity acts agreed to perform for free.

Spike Berenger found the two tickets delivered to Rockin' Security that afternoon. Carol's graciousness was admirable, considering he was working for the defense, and it was a good thing she had sent them before he had confronted her about the tax evasion. Now Berenger's dilemma was whether he should ask Rudy or Suzanne to accompany him to the black-tie event—and it was a no-brainer. Suzanne nearly fell out of her chair when he made the offer.

Security was tight around the theater. The street itself was blocked off from all traffic except for screened limousines and private cars delivering attendees to the front of the building. Barriers kept pedestrians a hundred yards away but close enough to scream at their favorite star. The network's trucks were parked across the street and several cameras covered the happening from many angles, both inside the theater and out.

Berenger and Suzanne took a cab to Broadway and Forty-fourth, then walked down to the Music Box. He was dressed in the tux he wore at least two or three times a year—it was one of the smartest investments he had ever made—and Suzanne looked stunning in a gown that might have come off a Hollywood actress en route to the Oscars. Berenger flashed his tickets at the security men and allowed one of them to wave a metal-detector wand around him before they went inside. Rudy was dismayed that Rockin' Security hadn't been hired to oversee the concert but Berenger figured Carol might not have considered it a good political move. Supplying a couple of tickets on the sly to an old friend was one thing, but publicly flaunting the firm representing the accused murderer of the night's honoree would not have flown.

"Wow, will you look at this," Suzanne whispered as they stepped into the theater. At first glance they could count twenty or thirty famous faces, from rock stars to film actors and actresses. Wealthy record executives and other industry types may have dominated the audience but Berenger commented that there was at least one celebrity for every three unknown rich patrons. Right off the bat, Berenger recognized Yoko Ono and her son Sean, David Bowie, Mick Jagger, Sir Paul McCartney, Peter Townshend, Jimmy Page, Ian Anderson, Jack Nicholson, Dustin Hoffman, Robert De Niro, Donald Trump, Madonna, Pamela Anderson, Meryl Streep, Kevin Kline, Tom Hanks, Steven Spielberg and his wife Kate Capshaw, and Martin Scorsese.

The seat locations were also a surprise—on the aisle, fourteen rows from the stage.

"Wow," Suzanne said. "I think that's going to be the operative word tonight. Wow."

"I guess I owe Carol one, even if she might be an embezzler," Berenger said. They sat and looked around the room, unable to resist gawking.

"I really appreciate this, Spike."

"Hey, the next time *you* get a free extra five-grand ticket to something, you can take me."

"Being in a room with this many celebrities must be old hat to you," she commented as she turned around in her seat to watch the people coming in.

"Not really. I went to the Grammys a couple of times and it was like this, only bigger. But I think there are more heavyweights here tonight than I've ever seen in one place."

"Are we going to any parties afterward?" she asked, wiggling her eyebrows.

"I'm afraid not, Suzanne. I made plans with Charlie. We're going to get together and jam at the studio tonight. Do you mind?"

"Oh, I guess not. Hey, look there."

She pointed to the two rows near the stage taken up by the Messengers. Reverend Theo was all smiles as he waved to people and took a seat next to his wife. Brenda Twist sat demurely as if she were the only person truly in mourning. Ron Black stood in the aisle, acting more like a bodyguard than a chauffeur.

A familiar feminine voice interrupted his inspection of the crowd. "Hello there."

Berenger turned to find Gina Tipton standing in the aisle. She looked ravishing in a black dress that accentuated her blond hair. It was impossible to view her as a grieving woman. Berenger stood and said, "Hello, Gina. How are you?"

They kissed on the cheeks and he said, "Do you know my assistant, Suzanne Prescott?"

"We've met before, haven't we?" Gina asked her.

"Yes, once," Suzanne said. They shook hands.

"This is quite a crowd, isn't it?" Gina said, wide-eyed.

"I'll say. Where are you sitting?"

She looked at her ticket. "It looks like I'm right in front of you! How nice." Gina and Berenger sat and then she turned around to continue talking. "I guess I have Al Patton to thank for this. Carol didn't want me here."

"Well, that's not right," Berenger said. "You have as much claim to be here as anyone. Are you one of the speakers?"

"No. Again, Carol wouldn't have me on the stage. Allowing me to attend was one thing. Letting me speak?— no way!"

"That's too bad," Berenger said.

"Speaking of Carol, there she is," Suzanne mentioned. They saw the grand widow with Joshua Duncan on the far side of the house, near the stage. She appeared to be chewing out her son about something.

"I need to talk to her for a moment," Berenger said. "Please excuse me, ladies?"

"Of course," Gina said. "Give her a kiss for me, will you?"

"No sarcasm, Gina," Berenger said, smiling. "Not tonight."

"Sorry."

He made his way through the mingling million-dollar fashions and was nearly five or six feet away from Carol and Joshua when he heard bits of their argument.

"You can't just *fire* Al, Mom. I need him," Joshua said.

"Quiet!" Carol said, shushing him. "This isn't the time or the place." Her eyes caught Berenger's and she gave

181

him a broad but insincere smile. "Look who's here. Hello, Spike!"

"Carol, Joshua," Berenger said as he stepped up to them. "Thank you so much for the two tickets. That was mighty generous of you."

"What are friends for?" She gave him a compulsory hug and Berenger shook hands with Joshua. "Now stop working for Adrian Duncan and help us prove what a guilty slimeball he really is!"

"Now, Carol," Berenger said.

"Forget it. I need to keep such thoughts to myself tonight. I'm just stressed out. It's been a hectic day, to say the least. Was it this morning when you were at my apartment? My God, it seems like I've been through a complete lifetime since then."

"How was your meeting with Patton?"

"That bastard. We had a huge fight over some of Flame's business affairs, just as I expected we would. He obviously can't wait until my son is in charge 'cause he thinks he can push Joshua around. I've got news for Al Patton—Joshua's going to be just as tough as me, right Josh?"

"Mom . . ." Joshua turned red and looked away.

"Look, Spike, I have to get backstage. Have a good time."

"Thanks, you too, Carol. Bye, Joshua."

They hurried away and Berenger headed back to his seat. Along the way he noticed Dave Bristol, Brick Bentley, and Moe Jenkins talking to Al Patton. Kenny Franklin and the boys from Flame's recent touring band were farther back. Apparently they didn't rate as highly. Berenger glanced up at the balcony and immediately noticed Lieutenant Billy McTiernan standing behind the rail, looking down on the crowd. Berenger figured it made sense that McTiernan had been invited.

The lights began to dim as he sat down. "Find out anything interesting?" Suzanne asked.

"Not really."

Gina turned around and said, "Here we go. I hope I can control my emotions." Berenger reached up and squeezed her shoulder. She patted his hand.

The crowd roared when the lights extinguished completely and the grand opening guitar chords of one of Flame's solo hits, "Burning Rubber," blasted through the house speakers. The curtains parted to reveal a still image of Peter Flame projected onto a movie screen. He was in his famous "David" pose, one as iconic as that of Jethro Tull's Ian Anderson standing on one leg and playing the flute. Right on the beat, the image became a live-action film as Flame burst out of his tableau to play his guitar. In sync with the soundtrack, Flame sang along with the words to the song and the entire house was rocking.

Berenger didn't remember getting to his feet. The excitement in the packed theater was contagious—not a single person was unaffected by the powerful opening. It was going to be more like a high-energy rock concert than a memorial service.

When the song and film finished a spotlight hit none other than Al Patton, who approached a microphone stand that appeared out of nowhere. The crowd was not ready to settle in their seats—the cheers and whistles went on for a couple of minutes. Patton mistakenly thought the response was for him as he smiled and waved. Finally, an announcer's voice boomed through the house, "Ladies and gentlemen, Liquid Metal Records'

CEO and the producer of some of the world's greatest musical acts, Al Patton."

Berenger noted that the applause tapered off and there were even a few boos in the background. Patton didn't notice, though. He spoke into the microphone with confidence. "Welcome everyone. It's great to be here, even though it's on such a sobering occasion as this. After all, we're here to pay tribute to one of the world's legends. If the tears flow tonight, it's with good reason. But I don't think that's what Flame would have wanted. He once told me he wanted a big party thrown when he departed this earth, so that's what I, as his manager, and Carol Merryman, his former wife and the current vice president of Flame Productions, set out to do. Tonight you're going to hear from some of Flame's friends and family, we're going to allow ourselves to get a little emotional for a bit, and then we're going to bring on the music."

A swell of cheers followed that announcement. Patton waved his hands to silence the crowd.

"That's right, yes, thank you. Some of the biggest names in rock 'n' roll are here tonight. We're being taped for a prime-time broadcast and Warner Brothers is filming the entire evening for a future feature film. It's all a testament to the status that Peter Flame held. He was a legend in his own time, if you'll pardon the cliché. Words can't express what Flame was to all of us. The world has lost a giant whom we'll never forget." Patton looked up and said, "Flame, wherever you are, this night's for you."

Patton walked off the stage. Music segued into the beginning of a short film that Martin Scorsese had put together chronicling Flame's career. There were the obligatory childhood stories, his first breaks in the music business, and the meteoric rise to fame as a member of

Hay Fever. Cheers from the crowd accompanied every milestone, especially when the timeline reached the days of Flame's Heat.

When the film was over, David Bowie took the stage. He received a standing ovation, of course, and then spoke humbly into the mike with his distinctive British eloquence.

"Good evening. I first met Flame in 1974, which was a particularly chaotic time in my life," the rock star said. "I had just come out of the *Diamond Dogs* tour, which was something of a financial disaster, and I was battling with the demons conjured up by that expensive white powder we all loved so much in those days."

More cheers.

Bowie laughed and continued. "One night in Los Angeles, I happened to get together with Flame and John Lennon for a night of debauchery, for lack of a better word. We were pretty tanked up and out of our minds, but we ended up in a recording studio around midnight and started to lay down some tracks."

Another response from the audience.

"Yes, yes," he said. "The rumors are true! John and Flame had some songs they'd been working on and also wrote some songs on the spot—I think I was too out of it to contribute much—but the three of us, and Dave Bristol and Harry Nilsson, we slapped together an album's worth of stuff that's never seen the light of day. It was a fantastic nine hours of high-energy, drug-induced euphoria that I was happy to be a part of. At the time I thought it was some of the most brilliant music ever recorded. Of course we were so stoned you'll have to take that statement with a grain of salt. I never heard the tapes after that night so I can't be entirely too sure of the quality. At any rate, Flame and I ran into each other a few times over the years after that. I'm happy to say he was a friend, a man with unlimited talent and fortitude." He went on to describe the man the public knew as an extroverted and innovative pioneer of rock 'n' roll. Bowie said he was particularly inspired by Flame and never lost his admiration for the man. He ended his short speech with, "You were the real rebel. Here's to you, Flame."

Suzanne whispered to Berenger, "Boy, I wish they'd release that album!"

Berenger nodded but his attention was focused on Carol Merryman, who was next to take the stage. She began by thanking Al Patton, Martin Scorsese, and Bowie, and then went into an overlong appreciation of her former husband. Even Berenger was beginning to get bored until she made intimations of what was going to happen with Flame Productions.

"I'm looking forward to handing the company over to my son, Joshua, per Flame's wishes," she said. "In the meantime, I'll be making some very important business decisions with regard to how we're going to deal with past and future contracts, as well as what's going to happen to some of those unreleased recordings that Flame had in his vault."

More cheers.

The testimonials took up nearly an hour of time. Sir Paul McCartney gave an eloquent speech about how Flame's music inspired even *him*, Eric Clapton put in his two cents' worth, and Bonnie Raitt—who was once linked romantically to Flame—presented a heartfelt tribute to the man.

Finally, the all-star jam began. Blister Pack took the stage and Dave Bristol received a standing ovation. They launched into one of the better-known Flame's Heat songs and the crowd went wild. David Bowie came on, picked up a microphone, and provided vocals in lieu of Flame. When it was time for the guitar solo, Eric Clapton appeared and did his best imitation of Flame's chops.

Over the course of the next two hours, a nonstop progression of rock stars joined the growing supergroup on stage. McCartney played and sang a couple of tunes. The Who's Pete Townshend showed up with his power chords. Bonnie Raitt traded licks with none other than Jimmy Page. Ian Anderson, the front man from Jethro Tull, stood on one leg and blasted away on his instrument during two numbers. Berenger had completely forgotten that Anderson had supplied a flute riff on one of Flame's solo albums in the days before Flame's Heat.

During the show Berenger could see that Gina was crying. She dabbed her face with a handkerchief, especially when some of the earlier numbers were performed. He figured they must have struck a nerve since that was the time she had been married to Flame. Once again he squeezed her shoulder and Gina held his hand there. Berenger glanced at Suzanne and his partner gave him a nod of approval. He wondered how the other wife was taking it, so he scanned the crowd for a glimpse of Carol. He found her sitting with Joshua in one of the boxes high on the side of the theater. She, too, appeared to be crying. Joshua, on the other hand, seemed curiously emotionless. He sat with his arms folded, eyes focused in his lap, unmoved by the music. For a fleeting moment, Berenger thought he was looking at the young man's half brother, Adrian.

Adrian Duncan. The son who wasn't there. The man accused of killing the rock legend to whom they were paying tribute. Did Adrian regret not being there?

A thought suddenly popped into Berenger's head. If Adrian wasn't guilty of the heinous crime, then it was quite conceivable the real killer was somewhere in the theater at that very moment, listening to the sounds of Flame's legacy.

If so, what could that person possibly be thinking?

19

Prove It All Night

(performed by Bruce Springsteen)

As the lucky and enlightened audience poured out of the Music Box, Suzanne told Berenger that he didn't have to take her home. She had picked up on what wasn't said between him and Gina Tipton and gracefully bowed out. "Take her for a drink," she whispered to Berenger and left him on the street with Flame's first wife.

"Where's she going?" Gina asked.

"She, uhm, had another engagement. Say, listen, I'm meeting up with Charlie Potts in a little bit. You remember Charlie?"

"Sure! How is he?"

"He's doing good. Anyway, we get together and jam every now and then at our office studio. Would you like to come and listen? We could have a drink or something before he shows."

"I'd love to. Lord knows I won't be invited to any of the after-parties."

They walked to Eighth Avenue to catch a taxi going uptown and within fifteen minutes they were on the Upper East Side in front of Rockin' Security. Berenger unlocked the door and held it open for Gina. They went upstairs to the recording studio and Berenger flicked

189

on the lights. He went to the makeshift bar to inspect what they had in stock as he removed his tuxedo jacket and tie.

"Gina, what can I make you?"

"What have you got?"

"Some scotch. Bourbon. Vodka. Whatever mixers you want. We have some beer and wine in the kitchen. I'll have to go in there to get some ice anyway."

"I'll have what you're having."

"Jack Daniel's and Coke all right?"

"Sure."

Berenger went to fetch the Coke and ice and brought back two full glasses. They clinked the drinks together and said, "Cheers." Gina sat on the sofa and crossed her legs. Her black dress was tight and slinky, showing off her well-toned figure. Berenger sat beside her and said, "Gina, how do you do it? You look like a million bucks."

She grinned. "Thank you, sir. It's nice to hear that when you get to be my age."

"You mean *our* age."

"I think you're a little older than me, aren't you, Spike?"

"A little. And I'm not as fit. I could stand to lose twenty-five pounds."

"Why don't you?"

"I try, believe me. See the Nautilus equipment over there? Suzanne and I are the only ones in the firm who use it. I work out religiously and I still can't lose the pounds."

"Maybe it's what you're eating."

"I *know* it's what I'm eating. Shoot, I just figure we're on the earth for such a limited time, why not enjoy it? We shouldn't *have* to limit what we like to eat."

"Famous last words."

"Whatever."

"Spike, you don't look bad at all," she said, moving a little closer. "You were always a big teddy bear. I like you that way."

"Aw, shucks, ma'am," he said as he put his arm around her. They were quiet for a few minutes as they sipped the drinks. Finally, he asked, "Gina, are you happy out there in California?"

"Sure am. You can make a lot of money in real estate in California."

"I'll bet you can. What about other things, though?"

"You mean men?"

He shrugged. "Just curious. You don't have to answer if you don't want to."

"There are men in California," she said. "Last time I looked."

"Okay, okay. I'm being nosy."

"It's all right. There was one man I saw for a few years but that ended about ten months ago. I'm not really looking for any kind of permanent relationship. What about you, Spike? What happened with your marriage?"

"Oh, you know. I wasn't ready to grow up and be a husband."

"But you were, what, in your thirties?"

"Yeah."

"That's old enough."

"I guess. I just wasn't ready. Linda and I are still friends, sort of. I see my kids as much as I can."

"Where are they? Aren't they twins?"

"Yeah. Michael goes to NYU and Pam's in Albany. Their mother lives over on the West Side."

Gina nodded and took Berenger's hand. Softly, she asked, "Do you think Adrian has a chance?"

"Sure he does."

"Do you believe he's innocent?"

Berenger didn't know how to answer that. He wanted to trust that her son was innocent but so far everything pointed to his guilt.

"Something's not right about the case," he said. "I haven't got a handle on it yet. We've been on the job for just three days, you know. Give me some time."

"Sure, Spike." She looked up at him and the green eyes he once knew so well mesmerized him. Her lips were moist and they parted expectantly.

Keep your professionalism! he told himself . . . but he kissed her anyway. Her tongue slipped into his mouth and he was aware of a powerful desire that had eluded him for months.

When their mouths separated, she whispered, "You used to be able to go all night, Spike. Can you still do that?"

"I don't know," he said. "It's been a while since I've tried." He chuckled. "I haven't had to use Viagra yet, knock on wood. Er, no pun intended."

"Prove to me you can still do it." She kissed him again but the door buzzer interrupted them.

"That must be Charlie," he said, breaking the embrace. He gently touched her cheek and she acknowledged his need to stand up. "I'll be right back."

Charlie Potts was the same age as Berenger. He had curly salt-and-pepper hair and wore glasses, and unlike Berenger, was thin and gaunt. He was dressed in a T-shirt and blue jeans and had a guitar gig bag over his shoulder.

"Geez, you guys," Potts said, eyeing the others' tux and gown. "I didn't know this was a *formal* jam session."

Gina laughed and stood. He gave her a hug as she said, "Charlie Potts, how are you? I haven't seen you in years."

"I'm okay. Gosh, Gina, you look fantastic!"

"We were at Flame's Memorial Service and Concert," Berenger said. "I told you I was going."

"I remember now. That explains the monkey suit. How was it?"

"Pretty incredible. A lot of big shots got on stage."

"I'll see the movie when it comes out. You got some more of whatever you're drinking?"

"Sure. Have a seat."

Potts and Gina caught up with each other while Berenger went for more ice and Coke. He returned with a full glass for himself and one for Potts. Gina was still working on hers.

They talked for ten minutes, reminiscing about old times, until Potts said, "Well, partner, are we going to make some music, or what?"

"Let's do it."

Potts opened his gig bag and removed a Gibson Les Paul/VG 88. It had been his pride and joy for over a decade.

Berenger opened the cases containing his prized possessions. The first was a walnut-colored Dean HardTail Professional electric guitar with an all-mahogany body and neck, rosewood fingerboard, abalone and sterling silver twelfth-fret inlay, the original Dean V Profile neck, and satin nickel hardware. The second was a beige hollow-bodied Dean Stylist Deluxe, made of flame maple, a spruce top, rosewood fingerboard, block inlays, Grover tuners, and gold hardware. Finally, for a nice bottom sound, Berenger played a Dean Edge 04 Bartolini bass guitar, made with a quilt maple top, basswood body, bolt-on maple and walnut neck, rosewood fingerboard, and Bartolini pickups. Berenger liked Dean's products ever since he had met the designer in Chicago several years ago. Dean Zelinsky made an impressive line of electric and acoustic guitars and basses that were sold across the United States in retail shops—but they were definitely upscale items. Among the rock stars that used Dean Guitars were Billy Gibbons, Sammy Hagar, Vince Neil, Pat Travers, and Michael Angelo Batio, among others. Berenger had used original V Standard and ML models when he was with the Fixers and he kept those classic guitars only for playing on special occasions.

They plugged into 50-watt Marshall stack amps, tuned up, and started. Berenger began on the bass, giving Potts a riff to work off of. Potts laid on an improvised melody that drew roots from the Cool Jazz of the fifties. Gina closed her eyes and allowed the music to take her away in a cloud of rapture. After ten minutes, Berenger switched to the Edge and worked with Cry Baby Wah-Wah and Fuzz Face pedals, complementing Potts's artistry on his Les Paul. It was obvious the two men were well attuned to each other. They traded licks like professionals and laughed like schoolboys when something surprised them.

Berenger switched on a drum machine that kept a steady beat and then the two men really let loose. Berenger picked up the HardTail and added effects from a Roland GP100 processor. The room was cooking and Gina got up to dance. She moved sensuously around the room, slowly swinging her hips to the beat and looking at Berenger the whole time. He thought about what was said earlier and wondered what the night held in store for him as he allowed the feeling to carry through in his playing. It was some of the most soulful music he had produced in months.

After nearly an hour, the two musicians launched into a couple of old Fixers tunes, including "Moonbeams on

Mars," which Berenger sang in his throaty, baritone voice. When he let loose vocally, people often told him he could do a mean Howlin' Wolf or Captain Beefheart imitation. The session finally ended with a fire-breathing cover of Deep Purple's "Highway Star."

"Whooo!" Gina cried. "You guys are *great!* Why aren't you playing Radio City Music Hall?"

"We're too good for Radio City Music Hall," Potts said as he gave Berenger a high five. Berenger stepped over to the deck and switched it off.

"You were recording?" Potts asked.

"I always record. Just in case something brilliant happens."

"It was all brilliant," Gina effused.

The three settled down for another drink and chatted for another half hour. When Gina snuggled against Berenger and closed her eyes, Potts stood.

"I'll, uhm, leave you two alone, I think," he said.

Berenger didn't protest. He gently moved Gina's head and let her lie on the sofa as he got up. He walked Potts downstairs and promised they would get together again soon. Upon leaving, Potts winked at Berenger and said, "Be careful, Spike. You know you two have some history."

"I know. It's pretty ancient, though."

Potts nodded and left. Berenger bounced back up the stairs and found Gina standing by the studio door.

"You want me to take you to your hotel?" he asked.

"I want you to take me to your place," she said. "Unless you've got a bedroom here."

He looked at her and smiled. "You sure?"

She put her arms around him and kissed him hard on the mouth. When she was done, she said, "Yeah. Are you okay with that?"

"I'm okay with that."

"Then let's go."

Berenger opened his eyes to the sunlight streaming in from the slightly open blinds on his bedroom window. First he turned his head and made sure that Gina was still there. She was under the covers next to him, her warm, naked body pressed against his. She was sleeping soundly. Next he looked at the digital clock by the bed and saw that it was a little after 7:00. He had slept for about an hour and a half. He felt fine now but knew it would catch up to him later.

By the time he and Gina had got to his apartment it was nearly three in the morning. As soon as the door was closed they had hungrily pulled at each other's clothing until they were rolling on his living room floor with nothing on. The lovemaking there had been desperate, as if achieving orgasms were the goals in a race for humanity's salvation. When they were spent, they laughed and cuddled, had another drink, and moved to the bedroom. On Berenger's bed they went slower, giving and taking so that the intensity of the sensations increased to an excruciating high. After a second, and then a third climax, they lay together as their bodies glistened in sweat. Berenger suggested taking a shower, so they both climbed into the small stall where they took turns soaping each other. When they were rinsed, Gina stooped to her knees and took him in her mouth. He was surprised to find that he could come a fourth time. When they had dried off, he carried her to the bed and they fell asleep within minutes. Berenger remembered the clock read close to 5:30 when he had shut his eyes.

The phone rang, jolting Berenger out of the dreamlike euphoria. Gina stirred and groaned lightly. He grabbed the phone and said, "Berenger."

"Spike! Did I wake you?" It was Rudy Bishop.

"Yeah. What's up, Rudy?"

"Sorry, but oh, man, you need to get over to Carol Merryman's place as quick as you can."

"Why? What's going on?"

"Early this morning she took a leap off the roof of her apartment building. She's dead, Spike."

20

Free Fallin'

(performed by Tom Petty)

By the time Berenger arrived by taxi, a swarm of onlookers had gathered in front of Carol Merryman's Madison Avenue building. Three NYPD patrol cars, an unmarked detective's vehicle, and an ambulance surrounded the site—an infallible advertisement for the curious that something grisly had happened. Police had partitioned off the crime scene with the familiar yellow tape but that didn't keep gawkers and reporters from attempting to sneak a better view.

Berenger approached the scene and saw the drape covering the body, which was sprawled across the dividing line between the sidewalk and the street. He also spotted Lieutenant Billy McTiernan among the policemen, plainclothes detectives, and forensic technicians hovering inside the yellow-taped space. McTiernan looked up, met Berenger's eyes, and curtly nodded. Figuring he couldn't get out of there without talking to his nemesis, McTiernan ducked under the tape and walked over to the private investigator.

"Whatcha doin' here, Berenger?" McTiernan asked.

"What do you think, McTiernan? I'd say this concerns Rockin' Security," Berenger replied. "What are *you* doing here? Isn't this a bit out of your jurisdiction?"

198

"Yeah, it is. It's not my fucking case. I'm simply here as an interested party. The guys in this precinct are friends of mine."

"You mind telling me what happened?"

"The lady jumped. It happened around six o'clock."

"Any witnesses?"

"On the ground, yeah. A bus driver saw her free falling and then—*splat*—right there. At least six other people on the sidewalk saw her fall. Everyone else in the area, well, they just saw the goddamned mess after the fact."

"Anyone see her on the roof and actually take the dive?"

"Nope."

"Then how do you know she voluntarily jumped?"

"Because there's no sign of a break-in at her apartment and it looks like she didn't even enter her home after the concert last night. The boys have already contacted some witnesses from the party she was at. They stated she left 'highly intoxicated' around five in the morning. Figures. It was full of fucking hippies."

"Where was the party?"

"Some loft in Soho. A bunch of goddamned rock stars were there. You know. We're looking for the cabdriver that brought her home. The thing is, we're not sure if she took a cab or got a ride from someone."

Berenger stood and stared at the drape. After the crime-scene photos were completed, the body was placed on a stretcher and put into the ambulance.

"She didn't commit suicide, McTiernan," Berenger said.

"Yeah? How do you know?"

"Because of what she said last night at the concert. She had big plans for Flame's company. She had a lot of business decisions to make and she was looking forward to seeing them through. She was about to spend a year preparing her son to take over. By the way, where *is* her son?"

"We can't find him. Detective Pollock over there left a message on the kid's answering machine. Where could he be this early in the morning?"

Berenger shrugged. "Joshua's a college student. Maybe he had early classes. He was at the concert last night, too. Maybe he was at the same party or a different one, got lucky, and went home with some dame."

"Well, we need to find him. He's the next of kin."

"McTiernan, tell your pals not to write it off as a suicide just yet. They need to look into it deeper. She was having some problems with the IRS but I don't think they were bad enough to kill herself over."

"Hey, Berenger, let us do our fucking job, okay?" McTiernan moved closer to Berenger's face. "Go on. Get out of here. We don't need your kind tellin' us what to do?"

"*My kind?* What the hell is that supposed to mean?"

"Come on, Berenger, do I have to spell it out? You know *professional* law-enforcement personnel don't like goddamned private investigators. They step on our toes and shit where they're not supposed to."

"You're a real charmer, McTiernan," Berenger said. He poked his index finger into the police detective's chest. "I'm a pro and you know it."

"Fine, you're a pro and I know it. Now get lost. I gotta go back over there."

"McTiernan."

"What?"

"Up until now I wasn't sure if Adrian Duncan was really guilty or not. As of this morning I'm beginning to think he's not. I strongly urge you to look into all this.

Carol—her jumping, or whatever happened—it's related. I know it."

"Look, Berenger, if you're so sure Duncan is innocent, then go find the evidence and give it to the guy's lawyer so it can be presented properly—in court." With that, McTiernan walked away and joined his cronies who were powwowing beside the unmarked cop car.

Damn, Berenger thought as he crossed the street to hail a taxi. He had liked Carol Merryman. She could be a snotty bitch at times and it seemed she was only interested in what was good for her and her son, but she didn't deserve this. Whatever *this* was. Had she really jumped? If so, why? It didn't make any sense.

He looked up at the roof and saw a couple of patrolmen still working that part of the crime scene. There was no way he'd be able to get up there to snoop around. By the time he could, any evidence he might find would have already been picked up.

As he walked toward Rockin' Security, Berenger realized he emphatically believed that Carol Merryman hadn't jumped to her death.

She was pushed.

21

Something to Believe In

(performed by The Ramones)

The team assembled in the conference room at Rockin' Security and for once there was no music playing through the speakers. Remix was tempted to put on Iron Maiden's *Dance of Death* but ultimately decided it would be in bad taste.

"There was no way in hell that Carol Merryman jumped off the roof of her building," Berenger announced, beginning the meeting. "Suzanne, last night at the concert, did Carol appear depressed to you?"

"No," Suzanne replied. "She looked pissed off about a few things and under a lot of stress, but I wouldn't say she was looking to check out."

"That's what I think," Berenger agreed. "Listen, folks, I'm convinced that if we can figure out what's behind her fall—in other words, who *pushed* her—then we'll also find out who Flame's killer was. It's got to be related. Okay, give me what you got. Danny, how's the hacking going?"

Remix cleared his throat. "Spike, it's done. I got into the Messengers' server about midnight last night and spent a few hours looking at Reverend Theo's e-mails. This morning I took a look at Brenda Twist's but I still have a lot to go through. I printed out some of the more interesting ones in the reverend's mailbox. He sure keeps in constant contact with a guy named Chucky in Jamaica."

"That would be Chucky Tools," Briggs interrupted. "He's the Messengers' main man at their church outside of Ocho Rios."

"Chucky *Tools?*" Suzanne asked.

"Hey, that's his name." Briggs shrugged.

"Anyway," Remix continued as he looked at a piece of paper, "Reverend Theo mentioned Flame in an e-mail to Chucky Tools two days ago. It says, 'Flame's contribution to us was generous indeed but someone in our organization has put us in jeopardy. I aim to find out who it is and I strongly suggest that you do the same.' To this, Chucky replied, 'Come on, Reverend, you know who it is. You remember who got very friendly with each other at the second retreat Flame attended? It seems obvious to me.'" Remix slapped the printout and added, "That's all I could find so far but I'll keep digging."

"I'm beginning to wonder if I need to take a trip to Jamaica," Berenger said. "This Chucky Tools might be someone I'd like to talk to."

"Jamaica? Can I go?" Suzanne asked.

Berenger looked at her and asked, "Any more on Brenda Twist, Suzanne?"

Suzanne laughed, made a *swish* sound as she sailed a flat hand over her head. "That one flew right by, didn't it? No Caribbean vacation for me! Uhm, okay . . . Brenda Twist. Nothing new, really. I've confirmed that she was diagnosed with substance abuse and addiction in 1998 and sentenced by a court to go into rehab. She was there for two years, found religion, got out, but went right back in four months later. It was during that stint when she met Flame. Oh, I also learned she was a problem teenager in Seattle, where she grew up, and was arrested twice for narcotics possession. There's an indication that she may have worked the streets as a teenager to support her habit. Her juvenile records are under lock and key, though. We can't get at them without a court order. The amazing thing is that she's been squeaky clean since she got out of rehab and became a member of the Messengers."

Berenger looked at Briggs. "You have something for me, Tommy?"

"Not much more either. I did find out about Chucky Tools, like I said. He runs the retreat there in Jamaica. I've been vetting all the known members of the Messengers for criminal backgrounds. Other than the reverend himself, I've come up with zilch. I did receive an interesting report from Plaskett at the bureau who got it from *his* contact in Jamaica. There was a lawsuit filed against the Messengers three years ago. It was dismissed for lack of evidence but I got a copy of the suit. It alleged that the Messengers use drugs in their so-called retreats and that these events are very ritualistic. Not sure what that means exactly. Anyway, the drugs apparently reduce inhibitions and affect the users psychologically, making them more open to suggestion."

"What is it, some kind of truth serum?" Berenger asked.

"Who knows? It could be a number of things. But if it's powerful stuff, then it's no wonder these people start pledging their lives and fortunes to the group."

"That does it," Berenger said. "I'm going to Jamaica. Tommy, who's the contact in Jamaica? Can I see him?"

"His name is Baskin. Steve Baskin. I'll see if I can arrange a meeting."

"Great. Ringo, see what kind of flights you can get me for tonight or in the morning."

Mel nodded and left the room, saying, "Okay, but you better bring us some T-shirts and some reggae CDs."

The best flight out wasn't until the next morning so Berenger had a day to kill. Mel found out from the Sixth Precinct that Lieutenant McTiernan was at New York Hospital, where Carol Merryman's body was taken for a postmortem. Berenger caught a cab there and found the officer in the mortuary waiting room with Joshua Duncan. The young man appeared pale and extremely shaken.

McTiernan saw Berenger approaching and winced. "Geez, Berenger, don't you have any tact? We don't want to talk to you right now."

Berenger ignored him and spoke to Joshua. "Hey, I'm really sorry to hear about your mom. We were friends, you know."

Duncan nodded but wouldn't look Berenger in the eye. He stood and mumbled, "You guys can go ahead and talk, I'm going to the washroom."

As he walked away, McTiernan shrugged and said, "Poor kid. Lost both his parents in less than three weeks."

Berenger sat by McTiernan and said, "Look, Billy, I'm coming right to the point. I really think Carol Merryman was forced to take that jump. There are too many weird things about this case."

"Berenger, I don't—"

"Just hear me out, will you?"

McTiernan frowned and folded his arms. "Okay, I'm listening."

"Reverend Theo—you know, the Messengers guy—he served time in Jamaica before founding their church and coming to America. He even had a murder rap but was acquitted. The Messengers have a retreat in Jamaica where they send all new members. I've learned that they use drugs and rituals during the retreats, causing the participants to lose control and become susceptible to suggestion. I'm going to Jamaica tomorrow morning to check it out."

"So?"

"So, the Messengers have a motive for killing Flame. *And* Carol Merryman. They wanted his money. And Carol was in charge of the money after his death. They wanted her out of the way."

"You can't prove that, can you?"

"Not yet, but I'm—"

"When you have something to show me, Berenger, I'll listen. Right now I'm up to my ears in shit. What makes you think Adrian Duncan didn't kill his father? We've got him dead to rights. There's physical evidence and eye-witnesses."

"I think he was set up. I really do."

"Look, Berenger, I'm all for justice and getting the right guy and all that. But until you can convince me otherwise, we've *got* the right guy. What else do you have for me?"

"Brenda Twist was a drug addict before she met Flame. She's not the Snow White she lets everyone think she is."

"So? Big fucking deal. Neither are you."

"Oh, come on, McTiernan!" Berenger stood. "Didn't your boys find *anything* on that roof or in Carol's apartment? Anything to suggest she wasn't alone last night?"

"Nope."

"How did she get home from the party?"

"We still don't know. But we haven't found everyone who was there. It's going to take a while."

In frustration, Berenger rubbed his head and said, "Okay, McTiernan. You win for now. I'll be back when I have something more substantial." He walked away but McTiernan stopped him.

"Hey, Berenger."

"What?"

"I *am* interested in what you find out about the Messengers. Those people give me the creeps, too. I'm not totally blowing you off."

Berenger nodded and said, "Thanks." He left the waiting room and turned the corner to walk toward the elevator. He saw the men's room and decided to look inside. Sure enough, Joshua Duncan was there, standing at the sink and staring into the mirror.

"You all right, Joshua?" Berenger asked.

Joshua's eyes darted around the room and then he immediately began to splash cold water in his face. "Yeah, I guess," he said.

"You mind telling me where you were last night after the concert?"

"I went to the same damned party my mom went to. I left early, though. I left at two o'clock and took a cab home. Mom was still there when I left. I told the detective that, too. You can check with Al Patton's secretary. She called the cab for me."

"This was Al Patton's party?"

"Yeah."

"Do you have any idea how your mom got home after she left, whenever that was?"

"*No.* If I did I would have told Lieutenant McTiernan. And I'd tell you, too."

"Okay, Joshua." Berenger stood next to him and gave him a light pat on the back. "Take it easy, all right? I'll . . . I'll be in touch."

Joshua didn't say anything as Berenger left the washroom.

Adrian Duncan looked at Berenger with disappointment.

"I thought you were going to be Patterson," he said.

"You're not glad to see me?" Berenger asked.

Duncan shrugged. He looked away but Berenger noticed the shiner.

"What happened?"

"Fucking guard hit me."

"Did you provoke him?"

"He says I did. He's a really big Flame fan and wanted some payback."

"Have you told Patterson about it?"

"Not yet. What do you want?"

Berenger sighed and said, "Look, Adrian. I haven't been totally honest with you and Patterson. Before, I wasn't convinced you were innocent. But I came to tell you that now I really do believe you're not guilty and I'm getting closer to finding out the truth about what happened that night."

"Oh yeah? Well, gee, thanks for telling me. I really don't give a fuck if you think I'm guilty or not."

Berenger's instinct to punch the man returned in full force. Adrian Duncan really was an ungrateful, miserable louse.

"Listen," he said. "The Jimmys sent me a death-threat package. And the other night one of them tried to kill me in a parking garage. You know of any reason why the Jimmys would want to put me on a death list?"

Adrian's expression turned to one of genuine befuddlement. "No. Because you're working for my defense? Is that it?"

"I don't see why. You'd think they'd want me to find the evidence that proves you're innocent. Or could it be they want *you* out of the way, too, for some reason?"

Adrian shook his head. "You got me. I don't understand any of it."

Berenger paused a moment and then asked, "You heard about Carol Merryman?"

"Yeah, it was on the news. They let us watch CNN here."

"Don't you see? Whoever killed her—"

"I thought she committed suicide."

"Do you believe that?"

He shrugged. "What do I know? I don't give a shit about her."

"Believe me, Adrian. She didn't jump off that roof by herself."

"How do you know? Were you there?"

"No, but I've been in this business a long time. I smell a big fat rat and I think it's the same big fat rat that killed your father."

"Well, then, you better find some big fat cheese and set a big fat trap."

Berenger gave up. "Fine, Adrian. I came here to give you a little encouragement. I came here to say I believe you and I'm trying to help you. But apparently you don't give a damn." He stood and walked away from the table. Berenger gestured to the guard, indicating that he was done.

"Hey," Adrian called.

Berenger looked at the inmate.

"Thanks, Mr. Berenger." Duncan tried to smile. One corner of his mouth turned up and Berenger figured it was the best the man could do.

"You're welcome. And call me Spike."

He waited and watched the guard lead Duncan out of the visitor's room. When Berenger was outside, he called the office.

"Hi, Ringo. Do me a favor. See if Al Patton is in his office. I'd like to spend a few minutes with him."

Mel phoned him back as soon as Berenger got in his car outside the prison.

"Spike, Al Patton is booked up the rest of the day," she said. "His assistant didn't know when he'd be back in the office."

"Damn," Berenger muttered. Patton was the only one on his list who hadn't been interviewed at length. "All right, thanks." He hung up and drove out of Rikers.

She answered the phone with a weary "Yeah?"

"Hi, Gina."

When she realized who it was, she paused and said, "Hello, tiger."

"I'm surprised to find you in your room."

"Yeah, I was just about to go to dinner. Actually I'd fallen asleep. I was wondering if I'd hear from you today."

"Well, it's been a long one. You got back to the hotel okay this morning?"

"I'm here, ain't I?"

"Whatcha been doin'?"

"Sleeping, mostly. You wore me out, Spike." She laughed seductively.

"Yeah, I'm a little raw, too. Speaking of raw, would you like to get some sushi? There's a nice Japanese restaurant near your hotel."

She laughed again and said, "Sureshi."

They met at the restaurant, where they had a quiet and unhurried meal spiced up with no small amount of wasabi. They spoke very little, preferring to gaze at each other with bewildered affection. Neither one of them understood the mixed emotions they felt about the previous night. Berenger figured that they were simply refusing to acknowledge the previously dormant sexuality that had rekindled between them, so it was best left unsaid. When they did talk it was about the quality of the tuna or how hot the wasabi was. At one point during the meal Berenger laid his hand upon Gina's and they smiled at each other for a couple of seconds. It was indeed an awakening, but Berenger wasn't sure what kind. They were both lonely and single middle-aged adults, and perhaps that's all it was.

After dinner, with sinuses cleared and stomachs filled, they walked to Gina's hotel and stood on the sidewalk in front of the building.

"I'm going to Jamaica tomorrow," he said. "I didn't know if you'd still be in town when I got back."

"How long are you going to be gone?"

"I don't know. A couple of days. I hope no more than that."

"I haven't decided what I want to do. I feel like I should stay as long as Adrian's in jail. So, yeah, I'll probably be here."

He looked at his watch. "It's still early. We could—"

"We could go upstairs to my room," she suggested.

"I thought you were worn out."

She shrugged. "Hair of the dog?"

Berenger blinked. "Somehow that doesn't sound quite right in this connotation."

She laughed again, took his hand, and led him toward the door. "Come on, you big lug. I'll show you what raw really is."

22

Night Moves

(performed by Bob Seger
and the Silver Bullet Band)

When Gina was asleep, Berenger slipped out of bed, dressed, and left the hotel. The anticipation of his early flight to Jamaica and the events of the past couple of days had produced a strong bout of insomnia. He figured he might as well continue to work on the case.

He stopped by his apartment and retrieved the Kahr P9 semiautomatic before setting out on what they used to call a "covert op" back in his army days. He dressed in dark clothing, put the gun in a shoulder holster that he wore beneath a black leather jacket, and set out for the street. He hailed a taxi that took him to Hell's Kitchen, a block away from the Messengers' church.

Sticking to the shadows, Berenger moved down the street toward Ninth Avenue to survey the front of the building. All was quiet but a couple of lights were on upstairs—perhaps Reverend Theo and Brenda Twist were burning the midnight oil again. Berenger noticed that a small set of stairs descended to a basement level in front of the church, which was standard for many of the buildings from that era. These stairs often led to single-basement studio apartments that had their own access from the exterior. In this case, the door below street level appeared unused; it was rusty and dirty from years of neglect. Berenger went down the steps and turned on a penlight so that he could examine the space. The steel door was locked, of course. There was a square window at the top that was reinforced with steel mesh. Berenger peered inside and saw nothing but darkness.

One of the tools of the PI trade was a set of lockpicks and skeleton keys. Despite how they were depicted in most spy stories, lockpicks were not infallible. Depending on the type of lock and how old it was, the use of lockpicks or skeleton keys to open a door was always a gamble. Maybe one of them would fit—more often not. Berenger pulled out the ring from his trouser leg pocket and held the picks and keys so that they wouldn't jingle. He began with the keys, trying one at a time, hoping for a minor miracle. When he got to number fourteen, the key slipped into the keyhole like butter. It helped that the door was old and was fitted with what was then a fairly standard lock.

Berenger turned the key and heard the *click* that allowed him to pull the door open. He winced when the hinges squeaked loudly. If anyone were in the building, Berenger hoped that they were far enough away and didn't hear the noise.

He stepped inside and quietly shut the door behind him. Utilizing the penlight, he looked around the room. The small room was full of junk—old broken folding chairs, pieces of furniture, paintings and decorations that hadn't been used in years, and ancient cans of paint.

Another door led to the rest of the building. He tried it and was surprised to find it unlocked. Berenger moved into the hallway and found himself outside the chapel that Suzanne had told him about. He took a quick look inside, shuddered at the ugly artwork, and moved on.

He carefully ascended the stairs to the ground floor. The foyer and office were dark. He went to the sanctuary doors, put his ear to them, and determined that the room was empty. Berenger began to move away but froze when he heard the sound of a door opening above him on the second floor. He heard footsteps and quickly skirted to the corner of the foyer, where the illumination was at its darkest. He waited until the footsteps diminished and he heard the sound of a knock and another door opening. Muffled voices. Male and female.

Berenger moved to the stairs and slowly took each step one at a time. If any of them creaked he'd be discovered, so he kept to the outer edges of the steps where the carpet had not been tread upon as much and was still thick. When he reached the top, Berenger's forehead was covered in sweat.

He flattened against the wall by Reverend Theo's office. The door was slightly ajar and the lights were on inside. He heard movement and more muffled voices— but they weren't words. It sounded more like . . . *no, it couldn't be!*

Berenger inched toward the door and positioned himself so that he could steal a look through the tiny open slit.

Sure enough, the noise he had heard was what he thought it was.

Brenda Twist was sitting on the reverend's desk, naked from the waist down. The good Reverend Theo was standing in front of her, his trousers dropped to his ankles. Her bare legs were wrapped around his waist as he continually thrust against her hard and fast. Brenda's eyes were closed in ecstasy and the reverend's head was tilted up, as if he were praying.

So much for Brenda's faithfulness to Flame's memory, Berenger thought. He knew she had been hiding something and he wondered how long this had been going on. If he were to venture a guess, Berenger would have bet that poor Flame had been a cuckold long before his death.

He quietly moved away and down the hall to another open door. It was an office, presumably Brenda's. The computer was on, work materials were spread over the desk, and the decor was decidedly feminine. Her heels were on the floor underneath the desk.

Berenger risked the time to examine some of the papers. Brenda had been working on a spreadsheet when she had decided to pay a little visit to her boss's office. With a cursory glance, Berenger determined that the document was an inventory of newly purchased supplies. They consisted of the usual items—paper goods, office materials, and other ordinary expenses needed to run an organization.

But one thing stood out that struck him as odd. Most everything was listed under the heading 44th STREET ADDRESS. There was another heading that read, 22nd STREET ADDRESS. *What the hell was that?* Did the Messengers have another property that Briggs or no one else knew about? What was even more perplexing was that nothing was listed below the heading. What could they use the space for?

Berenger took the liberty to open the drawers of the desk. He rummaged around the expected supplies until he found two sets of keys. One was marked "44." The other was labeled "22." He pocketed the latter set and left the room.

Once more he quietly moved toward the stairs. He paused long enough to peek into the reverend's office. They were still at it, but now Brenda was standing, leaning over the desk. The reverend was behind her, grasping her hips with his hands. Their animalistic grunts would have made Berenger ill if he hadn't found them so funny.

He carefully descended the stairs, went down to the basement, and exited through the door he had used earlier. When he was on the street, he quickly walked to Ninth Avenue to catch a taxi going downtown.

He didn't realize that he was being watched . . . and followed.

It was nearly one o'clock in the morning when Berenger reached the area of Manhattan known as Chelsea, although technically the place was too far west to really qualify as a Chelsea address. Being so close to Eleventh Avenue, the spot was next to the West Side Highway and, beyond that, the Hudson River. It wasn't a residential area, although there were buildings on the street that surely contained apartments and lofts. Eleventh Avenue was home to several warehouses and commercial businesses. The address Berenger had noted was indeed a commercial warehouse with a roll-up steel door in front of the pedestrian entrance. Another barrier also shut off a driveway leading into what he presumed to be a loading dock.

He went to work on the padlocks that secured the roll-up door. Brenda's keys weren't marked but he got the right one on the second try. Throwing caution to the wind, he then pulled the chain that raised the door. It was terribly noisy but at this point he didn't care. All he wanted was a look inside and then he would get the hell out.

Another key opened the front door. He scanned the street to make sure he hadn't aroused anyone's suspicions and then stepped into the building. Using the penlight again, he made his way along a corridor, through a door, and into an office. Berenger found the light switch and turned it on. There wasn't much there—just a desk and chair, filing cabinets, and a phone. He shut off the light and continued into the main warehouse area.

Bingo. The place was full of musical instruments and equipment. Guitars, amps, drums, microphone stands, power cords—whatever it took to put on an impromptu concert. Some of the stuff looked used and battered while the rest appeared to be brand-new. It was stolen merchandise—he was sure of it. Every now and then the music shops in town reported a break-in and theft of equipment and instruments. The police always thought it was the work of the Jimmys or the Cuzzins and sometimes the stolen stuff was recovered when one of the bands left it behind after a street show.

And here was a cache of it.

Berenger rummaged through the place, making a mental inventory of what was there. At the back of the space he found a padlocked trunk against the wall that aroused his curiosity. None of Brenda's keys fit it, so he drew his P9 and shot the lock off. The noise of the handgun echoed loudly in the warehouse but Berenger was certain he was alone. He kicked away the padlock debris and opened the trunk.

It was full of Jimmy masks.

The discovery felt so good that Berenger wanted to laugh. The Messengers owned the building and they stored equipment for the Jimmys. It was irrefutable proof that they were in bed together.

And then Berenger nearly jumped out of his skin when the sound of a second gunshot reverberated through the space. The round hit the open trunk lid next to where he was standing. Reflexively, the private investigator jumped to the side and hit the floor.

BAM! Another shot, a foot over Berenger's head. He quickly wormed around the trunk and peered across the room. Another blast of gunfire forced him back behind the meager cover. With the P9 in hand, he lifted his arm and blindly fired the gun over the top of the trunk. Then he bolted out from behind it and ran to a set of large Peavey amps that stood seven feet away.

Another shot missed him but now he was in a better position to defend himself. Berenger carefully looked around the amp and saw his opponent.

He was a Jimmy, although an unusual one. The man wore the grotesque mask, but he wasn't wearing the punk clothing. Instead he had on what appeared to be a long-sleeved dress shirt and black trousers. Was it the same man who had shot at him the other night?

Berenger raised his gun and squeezed the trigger. The Jimmy leaped behind a pillar, avoiding the shot, and returned fire almost immediately. The slug ripped into the amplifier in front of Berenger with a loud thud.

It was a stalemate. Both men were behind adequate cover and it was up to one of them to make a move to exit or try to gain a better position. Berenger looked at the ceiling and counted three work lights. He carefully aimed the pistol and shot out each lamp one at a time. The room was plunged into darkness.

He then squatted behind the amp and waited. All was silent. He thought he could hear his opponent breathing but it was unlikely—the man was thirty feet away at best.

Then there was scuffling across the room. The Jimmy was moving. Berenger peeked around the amp but couldn't see a thing. Nevertheless he pointed the Kahr and fired at the sound. Suddenly, the warehouse door flung open and the figure darted through it. Berenger leaped to his feet and gave chase.

Before he could reach the door, however, the loading dock door creaked and started to move. The thing was opening! Berenger froze like a deer caught in headlights. The heavy door continued to rise, revealing four teenagers dressed in jeans and T-shirts. Two of them had shaved heads, one had a blue Mohawk, and the other had a normal haircut. A van was backed up to the dock, its back door open and ready to receive a load.

"Okay, you get the guitars and we'll get the amps," Mohawk said. Then he saw Berenger standing there, the gun in his hand.

"Shit, who are you?" he asked.

The only thing Berenger could think of to do was to point the gun at them and shout, "Hands up!" All four boys raised their hands.

"What the fuck?" one of the shaved heads muttered.

"Don't shoot, mister!" Normal Haircut pleaded. They were truly scared.

"Are you Jimmys?" Berenger asked.

None of the boys answered.

"Well?"

"We didn't do nuthin'," Normal Haircut said.

"Yeah," the others mumbled.

"I don't care. Did you see one of your guys run out of here just now?" Berenger asked.

"No," Mohawk said uncertainly. He turned to the others. "Did you?"

They shook their heads.

Berenger stood for a moment, allowing their fear to build. Then he holstered his weapon and said, "Have a good show, boys, wherever it is."

He then walked past them, out onto the loading dock, and jumped down to the street. The four Jimmys watched him in confusion, shrugged, and proceeded to load the van.

Berenger ran to the corner of Twenty-second and Eleventh Avenue and saw the taillights of a car speeding uptown. It was too far away for him to determine the make and model. Was that his assailant?

He scanned the street back toward Tenth Avenue and saw no other movement other than the Jimmys loading their van. Berenger returned to the warehouse and approached Mohawk.

"Hey," he said. "You got room in the van for one more roadie?"

23

Dead Man's Party

(performed by Oingo Boingo)

The van drove north on Eighth Avenue with one of the shaved heads driving. The four Jimmys had loaded it with two amps, a guitar and bass, a drum kit, and a microphone stand.

"So, like, who are you, man?" Mohawk asked Berenger.

"I'm a private investigator," he replied. He sat on a spare tire in the back of the van, holding on to the side of the vehicle for support.

"Whoa, no shit?"

"No shit."

"What were you doing in there? You're not gonna bust us are you?" Normal Haircut asked.

"I don't have the authority to bust you. I'm not a cop. Like I said, I'm a PI. I'm not after you guys. But there's one Jimmy I'm looking for. He was using me for target practice tonight."

"You know, I thought I heard gunshots before we opened the loading door," one of the shaved heads said. "I thought it was just noise from the door or something."

"So you wouldn't have any idea who that might have been?" Berenger asked.

"No, man, we didn't see a thing," Mohawk said.

Berenger gestured to the instruments. "So what instruments do you guys play?"

"Oh, we're not the band," Normal Haircut replied. "We're just the roadies. The band will meet us at the gig."

"How are these things set up, anyway?" Berenger asked.

"We get orders down the pipe."

"Yeah, orders."

"From who?" Berenger asked.

"Look, man," Mohawk said, "I don't know if we should be talking to you like this. We could get into some deep shit."

Berenger held up his hand like a Boy Scout. "I swear I won't rat on you. It's for my own information. Like I said, I'm trying to track down a guy."

The teens looked at each other. Then Mohawk said, "Well, Jimmy is the one who decides when we put on a show."

"Jimmy?"

"The boss."

"His name is really Jimmy?"

Mohawk shrugged. "Hell if I know. That's what he goes by. That's why—"

"—why you're the Jimmys," Berenger finished. "I get it. What does he look like? Who is he really?"

"Never seen him."

"Nope, we don't know him."

"He's black, that's all we know about him."

Mohawk explained as he gestured to the gear around him. "He's above all this. He just plans stuff and helps with legal problems if any Jimmys get arrested."

"Kinda like the mafia," Berenger suggested.

"I guess so. Jimmy's supposedly real connected."

"So he has lieutenants and enforcers and so forth, and the orders get handed down to you guys?"

Normal Haircut nodded. "Us and a whole lot more like us. We're the street soldiers, you might say."

"And the Cuzzins, they work the same way?"

"Fuck the Cuzzins," Mohawk said. "Those guys are losers."

"Yeah, losers."

"Real shitheads."

Berenger smiled. He knew enough not to pursue that topic further. "So how do I find Jimmy if I want to meet him?"

"Beats me," Normal Haircut said.

"Nobody meets Jimmy," Mohawk replied. "Forget it."

"Yeah, forget it."

The driver spoke up. "Better put on the masks, guys. We're nearly there."

"Where's there?" Berenger asked.

Mohawk smiled broadly. "The Jimmys are playing Madison Square Garden tonight."

"Well, outside of it anyway," Normal Haircut said.

The four boys put on Jimmy masks as the van parked on Thirty-third Street. They opened the back and began to unload the equipment. Berenger got out and saw three other Jimmys waiting in the darkness.

"Who's this asshole?" one of them asked as he picked up the guitar. The three were obviously the band.

"Oh, he's cool, man," Mohawk said. "He helped us load the van."

"Are you a Jimmy?"

"No," Berenger replied. "Just came along for the ride."

"Shit, the guy's a cop!" another of the new Jimmys proclaimed.

"I'm not a cop. Don't sweat it. I'm just gonna observe and see who shows up."

Mohawk gestured to the large open area in front of Madison Square Garden that faced Seventh Avenue. "Take a look, man. That's who showed up."

Berenger turned and his jaw dropped. There were at least a hundred people standing in the darkness. The lights around the building cast unholy illumination on the motley crew of skinheads, punks, bikers, and just plain teenagers.

Someone shouted, "There they are! The Jimmys are here!"

The crowd roared in appreciation as if one of the world's supergroups had just pulled up to play a free concert.

The roadies quickly found the power outlets near the building and signaled the band that they were ready to go. The setup was remarkably fast. Berenger figured they had it down to a science. These guerrilla-style gigs had to get in and get out before the law noticed. Berenger knew it wouldn't be long with a crowd this size gathering in front of the Garden at this time of night.

The guitarist checked his mike and then counted off. The band launched into a metal-rap tune that incited the crowd to "burn down the Garden." The audience cheered and applauded.

Berenger stood near the van and laughed. The spectacle was simultaneously ridiculous and inspiring. Once again he was impressed with how the Jimmys had tapped into the pulse of the street and created what could arguably be labeled a new art form, albeit an illegal one. It was a party for the underworld.

The band launched into a grunge-punk number when Berenger noticed a tall thin man approaching the van. He was so tall that the shape was familiar, someone Berenger thought he knew. One of the roadies held up a hand in greeting and the two of them began to walk closer. Berenger drew back into the shadows until they came into better light.

Dave Bristol slapped the Jimmy on the back and handed him an envelope. In return, the Jimmy gave Bristol a small packet. They exchanged a few words and then Bristol walked away.

Berenger set out after him, keeping a safe distance. It was fairly simple to tail the drummer, even in the dark. Bristol walked toward the IRT subway station and went down the stairs. Berenger knew that Bristol lived on West Seventy-fourth Street, just west of Broadway. Perhaps he was going home.

For a scary moment Berenger entertained the notion that Bristol was "Jimmy." But the kids in the van had said that Jimmy was black. Tommy Briggs had also said that the Jimmys originated in the Caribbean, so a black leader made more sense. Added to that was the new-found revelation that the Messengers—another Caribbean operation—were tied to the Jimmys. In all likelihood the leader was indeed a black man. It couldn't be Bristol.

The drummer was most likely buying drugs from the Jimmys. That had to be it. The Jimmys sold to rock stars. But why would Bristol need to come to the concerts? Couldn't the Jimmys deliver the stuff directly to him?

Berenger heard police sirens approaching the area. The band had segued into their third number, right on cue. As if on a signal, the crowd began to run about and cause damage to whatever property they possibly could before the cops arrived. They overturned trash cans, broke the glass in bus-stop advertising displays, and threw debris at the Garden building.

It was time to split. Berenger looked up and saw a taxi slowly cruising along Seventh, the driver gaping at the marvel unfolding on the street. Berenger held up his hand and called for the driver to stop. At first the driver thought he was being accosted by one of the hoodlums until he realized that it was a middle-aged man flagging him down.

Berenger got in the backseat and said, "Broadway and Seventy-fourth, please."

The taxi let him off at the corner just as a handful of people emerged from the Seventy-second Street subway station. Berenger had been lucky. Bristol probably had to wait five or ten minutes for the train and the cab had beaten it uptown.

Berenger hugged the wall in the shadows and waited. After a moment, lanky Dave Bristol walked around the corner and headed down the street to his town house. Berenger bolted out of the darkness and approached the drummer.

"Dave."

Bristol shrieked and involuntarily leaped several steps sideways.

"Hold on, it's me, Spike," Berenger said.

Bristol shook his head and said, "Holy *fuck*, Spike! You scared the *shit* out of me!"

"Sorry, man. I didn't mean to." Actually he did but Berenger wasn't going to tell him that.

"What the hell are you doing? You were standing there in the dark, weren't you! Just waiting for me!"

"I need to talk to you, Dave, let's keep walking."

Bristol backed away from him. "Nuh uh, Berenger. This is no way to—"

Berenger shoved the P9 into Bristol's side. "Just shut up and keep walking, Dave."

"Wha—? Spike?" Bristol looked at the gun in shock and surprise.

"This is just to show you I mean business," Berenger said. "Let's go to your place and have a little talk." He holstered the gun. "Look, see, I put it away. Come on, Dave, we've been friends a long time. I need to talk."

"All . . . all right, Spike."

They walked together until they reached the brownstone that Bristol had bought with his music royalties. He wasn't a superstar in the same league as someone like Flame, but he did very well for himself. When he wasn't playing in a well-known band like Hay Fever or Flame's Heat, he was a highly sought-after session man.

Bristol unlocked the door and held it open for Berenger. They stepped into the foyer where Bristol paused to shut off the security alarm, and then he led the PI into the living room. The four-story town house was a beauty and Bristol had maintained it well.

"Would you like a drink, Spike?" Bristol asked.

"No thanks."

"Really? Spike Berenger refusing a drink?"

"Just sit down a minute, Dave."

Bristol gestured to the sofa. Berenger sat and Bristol took the armchair that faced it. "Okay, Spike. What's this all about?"

"What do you have to do with the Jimmys?"

The look on Bristol's face indicated that he hadn't expected the question. "The Jimmys? Why, I—"

"Don't lie, Dave. I've seen you twice with them. I saw you buy something tonight down at the Garden. What's going on? Are you on horse again?"

Bristol looked at his feet. He was busted. After a pause, he said, "It's not H. It's coke. H brings me down too much. Coke mixes better with the booze."

"How long have you been dealing with the Jimmys?"

"Not that long. About a year."

"How did you hook up?"

"You know. Word of mouth. A friend of a friend of a friend."

"So why do you go to them? Why don't they deliver the stuff to you right here?"

Bristol shrugged. "Uhm, my, regular dealer, he's out of town. So I have to go to the shows until he, er, gets back. I'm on the network, you see."

"Network?"

"There's an e-mail list—you know, Listserv—it goes out to customers and fans whenever there's going to be a Jimmys show. The roadies know me. I go, conduct my business, and I'm out of there before the cops show up."

"That's damn risky, Dave," Berenger said. "Suppose you got popped?"

"I know, it's stupid. What can I say?"

For a moment the two men stared at each other. Berenger could see that the normally volatile Bristol was humbled and embarrassed.

"Why, Spike?" the drummer finally asked. "What's it to you?"

"The Jimmys have tried to kill me twice in the last week. I want to know why."

"What?"

"You heard me. Do you know anything about it?"

"Of course not! Why would they want to kill you?"

"That's exactly what I want to know. I think it might have something to do with Flame and Adrian Duncan. Adrian was dealing for the Jimmys, did you know that?"

"Actually . . . yeah, I did know that. It was Adrian that hooked me up. That's why I have to go to the shows to get my shit. Adrian's in jail."

"Oh, geez," Berenger said. "Okay, how about this? Are you aware that the Jimmys are doing business with the Messengers?"

Another look of incredulity passed over Bristol's face. "What? No! I don't believe it!"

"It's true. All right, look. I want to talk to someone in charge. I want to go as high up as I can. I want to meet Jimmy."

"Jimmy!"

"I want to have a conversation with him."

"Nobody meets Jimmy, Spike," Bristol said. "I've never met Jimmy!"

"You've got the clout, Dave. You're a major player in the music biz. I think if you had enough of a reason to want to meet the guy, you could do it. I want you to set up a meeting in the next couple of days. Will you try?"

"Spike, I don't know . . ."

"I'm going to Jamaica—" He looked at his watch. "—in a few hours. I hope to be back the next day or possibly the day after that. I want to meet Jimmy as soon as I return. Otherwise, Dave, I can make things pretty difficult for you."

"What do you mean?" Bristol furrowed his brow. Berenger could see the anger building.

"You, the cocaine, the Jimmys. You know what I do for a living."

"You wouldn't dare."

"Look, we're talking about a death threat on my head, Dave. I have to get to the bottom of it. I'm asking you as a friend. If you won't do it as a friend, then I have to play it like a hard-ass. Now are you going to help me or not?"

Bristol rubbed his gnarly chin. He stood and went to the bar that spanned one side of the living room. He took a bottle of bourbon and poured a tumbler full. He downed it in one gulp.

"All right," he said. "Call me as soon as you get back from Jamaica."

24

Stir It Up

(performed by Bob Marley and the Wailers)

The Air Jamaica flight landed on time at the Montego Bay airport, where Berenger rented a car for the drive along the northern coast. Berenger never liked Jamaica much. He believed it to be an island vacation spot that had seen its day and had sadly deteriorated. Because it was generally considered dangerous to step outside of the resort hotels into the poverty-stricken communities, the hotel managers fenced their grounds as if they were stockades. Berenger always felt he was a prisoner when he stayed in one. The resorts were nice, had great food and other amenities—but it was all an illusion. The hotels weren't *Jamaica*. They were miniature Disneylands where mostly white, middle- and upper-class clientele could go and *pretend* they were on an island paradise. It was easy to ignore the country's crime and poverty while sequestered inside a resort hotel. Berenger preferred the Bahamas and many of the other West Indian stops.

Still, a Caribbean island was a Caribbean island. The sun was hot, the ocean was deep blue, and reggae music filled the fresh air. As he drove eastward along the coast, Berenger rolled down the window and did his best to turn a blind eye to the squalor of the shanty-towns along the way.

He eventually reached Ocho Rios, one of the three major tourist areas on the island. Berenger pulled into the Jamaica Grand, a four-star all-inclusive resort. He had stayed there before and he figured it was as good as any of the others. After checking in, he dropped the overnight bag in his room and went straight to the bar. The place was already crowded and it wasn't quite noon. Men and women wearing swimming attire—some of them were *barely* wearing it—lounged around with their frozen piña coladas, daiquiris, and margaritas. Berenger was dressed in Bermuda shorts and a Hawaiian shirt, sandals, and dark sunglasses, so he looked as if he belonged.

He took a stool at the bar and ordered a piña colada. When in Rome . . .

"Mistah Berenger?"

The voice had the familiar musical lilt of a Jamaican accent. Berenger turned to see a tall, thin black man with graying short hair. He, too, wore a Hawaiian shirt, shorts, and sandals.

"Yes?"

"I'm Steve Baskin." The two men shook hands.

"Spike Berenger. I hope you weren't waiting long."

"Not at all. I checked your flight arrival and allowed time for you t' drive over dis way."

"Let's go over here where we can have some privacy." Berenger hopped off the stool and carried his drink to a table away from the crowd.

"I understand you're with the FBI?" Berenger asked.

"No more. I used t' be. I'm retired. But I still maintain contacts."

"You know Tommy Briggs?"

"No, never met him. I know of him. My contact in New York knows him."

"Tommy's my colleague. We work together. How much do you know about why I'm here?"

"Only dat you're interested in investigatin' the Messengers and their church."

"Can you take me there?"

"Sure. Their property is about ten minutes away from Ocho Rios. Security is very tight there. It's like one of deez resorts."

"I don't doubt it. What can you tell me about them?"

Baskin shrugged and said, "Not too much. Dey a reclusive bunch. It's a small staff residing there when no retreats go on."

"Do you know Chucky Tools?"

"Yes, I have met him."

"What's he like?"

Baskin shrugged again. "I never figured him t' be anythin'. He stays out of trouble. He's not a tough guy."

"Was it you that told our people in New York that the Messengers use drugs at these retreats?"

"Dat's right, man. Dey drink a special wine dat's made here on de island. Dey lace de wine with some drug dat loosens up people. Makes dem easy, you know what I mean?"

"Yes. I'd like to try and get a sample of it. Oh, and have you ever heard of a gang called the Jimmys?"

Baskin frowned. "No, I don't think so. Who are dey?"

"They're in New York but supposedly originated in the Caribbean."

He shook his head. "Can't say I know dem."

Berenger nodded. "Okay. You think Tools will talk to me?"

"Dey don't like strangers on de property. Dey prob'ly turn you away."

"Well, let's try it the polite way first. Then if that fails, we might need to do some sneaking around after dark. Are you up for that?"

Baskin grinned, revealing pearly white teeth. "Whatever you say, Mistah Berenger."

"Call me Spike."

The property was off the main highway, marked with a sign proclaiming THE MESSENGERS—A RETREAT FOR THE ENLIGHTENED. Baskin drove an old Ford Pinto onto a dirt road that went about a hundred yards in and then forked. Another sign indicated that the path to the left went to the church. The path to the right was marked PRIVATE—NO TRESPASSING.

"De church is open t' de public, of course," Baskin said. "Anyone can go t' de services, every Sunday."

"Just one service a week?" Berenger asked.

"As far as I know."

"In New York they hold them every day, I think. Sometimes twice a day."

"When Reverend Theo is in town de services are more frequent."

"What's the other road lead to?"

"Dat's where de offices are and where de retreats are held."

"Let's see the church."

Baskin drove to the left and followed the road a half mile to a small schoolhouselike structure that was painted white. A large cross adorned the eave. The parking area was empty.

"Looks deserted," Berenger said.

"You won't find anyone here at dis time of day. Dey at de other place."

Baskin drove around the building so Berenger could see all sides of the modest church and then drove out toward the other fork. About a half mile from the cross-road they came upon a barbed-wire fence and a gate. Baskin rolled down the window and pressed the call button on an intercom built next to the gate.

"Yes?" came a smooth male voice.

"We like t' see Mistah Tools, please."

"Who's calling?"

"Mistah Spike Berenger, from New York City. I'm his driver, Steve Baskin."

"What's this about?"

"Mistah Berenger is with a security firm in New York. He has some questions about de Messengers."

"Just a moment, please."

Baskin looked at Berenger and said, "I'm not sure tellin' de truth was de right thing t' do in dis case."

Berenger replied, "I always try to be honest about who I am unless special circumstances dictate otherwise. At this point I can't find a reason for special circum-stances."

The voice came back. "I'm sorry but Mistah Tools not here."

"He's not?"

"No, sir."

"When might he return?"

"Can't say. Probably not today."

"I see. Well, thank you. We try another time."

Baskin reversed, turned the car around, and headed out. "Now what?" he asked.

"We go to Plan B," Berenger said.

It was shortly after 11:00 P.M. when Berenger and Baskin parked the Ford in the brush off the main highway.

Baskin had supplied Berenger with boots, a soldier's camouflage outfit, and a backpack full of various tools he might need. Baskin also let the private investigator borrow a SIG P239 9mm semiautomatic. Berenger liked SIG and thought the company made excellent firearms, although for a semi he preferred his personal Kahr P9 that he had to leave at home.

They hiked through the thick junglelike terrain using small flashlights for illumination. Berenger asked Baskin about the possibility of stepping on snakes or other dangerous animals and Baskin replied that it was "entirely possible." That answer didn't bother Berenger. His time in Southeast Asia had forever immunized him against fear of the wild. He had performed many missions that involved traipsing through the jungles of not only Vietnam but also Laos, Cambodia, and the Philippines. Moving through the brush brought back memories—not always unpleasant ones—of the two years he had spent in the military as a criminal investigations special agent. The smell and feel of the jungle, the humidity, the crunching of branches beneath the boots, the constant chirping of insects, and the bright moon in the night sky served to remind Berenger that he was still a soldier, albeit an older and heavier one.

When they reached the barbed-wire fence, Baskin whispered, "Here we are. You sure you don't want me t' come in wit' you?"

"No, Steve, I want to do this alone. But thanks. Go on back to the car and wait. If I'm not back by dawn, bring in the cavalry."

"Okay, you're de boss. By de way, if you find Mistah Tools, just lean on him a little. I think he be somebody dat don't like t' get hurt." The men shook hands and Baskin took off into the dense thicket. Berenger removed the backpack, opened it, and found the wire cutters Baskin had placed inside. With four snips, he cut the wire wide enough for him to slip through. After donning the backpack once again, Berenger crawled through the hole and surveyed the property below him.

He was on the top of a slope that overlooked the retreat. A large farmhouse was the main focal point. It was a two-story structure that appeared to be fifty or sixty years old, built in the grand British Imperial style from the era when the UK was Jamaica's caretaker. Berenger suspected that a wealthy Brit who grew tobacco or coffee beans originally owned the property.

An armed guard sat in a chair on the front porch of the main house. Berenger wondered why a church organization would need an armed guard; in his opinion, this was further evidence that the Messengers were up to no good. The guard didn't appear very alert. His chin was on his chest and the rifle lay in his lap.

Berenger moved slowly and quietly out of the brush and then darted down the slope to the side of the building. He peered through a window into a dark room. He tried to open the window but it was locked. Berenger skirted along the wall to another one and tried it. It opened freely.

He climbed through the opening, softly shut the window, and found himself in an office. There was a photocopier in the corner, mailbox slots on the wall, a postage machine, stacks of copy paper, and boxes of Messenger literature. The mail room.

Berenger peeked into the corridor and found it empty. Somewhere in the distance Bob Marley and the Wailers were singing one of their many hits on a CD player. He snaked down the hallway, his back to the wall, and eventually came to a large open foyer facing the front door.

A long reception desk was unmanned but Berenger could see small mailboxes with corresponding keys hanging over each opening. Apparently the place served partly as a hotel—guests stayed in assigned rooms during the retreats. A stack of maps showing both floors of the building lay on the desk; Berenger picked one up and studied it for a moment. The guest rooms occupied the second floor while the first floor had a sanctuary, a dining hall, a recreation room, a kitchen, and several offices.

Berenger made his way toward the kitchen, which was around the other side of the foyer and down the hall, next to the dining room. Luckily, it was empty. Using the flashlight he examined the cabinets and refrigerators and found only food supplies and dining ware. A door next to the refrigerator was not on the map. A storage room, perhaps? He tried the knob but it was locked. Not about to let that stop him, Berenger reached into the backpack and removed a putty knife that Baskin had given him. It served as a lockpick but the going wasn't easy. The bolt was sturdy and old—it didn't give without a good deal of force on Berenger's part. He finally got the door open to reveal a staircase leading down into darkness.

He stepped through the door, closed it behind him, and felt an abrupt decrease in temperature. Shining the flashlight on the steps in front of him, he descended to the bottom and realized he was in a wine cellar. Bingo.

There were nearly fifty bottles lying horizontally in cubicles on one wall. He took one and examined the label. It was a cabernet made by Jamaican Spirits, a company he had never heard of. He stuck the bottle in his backpack, turned, and saw two large kegs occupying the other half of the room. Empty bottles sat in crates on a table. They obviously made and bottled the wine on the premises.

Berenger took an empty bottle, held it under a keg spigot, and poured a little of the red liquid into it. He smelled the stuff but couldn't discern anything other than a fruity wine with a hint of charcoal. He wasn't much of a connoisseur but to him the aroma was quite nice. At any rate, the drugs were either mixed into the wine before bottling or they were added after the wine was opened for serving.

He poured the wine into a slop sink and replaced the empty bottle. He then ascended the stairs to the kitchen. Berenger went back into the corridor and headed toward the sanctuary. The Bob Marley music grew louder as he approached the room. First making sure no guards were about, Berenger opened the double doors slightly and looked inside. The sanctuary was a near carbon copy of the Messengers' place in New York. A little larger, able to hold a hundred people or so, it was decorated in the same grisly religious iconography that he and Suzanne had found so disturbing.

A black man with dreadlocks stood at the altar preparing something, his back to Berenger. He hadn't heard the doors open, for a portable CD player on the floor was blasting out the reggae music. Berenger quietly let the doors swing shut behind him and he walked softly down the center aisle.

"Are you Chucky Tools?" he finally asked in a loud, commanding voice.

The man jumped and turned. "Damn, man! You scared de *shit* out of me!" He was in his forties, wiry, and looked more like a reggae musician than a church employee. Like Baskin, he also spoke with a pronounced Jamaican accent. "Who *are* you, man? How did you get in here?"

"Answer the question," Berenger said. He grabbed the man by the shirt, turned him around, and forced him against the altar. Berenger quickly patted him down and found no weapons.

"What is dis, man? Are you de police?" he wailed.

"Are you Chucky Tools?"

"Ya man! Ya!"

Berenger turned him around and said, "I'm not the police. I'm worse. I want some answers and I want them fast. If you cooperate I'll leave and you'll never know I was here. I warn you, though, I'm known to play rough if I don't get what I want."

"Sure, man, sure. What do you want t' know?"

"Tell me what goes on at the Messengers' rituals. How do you brainwash the members?"

"Brainwash? We don't brainwash—"

Berenger slapped the man hard. "Don't lie. I know how you lace the wine with drugs. What are they?"

"Shit, man." Tools rubbed his cheek. "Dat hurt."

"That was just a love tap because I like you. If you make me mad I can't be responsible for what happens next."

"Okay, okay. We put Reverend Theo's special mixture in de wine. But only for de members we want t' influence. You know."

"No, I don't know. What's in the special mixture?"

"Mostly X, man." Ecstasy. MDMA. A powerful and illegal drug that breaks down inhibitions and encourages emotional responses from the users.

"What else?"

"Sodium Pentothal. De reverend mixes it just right."

Berenger thought as such. Sodium Pentothal, the so-called "truth serum," most likely exacerbated the symptoms produced by the Ecstasy. After an extended and

241

carefully dispensed regimen of such a mixture, users would believe anything they're told.

"And what happens when the members are thoroughly stoned on the stuff?"

Tools held out his hands. "Man, de reverend does all dat. He's de master. During de sessions he treats dem like patients, man. You know, like he's a psychiatrist or somethin'. He lays all kinds of guilt trips on dem and dey have what he calls emotional breakthroughs. Most of dem end up in tears and beg de reverend to let dem help de Messengers any way dey can."

"I take it the drugs are used only on rich members? The ones who'll give money to the Messengers?"

"Pretty much." Tools was truly frightened and wasn't about to lie now. "What are you going t' do t' me?"

"Tell me about Flame. Do you remember Flame?"

"Sure, everyone knows Flame here. He's de biggest star dat ever came t' de Messengers."

"Tell me about his visits."

"Well, dat was a long time ago. I don't know. Four or five years, maybe six . . ."

Berenger opened the backpack, removed the SIG, and stuck it in Tools's face. "You better start remembering."

"Okay, okay!" Tools raised his hands. "Flame came and was here, I don't know, two or three weeks de first time. He came back with some of his people de second time and stayed longer. He went through de treatments just like everyone else and came out a true believer. He pledged his life t' de Messengers."

"The reverend just wanted Flame's money, right?"

"I guess so."

"Who came with Flame that second time?"

"I don't know. His manager, I think. Bald guy."

"Al Patton?"

"Dat's him. Ya, Al Patton."

"Who else?"

"Well, by dat time he was with Brenda. Dey never left each other's sides."

"Who else came with him from New York?"

"Dat's it. Just her and de bald guy. Mistah Patton couldn't get into it. De drugs didn't affect him and he left after a couple of days. That happens with some people. Anyway, he said he felt sick or somethin'. He never came back. De driver took him back t' Montego Bay t' catch a plane back t' New York."

"The driver? Flame's driver? You mean Ron Black?"

At the mention of the Black's name, Tools's eyes widened. It was as if he had let something slip and regretted it. "Er . . . Ron Black? No, I don't think I know dat name."

Berenger thrust the barrel of the SIG into Tools's nose. "Yes, you do," he said.

"Er, ya, I guess I do. He worked for de Messengers. Long time. But he started workin' for Flame by de time Flame came back dat second time."

"And now he's back with the Messengers. Okay, Mr. Tools, I have one more question to ask you. Very recently Reverend Theo sent you an e-mail and he said someone in your organization was messing up. You replied, saying that he should remember who became 'very friendly' during a retreat. Who exactly did you mean?"

Tools winced and almost started to cry. "Oh, man, if I tell you dat, my life, it be worthless!"

"If you don't tell me, in a minute from now you won't have a life at all."

Tools's eyes darted back and forth furtively as he made sure no one else was listening. "It was Mistah

Patton and Ron Black. Dey hung out t'gether de two days dat Patton was here."

Berenger lowered the gun. His instincts told him that Tools was telling the truth.

"Just who the hell *is* Ron Black, anyway?" he asked.

Tools gulped loudly and whispered, "A very bad man."

25

Black Limousine

(performed by The Rolling Stones)

On the morning after Berenger had infiltrated the Messengers' Jamaican headquarters, Suzanne Prescott sat in her Rockin' Security office, intently studying several photographs of Flame that she had spread out on the desk. Of the eight pictures, seven were recently shot candid group settings. Brenda Twist was with him in every pose. She clung to his arm like a dutiful companion but there was something about the body language that wasn't right. Having studied a number of Eastern philosophical tenets, Suzanne was in tune with the various emotional signals the body exhibited. It went hand in hand with yoga and martial arts.

The couple's body language indicated that she was the one in control of the relationship. Brenda was the dominant force working between them. Suzanne wondered how such a young woman could have that kind of influence on a powerful and famous rock star like Flame, but there it was.

Another photo showed Flame posing with Al Patton, one of the most famous manager/producers in the music business. The two men had their arms around each other and were smiling for the camera. The flash had produced a shiny glare on Patton's bald head. Suzanne found it funny and chuckled.

Flame was with Reverend Theo in another shot, surrounded by other members of the Messengers. None of the sycophants faced the camera but instead focused solely on the reverend and his star recruit. Theo was smiling his award-winning grin and Flame appeared to be in awe of the man.

Suzanne squinted when she noticed the other bald head at the back of the group. It was Ron Black, the driver. She reached into a desk drawer and removed a magnifying glass. Holding it above the photo, she examined the man more closely. It struck her as odd that Black's head was very similar to that of Al Patton's. Both men were bald and the shape and size of their skulls were strikingly similar.

That wasn't all that impressed her about Black. He was the only one in the group, other than Flame and the reverend, who was looking at the camera, and there was a snarl on his face.

I've seen that snarl before, Suzanne thought. *But where?*

She looked over the photos to see if Black was in any of the other shots but that was the only one. She needed to see him again in person, close up if possible. The first time she had met him there was something familiar about the guy that gave her the creeps. What was it?

She had to find out.

Flame's limo wasn't parked anywhere near the Messengers' church so she decided to go into the pizza parlor across the street and wait for a while. Perhaps Black was out on an errand or something. She got a slice and sat where she could watch through the window and monitor the comings and goings. Twenty minutes went by before the limousine pulled up in front of the church.

Ron Black got out of the driver's seat, trotted up the steps to the front door, and went inside. Suzanne stood, waved good-bye to the pizza chef, and left the restaurant. She was determined to talk to the man even though he frightened her. But that was the point—Suzanne needed to know why he scared her.

Before she could cross the street, however, Black emerged from the church and ran down the steps to the limo.

"Mr. Black?" Suzanne called, but the man didn't hear her. He had already slammed the door and started the engine. The limo rolled out into the street and picked up speed.

At that moment a taxicab was approaching from the end of the block. Suzanne thanked her lucky stars and raised her hand. When the driver pulled over, she got in the backseat and said, "Can you follow that limousine without being seen?"

The Middle Eastern driver shrugged.

"There'll be an extra twenty in it for you on top of the meter plus a generous tip."

The driver sped after the limo, which drove east across Eighth Avenue, through Broadway, and then past Seventh. At Fifth Avenue it turned south and the cabdriver deftly did the same. When the limo reached Forty-second Street, it slowed slightly and moved over to the east side of the avenue. It eventually stopped in front of the Liquid Metal Records building.

Al Patton came out the front door and rushed to the limo. He got in the front passenger seat and Black drove away.

Holy moley! Suzanne thought. Ron Black and Al Patton together? What was *that* all about? She doubted they were going to a convention for bald men.

"Keep on them," she told the driver.

The driver nodded. He obviously enjoyed the challenge.

The limo turned west to Sixth Avenue and then headed north. The taxi stayed a good hundred feet or more behind it. When the limo reached Central Park, it made a left and then turned north on Broadway. At one point the taxi driver almost lost them because of a sudden red light he was unable to run. The limo drove nearly six blocks ahead of them before the light turned green. The cabdriver stepped on it to make up for the lost ground by speeding through three yellow lights.

"You're doing great," Suzanne told the driver.

The limo eventually reached the area around Columbia University. At the corner of Broadway and 114th Street, it pulled to the curb and stopped.

"Pull over," Suzanne ordered her driver. "Don't let them see you." The driver complied and moved into a loading zone four car lengths behind the limo. For a few moments nothing happened. No one got out of the limo.

Then, out of nowhere, Joshua Duncan appeared on the sidewalk. He looked into the passenger side of the limo, spoke a few words, and then got into the back. Then the limo moved into traffic and turned east.

"Follow them!" Suzanne commanded.

Jumping jackrabbits, she thought. Joshua Duncan, Al Patton, and Ron Black together in one place. How could these three diverse people be friendly with each other? It was true that Joshua was going to be the owner of Flame's business. Perhaps Patton was courting him?

Some kind of major deal was taking place? But why was Ron Black involved? Was he merely a chauffeur? But that didn't make any sense because *he* worked for the Messengers now. Didn't he? And why couldn't Joshua and Patton meet in Patton's office?

The limo entered Central Park. The taxi driver did his best to follow them along the winding roads without alerting Black that the limo was being followed. When the limo backtracked and began retracing its route, Suzanne realized that Black was aimlessly roving through the park, making circles. The men inside *were* having a meeting and they were doing it in private.

At one point the limo sped under an overpass just as a flock of bicycles soared across the road in front of the taxi. The driver was forced to stop as the cyclists waved in gratitude. But the damage was done. When the cab finally slipped under the overpass and saw the three-pronged fork in the road and no limousine, Suzanne knew they had lost it.

"Damn," she said.

"I am sorry, madam," the driver said. "Maybe they went that way?" He pointed to one of the forks and Suzanne replied, "No, forget it. Just take me back to the spot on Sixth Avenue where the limo picked up the first man. Okay?"

The driver nodded and made his way out of the park.

Twenty minutes later, the cab sat across from Patton's building as Suzanne kept one eye on the street and one on the meter. This was going to be an expensive surveillance. Suzanne decided to cut it off when the meter reached $350.

She was gathering her purse and preparing to pay the driver when the limousine suddenly appeared on the avenue. Suzanne had the driver stop the meter—she paid him the fare, a tip, and the promised twenty-dollar bonus. "Wait just a second, would you?" she asked.

"No problem."

Suzanne watched as Al Patton got out of the limo. She caught a glimpse of Ron Black at the wheel for the brief second the passenger door was open. His head was turned in her direction. Patton closed the door and went inside his building, and then the limo drove away.

Had Ron Black snarled at her? Surely it was her imagination, since the limo was really too far away for her to adequately see his expression. That photo at the office had shaken her. What was it about Ron Black that set off alarms in her head? *Think, Suzanne, think!* She closed her eyes and let the images flow.

That snarl.

The bald head.

A jail cell came into view.

A frightened teenage girl sat on a bench.

Oh my God!

The memory burst through the wall in Suzanne's mind as her heart rate increased dramatically.

She quickly got out of the cab. Getting back to the office was a priority but she was flat broke. She needed to find and access an ATM for more cab fare—or even bus fare. Suzanne remembered that a branch of her bank was up at Fiftieth Street and Madison Avenue, so she walked a block east and headed north. As she moved purposefully across Forty-second Street, she punched the speed-dial number on her cell phone and put the instrument to her ear.

Melanie Starkey answered. "Rockin' Security."

"Ringo, it's me."

"Hi, Suzanne. Spike called, says he's on the way home."

"Great. Listen, I've just completed a surveillance of Ron Black, the limo driver. I have some very interesting news. Is Tommy Briggs around?"

"No, he's out. You have his cell number?"

"Yeah. I'll call him. In the meantime, if Spike calls again, tell him I may have a break in the case."

"Wow, can you tell me?"

"Not now. I have to put some things together first. In my head."

"Oh, well in that case, I'll start a good novel like *War and Peace* or something."

"Very funny. I'll be there soon."

"Bye!"

Suzanne was nearing Forty-third Street. She began to look up Tommy Briggs's number in her phone's address book when a dark shape moved into her peripheral vision.

She gasped when she saw that the black limousine was cruising slowly beside her. The driver's window was down and Ron Black stared at her.

"Ms. Prescott," he said. Suzanne stopped walking and the limo halted as well. She was too shocked to react. By the time it registered in Suzanne's brain that Black was pointing a handgun at her, the weapon had already fired.

26

Doctor Rock

(performed by Motörhead)

The Air Jamaica flight landed at JFK Airport mid-afternoon. Berenger was glad to be back but he was more interested in turning on his cell phone and checking his messages, and then grabbing a bite to eat. He had neglected to have a good breakfast and of course there was nothing served on the plane. As soon as the flight attendant announced that portable electronic devices and cell phones could be used again, Berenger whipped out his Motorola and powered it up. He quickly punched the speed-dial number to access his voice mail and found two very disturbing messages.

"Mr. Berenger, this is Betty Samuels at Franklin Village. Please give me a call as soon as you can. I've tried to reach you at home as well. Your mother has suffered a mild stroke. Don't be alarmed, she's going to be fine. She's at Franklin Hospital Medical Center in Valley Stream undergoing some tests." The woman left her office and cell phone numbers.

When he heard the message, Berenger experienced that tingly sensation produced by a combination of fear, adrenaline release, and worry. Suddenly he wasn't hungry anymore.

The second message was worse. The shaky timbre of his assistant's voice immediately sent up the red flags. "Spike, it's Mel. Call me as soon as you can. Something's happened. It's Suzanne. She's . . . she's been shot, Spike. They've taken her to New York Hospital and she's in surgery. Oh, God, Spike, we don't know if she's going to make it. It's pretty bad. Call me as soon as you get this."

As the plane pulled up to the gate and the passengers leaped to retrieve their things from the overhead compartments, Berenger remained in his seat, completely stunned. For several minutes he was unable to move.

How could this have happened? What the hell was going on? Suzanne? Shot? By whom? And his mom? A stroke? *My God!*

When he realized that he was one of the few remaining passengers on the plane, he stood, grabbed his overnight bag, and ran into the terminal. As he walked toward the airport exit he quickly dialed Betty Samuels's number. He got her voice mail and left a message that he was coming to Long Island and would go straight to the hospital. Berenger then called Mel.

"Rockin' Security."

"Mel!"

"Oh, Spike." She sounded very upset. "I'm glad you're back."

"Me too. How is she?"

"Not good. She's in surgery right now. We're not going to know anything until later. Probably not until tonight."

"What happened? Who did this?"

"No one knows. She was on Madison Avenue, midtown, walking on the street. There weren't any witnesses but several people heard the shots. A pedestrian called 911 as soon as it happened. She was lucky, the ambulance got there really fast."

"Aw, man." Berenger rubbed his eyes. "Do you know where she was hit?"

"In the chest, Spike. Twice."

"All right. Listen. My mom has had a stroke."

"Jesus, Spike!"

"Yeah. I'm gonna run out to Long Island and check on her. Since we're not gonna know anything about Suzanne until later, I'll take care of my mom first. Is anyone at the hospital with Suzanne?"

"Rudy went over there. The doctor told him it would probably be hours, so he got Rudy's cell phone number and told him he could leave if he wanted to. He's back here now and we're waiting for a call."

"I see. All right, I'll speak to you soon."

"What should we do, Spike?"

"Pray, I guess."

Berenger retrieved his Altima from the long-term parking lot and drove out of Queens to Long Island. Traffic was moderately heavy, typical for midday. Berenger drove like a demon, though, zipping in and out of the lanes to bypass the slower vehicles. He didn't care if a patrolman stopped him. He didn't care much about anything except reaching the hospital and seeing his mother.

The hospital wasn't far from Franklin Village. Valley Stream was a small community that resembled all the other municipalities that blended together in Long Island. Berenger knew that the medical center was a good one, although it was overcrowded and understaffed like every other hospital in the country. As he pulled into the parking lot, his cell phone rang. It was Betty Samuels, returning his call. She was there, at the hospital, checking on Ann Berkowitz's progress. Berenger told the woman that he'd meet her in ICU, where his mother was residing.

He took the elevator to the appropriate floor and found Mrs. Samuels in the ICU waiting area speaking to a middle-aged woman wearing a white coat.

"Hello, Mr. Berenger. This is Dr. Stephenson. She's taking care of your mother."

Berenger shook hands with the woman. "How's my mom?" he asked.

"She's stable," the doctor said. "We're moving her out of ICU in a little bit. You can go in and see her. It was a mild stroke. There was no damage to any brain functions that we can see, so far anyway. I think we might need to do some more cardiovascular testing in the coming weeks after she's fully recovered."

Berenger sighed. "Well, it's good she's okay. She can talk and everything?"

"She's a little groggy from the sedative we gave her, but yes, she's lucid. The Alzheimer's isn't helping but I think you'll find there's very little change from when you last saw her."

Berenger nodded. "Okay."

"One other thing," the doctor said. "I was just talking to Mrs. Samuels about this. Your mother will need some extended care at Franklin Village. You're going to have to think about hiring a part-time nurse to be with your mom from now on."

Mrs. Samuels spoke. "We just don't have the staffing for full-time care, Mr. Berenger. A lot of our residents have personal nurses that come in. We work with a very reputable agency that can provide someone if you don't know of any."

"I guess that can get expensive, huh?" Berenger said.

"It can, I'm sorry to say."

He shrugged. "Well, we gotta do what we gotta do. Whatever's best for my mom. Can I see her now?"

"Sure."

He went through the ICU ward doors with the doctor and walked down the corridor that was lined with small individual rooms, each containing a patient hooked up to monitors, tubes, and machines. Every intensive care patient was closely watched from the central operations area, located in the middle of the ward. The doctor led Berenger into Ann Berkowitz's room and whispered, "I'll leave you alone for a few minutes. Try not to get her too excited. I'm sure she'll be glad to see you."

The doctor left and Berenger approached the bed. His mother's eyes were closed. A heart monitor beeped rhythmically next to the bed.

"Mom?"

The woman opened her eyes and focused on him. "Abe? Is that you?"

"It's Spike, Mom. Your son."

"Oh, Spike. For a minute I thought you were Abe. Where is Abe?"

"Abe's dead, Mom. Remember?"

She didn't answer. Instead she said, "Spike, how are you?"

"How are *you*, Mom? You doing all right?"

"I think so. Something strange happened to me."

"Yes, but it's nothing to worry about. They're doing some tests and stuff. You'll go back to Franklin Village pretty soon."

"Go back where?"

"You know, where you live."

"Oh. Yes. I'd like to go home."

"You will. Listen, I want you to get some rest. I'm gonna call Carl and tell him what's going on, okay?"

"How is Carl?" she asked.

"I'm sure Carl's fine. I'm gonna call him."

"Okay." She closed her eyes.

"You sleep now, Mom." He patted her hand and quietly walked out of the room.

"Carl?"

"Spike?" His brother was three years younger but they had always been close. It was hard on both of them when Carl had moved from Texas to New York with their mother when she remarried. Berenger had stayed behind to live with his father and finish high school.

"Yeah, it's me. Listen, Mom had a small stroke."

"Jesus!"

"It's okay, don't get excited. She's fine. No damage that they can see. They're doing some tests, you know, and pretty soon she'll be going back to Franklin Village."

"When did this happen?"

"Last night or this morning. I'm not really too sure."

"Are *you* okay?"

"Yeah, I'm fine. I've been busy on a case and I also just learned one of my people—well, you remember Suzanne, don't you?"

"Sure. The good-looking brunette?"

"Yeah. Well, she got shot today."

"Oh my God! Spike!"

"I've got to rush over to see her now. Two in one day. Sheesh."

"Anything I can do?"

"Well, actually, yeah. They say Mom's gonna need some extra help at Franklin Village. You know, a hired nurse to work part-time. It might be expensive."

"You know I'll help with the cost, Spike."

"I know. I'm just telling you. The thing is, I'm really busy on this case and with Suzanne in the hospital and all—"

"I'll hop on a plane and be out there tomorrow."

"Can you? It would really be a big help if you were here with Mom."

"No problem. I don't have anything on my plate that can't wait." Carl Berenger was an entertainment lawyer who had done pretty well for himself.

"You sure?"

"Hey, I handle movie stars and their agents. I can *always* put them off!"

"What about Sarah and the kids?"

"They'll be fine with it. Let me make the arrangements and I'll call you back in a jiffy to let you know when I'm coming."

"Thanks, Carl. You're a pal."

"Pal, shmal, Spike, I'm your brother."

It was nearing sundown when Berenger drove into Manhattan. He went straight to the Upper East Side and found a street parking space a block away from New York Hospital. As he walked toward the massive structure, he phoned Mel at the office to get an update. She told him that the five-hour surgery was a success. She also gave him the name of the surgeon and said he was still in the ICU. Berenger made his way into the building, up to intensive care, and found the surgeon.

"I'm Dr. Chang," the man said. He was Chinese, obviously, and appeared to be ten to fifteen years younger than Berenger.

"Spike Berenger. I'm Ms. Prescott's employer and friend."

"Yes, your office called. I've been expecting you."

"This is the second ICU I've been to today," Berenger said.

"I'm sorry?"

"Never mind. How's Suzanne?"

Chang nodded. "Doing very good, all things considered. She was very lucky."

"How can being shot be lucky?"

"I meant she was lucky that the bullets didn't hit her heart or the larger portion of the lung, which might have resulted in massive hemorrhaging."

"Bullets? Plural?"

"Two. Both in the chest."

"So she's gonna make it?"

"Yes, I think so. But she's going to be out of action for at least a couple of months, maybe more. We had to repair one lung and remove the bullet. The other bullet entered just below her left collarbone and exited out her back."

"So you retrieved one of the bullets?"

"Yes. The police already have it. I can give you the detective's name and number. He gave me his card."

"Thanks. Can I see her?"

"I'm afraid not. She's still under and will be for some time. Maybe tomorrow for a brief time. We have to keep her very still and very calm. You understand."

"Of course. Just one other thing—was she able to talk at all? Did she say who did this to her?"

"No. She was unconscious when she was brought into the ER. I imagine she won't be able to have a conversation of any kind until tomorrow."

Berenger shook the man's hand. "You rock, Doctor. Thank you. You saved her life."

"Like I said," Chang said. "She was lucky."

27

Higher Ground

(performed by The Red Hot Chili Peppers)

Berenger met Dave Bristol at Washington Square in
Greenwich Village at 11:00 P.M. Since there was nothing
more he could do that night about Suzanne or his
mother, he had called the drummer to inquire about the
status of the meeting with the mysterious Jimmy and
Bristol replied that he had been successful in setting it
up. Bristol told the PI to meet him downtown and they
would go together from there.

"Do not come armed," Bristol warned him. "You will
be searched before you see him. If you're carrying so
much as fingernail clippers they won't let you in."

Berenger sat on a bench near the arch at the appointed time and waited. The usual crowd of NYU students, bums, and junkies that liked to loiter there still
populated the square. A small group of guys dressed like
punks hovered around a nearby bench. Berenger wondered if they might be Jimmys but the young men paid
no attention to him.

The drummer arrived five minutes late. Berenger immediately noticed that Bristol appeared extremely
nervous.

"Hey man," Bristol said. He and Berenger slapped
hands.

"You all right?" Berenger asked.

Bristol sniffed. "Yeah."

"So what's the score?"

"We wait here. Someone will come and pick us up." He sniffed again.

"You been using the candy, Dave?"

Bristol shrugged. "So?"

"Why don't you sit down?"

"I feel like standing." In fact, Bristol couldn't stop moving. Berenger could see that the drummer was very agitated.

They waited another minute and then Bristol abruptly kicked the side of the bench.

"Geez, Dave, take it easy," Berenger said.

"Fuck this," Bristol spat. "I don't like doing this. Why did you have to pick on me, Berenger? I thought we were friends."

"Well, we are. That's why I asked you."

"You didn't ask. You threatened me, remember?"

"Dave, that was just to get you to listen. You think I'd really fuck you over?"

"I don't know, Spike. I guess I'm just stressed out. Blister Pack is recording tomorrow starting at noon. Al Patton's producing us and I'm gonna be in the studio all day. It's gonna be hours and hours."

"Al Patton? That guy is never in his office. He's the only person I haven't talked to about Flame."

"Drop by Lightning Rod Studios tomorrow afternoon and you can catch him."

"Maybe I'll do that."

At that moment they both looked up and saw that two of the punks had walked over to them from the other bench. One of them suddenly produced a Colt .45 and pointed it at Bristol.

"You Bristol?" he asked.

Bristol swallowed, raised his hands, and answered, "Yeah."

They looked at Berenger. "And you're the PI?"

Berenger stood and held up his hands. "Uh huh."

"Put your hands down, both of you. Are either of you carrying?"

"No," Berenger answered.

"Then let's go." The punk gestured with the handgun toward the arch.

They started to walk out of the square but Berenger said, "Where are we going?"

The other punk turned and laughed. "If we told you, we'd have to kill you. You coming or not?"

Berenger stepped forward but Bristol didn't move. Berenger took him by the arm and said, "Come on, Dave. It'll be fine."

They followed the two punks to a decrepit Chevy Malibu that was parked on Fourth Street. Punk #1 unlocked the doors and gestured for the two men to get in the back. Punk #2 got in the passenger seat. Berenger and Bristol climbed into the back and the car took off, heading south. The driver eventually crossed Houston Street and then turned west. In five minutes they were in Tribeca.

Punk #2 leaned over the seat and handed the two men a pair of blindfolds. They were sleepers, the kind that airlines gave passengers for intercontinental flights. "You gotta put these on," he said.

Bristol protested. "Hey, I'm not gonna wear no damn—"

"Dave!" Berenger spat. "Do it." He put his on and made sure that it fit snugly. "See, I've got mine on."

Bristol quietly cursed and grudgingly put on the blindfold.

The car drove on and finally stopped at the corner of West Broadway and Chambers Street, although the two backseat passengers didn't know it. Punk #2 got out and opened the back door. "This is it," he said.

Berenger and Bristol stepped out of the car and the driver pulled away.

"This way," the punk said. He took both men by the arms and began to walk along Chambers, toward Greenwich Street. When they were halfway down the block, the punk led them into a brownstone. He pressed a call button.

"Yeah?" a voice asked through the intercom.

"It's Chief," the punk said.

The door buzzed and "Chief" led them inside. Two African American men came down the stairs and took over.

"Turn around," one of them told the men. "Gotta frisk you."

Berenger and Bristol submitted to the pat down and then they were told, "You're gonna climb some stairs. Take 'em one at a time. Hold the rail."

Berenger and Bristol ascended to the second floor with no problems. A pounding slap-bass line could be heard through the walls of the building and Berenger felt the vibration in the staircase. Wherever they were going, the music volume was pretty high.

The two men led them into a room and shut the door. "You can take off the blindfolds now," one said. He had to shout because the Red Hot Chili Peppers were rocking through "Higher Ground" at a tremendous volume.

They were in a large, immaculately decorated loft. Most of the light came from a vast aquarium that was built into one of the walls. Berenger estimated it to be ten feet in length and four feet tall. It was stocked with an amazing assortment of colorful, tropical fish. One part of the floor was occupied by expensive-looking leather lounge furniture. The pieces were arranged in front of a big-screen plasma television and a high-end sound system. The music was booming out of five-foot tall Bose speakers. Another part of the room contained gym equipment. The far side was a kitchen and dining area. Doors led to, presumably, the bathroom and bedrooms. But by far the most outstanding feature of the loft was the abundance of plants—mostly tropical ones, growing out of pots, in trays, hanging from the ceiling, and situated on the floor.

The two men were huge brutes sporting Mohawk haircuts. Bodyguards, no doubt. Berenger thought one of them looked like that actor/wrestler from the eighties, Mr. T, except he had a pink scar that ran from his forehead to the left side of his chin. The other guy was more of a Mike Tyson look-alike. He was playing with a strand of guitar string in his bulky hands, entwining it in his fingers. Both bodyguards packed semiautomatics—they appeared to be Brownings—in holsters on their waists.

"Have a seat," Mr. Scar said. He pointed to the lounge furniture.

Berenger and Bristol did as they were told.

"Nice place, huh?" he said in Bristol's ear.

"Fuck this," Bristol muttered.

One of the bodyguards disappeared through a door near the kitchen. After a moment he returned and pointed to Berenger.

"Jimmy will see you now."

Both Berenger and Bristol stood but the man shook his finger at Bristol. "Nuh uh. You stay." He indicated Berenger. "Just him."

Bristol grumbled again and sat. The bodyguard with the guitar string stood behind the drummer. He looked at Berenger and said, "If there's any trouble in there, your buddy here gets decapitated with a D string."

Bristol turned around, a look of panic on his face. "Hey!" he said.

"Be cool, Dave," Berenger said. "Everything's gonna be all right." He followed Mr. Scar through the door and into a small, dark room illuminated only by mood lighting built into the walls. It was an office containing a large mahogany desk, more leather furniture, and more plants. The walls were covered by four rather kitsch paintings of nude black women in tropical settings. The music was now muted, as if the office was sound-proofed to an extent.

A man sat behind the desk but he was bathed in shadow. Berenger could barely discern the shape of his head and broad shoulders.

Mr. Scar left the room. The man behind the desk said, "Mistah Berenger, please sit down."

Berenger took the chair facing the desk.

"I'm Jimmy," the man said. "I've heard a lot about you."

"You have?"

"Yes, I have. Your reputation precedes you. I know all about Rockin' Security. It's de best concert security outfit in de business. You never would have got in here to see me without dat."

"Thanks." Berenger once again recognized the musical lilt of a Jamaican accent. He cleared his throat. "You have quite an impressive loft here."

"Thank you. I worked hard for many years t' get it."

"I can see that."

"Shall we get down t' business?" the man asked smoothly. Berenger felt no threat from the man, but even Jimmy's silhouette exuded a powerful, menacing charisma. He was not a man that one wanted to cross. "I understand you wanted t' see me."

Berenger leaned forward. "I understand that the Jimmys have a contract out on me. I want to know why."

Jimmy took a moment to examine the fingernails on his right hand and then said, "I am de only one who can issue an order like dat. I have issued no such order on you."

"You . . . you haven't?"

"No. Why should I? I have nothing against you."

"But I got the guitar strings. You know, the package of broken strings. It was delivered to my office. And I got a threatening phone call. But more importantly, twice now, a Jimmy has tried to shoot me."

"If dat is true, de man who did dis is not a Jimmy. You are being deceived."

"Yeah?"

"I give you my word, Mistah Berenger. And my word means a lot."

Berenger wished he could see the man's face. Even so, there was something about the man's voice and manner that Berenger found sincere. Jimmy might be the leader of a peculiar organized crime outfit, but like the *mafiosos* of old he was a man of honor. Berenger believed him.

"All right."

"I suggest you focus your investigation elsewhere," Jimmy said.

"Okay. Thank you."

"Is dere anything else?"

"I'm working for one of your . . . dealers. Adrian Duncan."

"I know that. I hope you can help free him," Jimmy said.

"His lawyer will have to do that but I'm beginning to feel more confident that I'll be able to provide what he'll need to get Adrian off. The thing is . . . Adrian might not be in a position to work for you anymore. I hope you won't . . . hold that against him."

"I understand. If he had been arrested for dealing den I could have used my people t' obtain his release—and for dat he would have been in my debt. But seeing as how dis is a case dat doesn't involve de Jimmys, I believe I can turn a blind eye to his . . . resignation. I have other people dat can take over his territory. Is dat all?"

"Just one more thing. I understand you do business with the Messengers."

Jimmy paused a moment, as if he were thinking about what he should reveal. Finally he said, "Maybe."

"I need to know what business you have with them."

"Is dat really your concern?"

"It would help in my investigation."

Jimmy exhaled loudly and then shrugged. He said, "We pay de Messengers a tidy sum for a space where we store some equipment. Musical equipment. I understand you already know of dat place. Dat's why I'm telling you dis."

"Yes, I've been there."

"Dat's it, Mistah Berenger. Dat's our only connection wit' de Messengers." Jimmy chuckled, as if something amused him. "Dat Theo, he's one crazy bastard, ain't he?"

"Oh, you know the reverend?" Berenger asked.

"Know him? I shared a jail cell with him for four years!"

"In Jamaica?"

"Dat's right. He was a two-bit yardie dat got into some trouble. I was serving time for . . . well, a number of things. I got out in 1984. Theo, he was in a little longer after dat. He wasn't a preacher when I knew him back den."

"That explains the Caribbean connection. Do you know much about his operation? Or about his assistant, Ron Black?"

Jimmy paused and said, "Mistah Black I know about but I never met him. He came to de prison after I was out."

"So he was in the same prison dat you and Theo were in?"

Jimmy nodded. "Not only dat, but he occupied the same cell I once did. He was Theo's cell mate for a short time."

This jived with what Chucky Tools had told Berenger. "He's not who he says he is. Do you know his real name?"

"Well, I don't know if it is his *real* name, but when he was in Jamaica he was called Paul Daniel."

"Paul Daniel?"

"Dat's what I said."

"Okay. Thanks. That might help."

Jimmy stood in the darkness, indicating that the meeting was over. Berenger could see that the man was taller than Dave Bristol, and that was saying a lot. "Mistah Berenger, I do hope that in light of my cooperation wit' you dat I will have no trouble from you in de future."

"I'm not a police officer, Jimmy."

"But you could tell de police things about me."

Berenger said, "You have *my* word."

On cue, the door opened and Mr. Scar gestured for Berenger to exit. Berenger did so and found Bristol sitting nervously on the sofa. The Chili Peppers were still blaring out of the speakers at deafening decibels.

"Let's go! We're done!" Berenger shouted.

The two bodyguards outfitted them with blindfolds again and led them down the stairs to the street. Chief met them there and ushered the two men to the Chevy. Once they were in the backseat and the car was driving north, the driver told them they could remove the blindfolds.

He dropped them off at Washington Square.

There wasn't much that could be said. Berenger shook hands with Bristol. "Thanks, Dave. I appreciate this."

"Yeah."

"Listen, I know it's none of my business, but you should probably stop buying shit from the Jimmys."

"I know. I'm gonna try. I just don't know if I can."

Berenger nodded.

"I'll see ya, Spike."

"See ya, Dave."

The two men went their separate ways uptown.

28

Nothing is Easy

(performed by Jethro Tull)

After the trip to Jamaica and the emotional roller coasters of the previous day's hospital visits, not to mention the dramatic meeting with Jimmy, Berenger was dead tired. He slept hard for the remaining hours of the night and woke up surprisingly refreshed and ready to unravel the various mysteries surrounding the murders—for he was convinced they *were* murders—of Flame and his second wife Carol. Not to mention Suzanne's shooting and the two attempts on his own life. They were all related. He was certain of it.

The first thing he did was pick up the phone and order Tommy Briggs to find out anything he could about "Paul Daniel."

"How'd you find that out?" Briggs asked him.

"I'll tell you later. Just get on it. Any word on Suzanne?"

"No word on her condition but we heard from Detective Sharpe—the guy who's investigating the shooting—he says a witness came forward late last night to say that the shooter was driving a black limousine."

Berenger's heart skipped a beat. This prompted him to say good-bye to Briggs and then dial Lieutenant McTiernan.

"McTiernan," the gruff voice answered.

"It's Spike Berenger."

"Oh. What is it now?"

"You heard about my partner?"

"Yeah. Sorry about that. Is she gonna be all right?"

"It was touch and go, but it looks like she might make it."

"Glad to hear it."

"Thanks. Listen, a witness has come forward and said that someone in a black limousine did the shooting. A black limousine, McTiernan. What does that tell you?"

"That the shooter is a rich son of a bitch?"

"Ron Black, McTiernan. He drives a black limo for the Messengers. And he was Flame's driver for a few years."

"There are a lot of black limos in the city, Berenger," McTiernan said.

"Look, you gotta pull Black in. I just got back from Jamaica, doing some snooping. I talked to one of the Messengers' main men down there and he says Ron Black isn't the guy's real name and that he was in prison with Reverend Theo. The guy's got a criminal past. And I've learned, uhm, from another source that his name is Paul Daniel. That mean anything to you?"

"We had a couple of interviews with Ron Black, Berenger. The guy checked out okay. There was absolutely nothing that indicated he might be dirty. But I gotta admit, you're throwing some new light on all this. All right, Berenger. We'll see if we can find him."

"Great. I tell ya, Billy, if Ron Black is doing all these killings, who knows who might be next? Joshua Duncan? He's the heir apparent to Flame's estate."

"Yeah. I'll see if I can find the kid today, too."

"Thanks, Billy."

"Sure." The men were silent for a few seconds. It was the first time they had actually seen eye to eye on something.

"You still think Adrian Duncan is guilty?" Berenger asked.

"I don't know. You've raised some doubts."

"Good."

They signed off and Berenger looked out the window onto Sixty-eighth Street and considered everything he knew about Ron Black. Why would the guy want to kill Suzanne? And if he was responsible for the other murders, what was the motive? Flame was his employer. Carol Merryman was no threat to him. It didn't make a lot of sense but did it have to?

Another thing puzzled him. What was Ron Black's connection to Al Patton? Tools had told him that Black and Patton were very "friendly" during Flame's Jamaican retreat with the Messengers. Berenger remembered Patton speaking to Black after the reading of Flame's will. Patton had leaned into the limo window and had a conversation with Black. Berenger didn't tell McTiernan about the Patton angle because he wasn't sure what to make of it. He wished to hell he could find Patton and have a face to face but the record mogul had a convenient knack for avoiding him.

Berenger looked at his watch. It was way too early for Patton to be at the recording studio with Blister Pack but maybe he was at his office. He picked up the phone and dialed the Liquid Metal office. When Patton's personal assistant answered, Berenger said, "This is Spike Berenger. I need to talk to Al as soon as possible. Is he around?"

"No, sir," she said. "He's on vacation."

"Vacation? I thought he was producing today."

"No, sir, he's away. Out of town."

So who was lying? Patton, his assistant, or Bristol?

"Well, can I call him, wherever he is? This is really important."

"I'm not allowed to give out his cell number. I can get a message to him, though, and ask him to call you."

"Please do." Berenger gave her his number and hung up.

Nothing was easy in this business. Berenger stood and paced his office a couple of times and then made a call to Derek Patterson. He needed a visitor's pass to Rikers Island.

Adrian Duncan looked better than he had the last couple of times Berenger had seen him. The black eye had diminished in intensity somewhat and there were no other visible signs of prison abuse.

"I guess Patterson's complaint did some good," Berenger said.

Duncan shrugged. "I guess. The guard who hit me ignores me now. He gives me dirty looks but they assign other guys to me."

"You're looking better."

"I'm getting used to this place, I'm sorry to say," Duncan said. He actually managed to smile.

"Listen, things are moving along nicely," Berenger said. "I need to ask you something."

"Go ahead."

"Would Al Patton have any reason to kill Flame?"

"Al Patton?" Duncan was genuinely surprised by the question. "I don't think so. Geez, Patton was my dad's friend and manager for, like, forever."

"I know he was not happy about Flame's conversion to fundamentalist religion and becoming a Messenger."

273

Duncan shrugged again. "Nobody was happy about that. Dad's music changed and didn't make the kind of money it used to. You think that might be it?"

"I don't know. Patton makes plenty of money. He's got other acts and he still makes a fortune from Flame's earlier recordings. It shouldn't matter that much, not enough to commit murder for, anyway."

"Well, one thing that's always impressed me about Al Patton was that he sure *loves* his money," Duncan said. "I mean, he'll do anything to make another buck."

"So how does making another buck translate into killing one of his biggest stars?"

"You got me. I don't know."

Berenger drummed his fingers on the table and mulled over the puzzle pieces before him. "Was Flame holding back anything that could have made Patton a lot of money?" he asked.

"I don't know. I wasn't taken into my dad's confidence very much, if you remember. You'd have to talk to Carol Merr—oh. I forgot. She's dead."

"Doesn't Liquid Metal Records own Flame's recordings?"

"Yeah, I think so. Everything he recorded *for* Liquid Metal Records."

"You mean there's stuff that he didn't record for Liquid Metal?"

"Sure. There's some stuff. I told you about that album I wanted to produce and release. Remember? Dad wouldn't let me."

"What was that?"

"That crazy recording he did with John Lennon. And David Bowie. Back in the seventies."

Berenger rubbed his chin. "Bowie mentioned that at the memorial service. Tell me more about that."

274

"Let's see, it was in 1974. Lennon was in L.A. at the time. Bowie was passing through after one of his big tours was a financial bust."

"That would have been *Diamond Dogs.*"

"Yeah. One night the three of them got together in some studio. They were smashed out of their heads but they turned on the recorders and made some incredible music. Dave Bristol was there. Harry Nilsson was there. I forget who else. The material was all by my dad and Lennon. Bowie sang some backup vocals. It's really great stuff. I heard it when I was pretty young but I remember it being phenomenal."

"Why wasn't it ever released?"

"Dad and Lennon didn't want it released. For some strange reason, they thought it was crap. That very night they signed a pact agreeing they would hold on to the tapes until after they were dead and buried. They had this idea that the tapes would be unearthed like some archeological relic."

"Who's got the master tapes?"

"Dad always hung on to them. They're in his vault. I wanted to take them and do some remixing because, as you can imagine, some of it is pretty rough. After all, they were jamming and were real stoned. Still, it's about nine hours of fantastic stuff. It would make a great box set."

"And quite a lucrative one for whoever released it."

"You can say that again."

Berenger stood and held out his hand. "Thanks, Adrian. Hang tight. This ain't over yet." They shook hands and Berenger said, "Oh, by the way. The Jimmys don't expect you to continue dealing for them. When you get out, I hope you'll consider leaving them alone."

"How do you know that?"

Berenger winked at him and pointed at his temple. "I know things." He then signaled the guard that they were done.

Berenger left Rikers Island and drove back to Rockin' Security in record time. He had two phone calls to make—the first one to David Bowie, a man he had met a couple of times but didn't know well.

The second, more difficult call would go to Yoko Ono.

29

Danger Zone

(performed by Kenny Loggins)

At noon, Mel received word that Suzanne was alert and had asked for Berenger. He dropped everything and rushed over to see her. Dr. Chang met him in the ICU waiting area and cautioned him to keep the conversation short.

"She's drifting in and out," the doctor said. "She already had one visitor today—the detective working her case. I would have preferred that we wait another day before you talk to her but she's very persistent. She insisted on talking to you today."

"Suzanne's very stubborn," Berenger said.

Chang smiled. "It's the stubborn ones who survive. Go ahead but please try not to upset her."

Berenger entered the little room and saw his partner and long-ago lover in the most vulnerable and heartbreaking condition he had thought possible. She was covered by a sheet and blanket, from under which several tubes ran to various machines positioned around the bed. A heart monitor, much like the one he had seen in his mother's room, transmitted a steady, slow pulse. Suzanne's neck and shoulders were in bandages but her arms lay on top of the blanket. A drip was attached to one hand and the heart monitor was clipped to one of her fingers.

Despite all of that, she was still Suzanne. Her face, though pale, hadn't lost any of her natural beauty. Her eyelids drooped over her large brown eyes, but they retained the sparkle he had found so endearing ten years ago.

"Hey, sport," he said softly.

She smiled weakly. "Hey there," she whispered. Her voice was still hoarse from having a tube down her throat.

"How are you feeling?"

"Okay. I'm pretty doped up."

"Any pain?"

"Not right now. I'm just real . . . groggy."

"The doc says I can't stay long anyway. You can get back to sleep in a minute."

"I . . . I have to tell you . . ."

He put a hand on her arm and said, "Take it easy, Suzanne. Go slow, it's all right."

"Ron . . . Black. He shot me."

"I thought so."

"Did they get him?"

He shook his head. "Not yet. Detective Sharpe, he's handling your case—"

"He was here . . . this morning."

"You told him about Black?"

"Yes."

"Then I guess they're looking for him."

"I . . . I figured out . . . who he is," she struggled to whisper.

"Oh?"

"In California. When I was arrested." She closed her eyes and swallowed. Berenger handed her a cup of water from the bedside table and placed the straw between her dried lips. She sucked some liquid into her mouth and nodded. He put the cup back and she continued.

278

"When I was fifteen . . . you know . . . 1985 . . . when I was arrested for drugs?"

"Yeah."

"He was in one of the jail cells. When I spent the night there. He was in one of the holding cells all night. I remember him . . . looking at me. I remember being more scared . . . more scared of *him* than I was of the arrest."

"You don't know why he was in there, do you?"

"No. But I don't think Ron Black is his real name."

"It's not. I learned pretty much the same thing in Jamaica. Does the name Paul Daniel ring a bell?"

She closed her eyes and shook her head. "Maybe. I don't know."

"Never mind. This helps a lot, Suzanne. With this information it'll be easier to find out who the hell this wacko is."

"Another thing . . ." She winced and paused a moment. "I was tailing him . . . in the limo. He picked up Al Patton. Then . . . he picked up Joshua Duncan. They drove around Central Park for a half hour . . . and then I lost them. Those three . . . the three of them . . ."

"Don't say any more, Suzanne," Berenger said. "I get the idea."

Dr. Chang stuck his head in the door. "I'm afraid I must interrupt you now, Mr. Berenger. We don't want to overexert our patient."

"We're just finishing, Doctor." Berenger leaned and kissed Suzanne on the forehead. "Get some rest, honey. You'll be back with us in no time. Don't worry about a thing."

Her eyes closed and she seemed to drift away as he stood there. Berenger nodded at the doctor and followed him out of the room.

* * *

Berenger sat on the front steps of the hospital and phoned Tommy Briggs. He relayed what Suzanne had said about Black. He then phoned Detective Sharpe but got voice mail. So instead he called McTiernan, who answered with his gratingly rough voice.

"Hey, it's me," Berenger said. "Suzanne has definitely ID'd Ron Black as her shooter."

"I know. I spoke to Sharpe an hour ago. They're out looking for the goddamned guy now. The thing is, he's disappeared. The limo's at the Messengers' place but no one's seen Black since yesterday. I hope to fuck he hasn't skipped town."

"Where does Black live?"

"He has a small apartment in Queens. They raided the place just a little while ago. No sign of him."

"Crap. If he's flown the coop . . ."

"He'll be found, Berenger."

"What about Joshua Duncan? Did you find him?"

"Yeah, I spoke to him. He's fine, he's going to his classes. Nothing seems amiss there. Listen, I gotta run."

"Right. Talk to you."

"Yeah."

Berenger hung up and wondered what his next move should be. If Ron Black had run away and Al Patton was supposedly indisposed all day—either on "vacation" or at Blister Pack's afternoon recording session—what else *could* he do? He didn't really have anything on Patton . . . yet. Should he interrupt the recording session and have a talk with him? That probably wouldn't sit well with the producer and he'd be uncooperative.

Berenger stood and began the walk back to Rockin' Security. It wasn't far and the air would help clear his head. He detested the smell of hospitals. It was painful to see Suzanne in that condition but he was confident that she'd be out of there sooner than the doctors predicted. She was a fighter.

As he walked he placed a call to Gina Tipton. He hadn't spoken to her since returning from Jamaica. He got her cell's voice mail, left a short and sweet message, and asked her to call him.

He was nearing First Avenue and Sixty-eighth Street when his phone rang. It was Tommy Briggs.

"Spike, I got it."

"What?"

"Ron Black. I got the scoop. Suzanne's info made it easy."

"Talk to me."

"Okay, you were right. The name he was using before Ron Black was Paul Daniel. In the seventies he worked for a casino in Vegas, but you know what that means. He worked for the mob, probably as a hit man. In 1974 there was a murder in Los Angeles—a mobster named Charlie Spinoza was found in his hotel room, *hanging by the neck*. The police wrote it off as a suicide, but whispers in the underworld told a different story. Paul Daniel allegedly killed Spinoza and staged the suicide. He was arrested for murder in L.A. but was convicted of manslaughter—they couldn't get the murder charge to stick. So he served eight years in a California prison, between 1975 and 1983. Got paroled. He was arrested again in L.A. in March of 1985 for racketeering and suspicion of murder, but he was released two days later. That was when Suzanne saw the guy in a holding cell. Then, get this—he skipped parole and left the country. He went to *Jamaica*. Not sure how he got there. Probably some kind of passport creativity going on with that. Anyway, he's there in Jamaica and gets arrested *again* in 1986 for drug-related charges and assaulting a police officer. He was trying to smuggle a ton of marijuana to the States and got caught. He was sent to the same prison where Reverend Theo was residing, and that's where they met. Theo got out in 1987 but Daniel was there until 1990. He apparently got in contact with Theo upon his release and was supposedly a changed man. Found religion and all that shit. That's when he changed his name to Ron Black. Next thing you know, Theo and his wife move to America and Black follows them. He's the first permanent employee of the Messengers in New York. I'm having Black's files with all the details sent to me overnight. Should provide some interesting reading."

"Great work, Tommy," Berenger said.

"Wait, wait, that's not all."

"What?"

"Well, after I found out all that, I talked to Plaskett at the bureau, who then talked to *his* guy in Vegas. I wanted to find out a little more about Paul Daniel, and it turns out they have quite a file on the guy. Paul and Daniel are just his first and middle names. You know what his real surname is?"

"Do tell!"

"Paul Daniel *Patton*."

Berenger stopped in his tracks. "Get out of town!"

"I kid you not. Paul Daniel Patton is Al Patton's big brother."

Of course. The two bald heads. They *did* resemble each other.

"Spike? You there?"

"I'm here, Tommy. I just thought of something."

"What?"

"If Ron Black, aka Paul Daniel Patton, has disappeared, then he could just be hiding out somewhere. He shot Suzanne because he realized she was about to figure out who he was. Damn, I'll bet the farm that *he's* the guy who was shooting at *me!* He was impersonating a Jimmy and had the means to do it because of the connection between the Jimmys and the Messengers. That means he's possibly bumping off anyone who might know things about him or know what he's done. Tommy, now I think I know why he killed Flame. And I know why he killed Carol, too."

"And?"

"Joshua Duncan has to be next," Berenger said. "I think the kid's in a shitload of danger."

30

Barrel of a Gun

(performed by Depeche Mode)

Joshua Duncan left his corporate law class early and decided to cut the rest. The events of the past few days had left him weakened and upset. With his father's death, followed within a month by his mother's, he simply didn't know how to handle himself. He couldn't concentrate on his schoolwork and had no desire to be in public.

It had all gone so terribly wrong. None of it was supposed to happen the way it did. They had lied to him and used him. And things just kept getting worse. Now with that private detective's partner being shot and all, the heat was surely going to come down hard and fast.

Duncan considered leaving the city. But where would he go? He knew no one outside of New York. And wouldn't it seem suspicious if he left? No, he had to stick it out. So far, he was safe. He had to carry on with his normal life, as depressing as that was. He couldn't do anything that might attract unnecessary attention.

Damn it to hell, he thought. Why did he have to be the son of a famous rock star?

Duncan walked down West End Avenue and entered his fourteen-story building between 103rd and 104th streets. Freddie, the doorman, gave him a smile and a wave. Duncan often wondered why the building management bothered to employ a doorman. He was supposedly there for security purposes but all the guy ever did was sit and read magazines. Duncan didn't think Freddie could stop a criminal even if he was armed, which he wasn't.

The elevator reached the twelfth floor and Duncan got off. He walked down the hall past the stairwell to his apartment, fumbled with his keys, and unlocked the door. If he had been quick enough, he might have noticed the movement behind him as he swung open the door. Perhaps he could have done something to prevent the attack, even though Joshua Duncan was ill prepared to handle a self-defense situation.

Ron Black body-slammed Duncan, knocking the young man into his apartment and onto the wood floor. Black followed quickly, slammed the door shut behind him, and turned the dead bolt.

"What the—?" Duncan stammered. "Hey, that hurt!" He rubbed his arm and then stared up at the bald man in fright. Black's face contorted as if he were possessed by some kind of demon. His eyes were red and he was practically frothing at the mouth.

"I'm closing loose ends," Black said breathlessly. "Then I'm getting the hell out of Manhattan. Do you know where my brother is?"

"Your brother?"

"My *brother!* Patton! Al Patton!"

"Al Patton is your *brother?*" Duncan slowly crawled backward away from the manic killer.

"Yes, he's my fucking brother. Where is he?"

"I . . . I don't know! I haven't seen him since the other day!"

"His people at his office say he's on vacation. That's bullshit. He's hiding somewhere in the city. I know it."

"I don't know where he is! Honest!"

Black slammed a fist into the wall, cracking the plaster. He stood, panting, staring at Duncan with menace.

"Things have gotten too hot for me and it's all yours and Al's fault," he said.

"What do you mean? What did we do?" Duncan was now backed against the wall of the apartment foyer. He had no other place to retreat.

Black reached behind his back and drew a Colt Cobra .38 revolver. He aimed it at Duncan, causing the young man to scream.

"No! Please don't!" Duncan cowered, covering his head with his arms as he started to sob uncontrollably.

"Shut up, you little shit!" Black said.

The door buzzer sounded. Black froze.

"Joshua?" The voice came from the other side of the locked front door. "Are you in there?" The buzzer rang again, followed by loud knocking.

Black crouched beside Duncan and whispered, "If you make a sound I'll blow your head off." He then went to the door and looked through the peephole.

It was Berenger, the PI.

"Joshua, open up! It's Spike Berenger! The doorman said he saw you come up." More knocking.

Black moved to Duncan and pulled him to his feet. "I want you to answer him, tell him that you're sick, and for him to go away." He stuck the pistol's barrel in the back of Duncan's neck and shoved him toward the door.

Sweat poured off Duncan's head as he nodded in compliance. Trembling, he faced the door and said, "Mr. . . . Mr. Berenger?"

"Joshua! Are you all right?"

Perhaps it was the disparity of Duncan's situation that motivated him to take the risk he did. Or maybe it was the lifelong fatalism that he had always possessed and never attempted to combat. Whatever it was, the young man steeled his nerve and unexpectedly shouted.

"Black is here, he's got a gun!"

Simultaneously, Duncan slammed his elbow into Black's chest and did his best to shove the man away. He then ran toward the back of the apartment—if he could just make it to the bedroom, he could lock the door and go down the fire escape.

Black's Colt fired twice.

Duncan's body propelled forward through the arch dividing the foyer from the living room. He slid across the smooth wooden floor, two slugs in his back.

Out in the hallway, Berenger heard the shots, drew his S&W Bodyguard AirWeight, released the safety, and fired at the doorknob. The lock mechanism blew away and Berenger kicked in the door. He crouched in a firing position, arms stretched forward and both hands on the gun.

The foyer was empty.

He moved quickly to the arch, peered into the living room, and saw Joshua Duncan lying in a puddle of his blood. No one else was in the room. Berenger skirted quickly across the space to the back hall, taking the necessary precautions to look first and move second. The hallway and bathroom were empty. The bedroom door was closed.

Berenger kicked it open and crouched with the gun in front of him.

The room was empty. The large window by the bed was open and the white drapes blew in the breeze.

Black had gone down the fire escape.

Berenger looked out the window and didn't see the man. He moved back into the living room, stooped beside Duncan, and felt his pulse.

"Did . . . did . . . you get him?" Duncan rasped.

"Hush, Joshua. I'm calling for an ambulance."

Berenger flipped open his cell phone and dialed 911. When the dispatcher answered, he relayed the details and address of the shooting.

"They'll be here in a few minutes, Josh. Just hold on." Berenger examined the two wounds. They looked bad. One had surely punctured a lung and there was no telling what damage the second one did. It was near the center of the young man's back.

"Go . . ." Duncan whispered.

"What?"

"Go get him."

"I shouldn't leave you."

"Go get him. He killed my parents. Don't let him . . . get away."

Berenger frowned. Duncan was right. There was nothing Berenger could do to influence Duncan's pendulum of fate.

"Hang on, Joshua. I'm going after him," he said.

Berenger ran to the bedroom and climbed out onto the fire escape.

31

Run Like Hell

(performed by Pink Floyd)

Berenger stood on the platform and looked down.

How come he couldn't see Black? It was twelve flights to the ground. There was no way the killer could have made it down so quickly.

As if in answer to Berenger's thoughts, a gunshot thundered above him and the bullet struck the metal bars on the fire escape with a loud *clang*. Berenger threw himself back to the side of the building and remained flat. It was times like this when he wished he could get rid of some of the gut that protruded over his belt buckle.

He raised his head and squinted into the sun, which was directly overhead. It was impossible to focus on anything but it was obvious that Black had climbed *up* rather than down the fire escape.

Fine, Berenger thought. If a chase was what the guy wanted, then that's what it would be. He holstered the S&W and boldly took hold of the ladder rungs. Berenger climbed halfway to the fourteenth floor—there was no thirteenth—when another shot zipped past his head. He hugged the ladder, waited a moment and then continued his ascent.

"Give it up, Black!" he shouted. "Or is it Patton? We know who you are now!"

Berenger saw the killer quickly peer over the edge of the roof and then vanish. He continued to climb—the fire escape ladder reached all the way to the edge of the roof. Berenger carefully looked over the ledge and saw nothing but a small maintenance structure that was also the entrance to the stairwell running through the center of the building. It stood about thirty feet away.

He climbed over and crouched, the S&W once again snug in his hands.

Another shot came from behind the structure. Berenger leaped sideways and fired two shots. Another round chipped off pieces of brick inches above his head. Reflexively, Berenger catapulted over the roof edge and back to the fire escape platform—it was safer there.

He attempted to climb the ladder, raise his gun, and shoot again, but Black had managed to reload and fire first. Berenger felt the bullet's heat as it missed his left cheek by an inch. He didn't stop his momentum, though. Berenger quickly reached over the ledge, took a bead at the shape behind the maintenance structure, and squeezed the trigger. Bits of the building flew like shrapnel.

Black suddenly appeared in the open. He fired twice as he moved to the stairwell door. Berenger was forced to duck for cover; by the time he could raise his head, Black had disappeared inside the structure.

Berenger climbed over the ledge once more and ran after Black at full speed. He flattened his back against the wall next to the steel door and then yanked it open. He swung around with gun ready but the landing was empty. Berenger leaned over the rail and heard running steps descending through the building. There was only one thing to do. Berenger climbed on top of the rail and jumped to the fourteenth-floor landing below him. His military training had taught him to land flat-footed with knees bent so that his hefty weight wouldn't cause him to lose his balance or, even worse, break his legs. With one floor down and twelve to go, Berenger once again climbed onto the rail and jumped to the landing below.

Now Black's steps were louder. Berenger leaned over the rail and glimpsed the man's arm and leg as the killer ran down the stairs. Berenger pointed the S&W at the rail, slightly ahead of his prey, and squeezed the trigger. The rail exploded into bits as the gunshot echoed robustly in the stairwell. Black, enraged, stopped and looked upward through the gap between flights and aimed his Colt. Berenger pulled back as two shots tore into the wooden rail in front of him.

The chase resumed. Berenger took the stairs two at a time and passed a few floors when he finally heard the sirens outside.

It's about time! he thought.

Once again he climbed onto the railing and leaped to the landing below. Only seven more floors to the bottom. He rounded the corner and started to descend the stairs but was halted by the sight of Black standing at the bottom of the flight, gun in hand. Berenger simply fell back onto the steps as the Colt recoiled and the bullet whizzed over his chest.

Shit! He was surely a goner. There was no way he could scramble out of the way now.

Black pulled the trigger again but the gun only clicked. He was out of ammo!

Berenger sat up, pointed his gun, and fired. But Black had already begun the next descent and the bullet simply bore a hole in the plaster.

Where were the goddamned cops?

He got to his feet and resumed the chase. Floor 4 . . . Floor 3 . . . Was Black completely out of bullets? Was he reloading as he ran? Berenger always kept a spare magazine with him when he carried his weapon. He had lost count of how many shots he had fired—did he need to reload as well? There was no time for it, for he heard Black opening the door to the ground floor, followed by shouts.

One last time, Berenger climbed onto the rail of the second-floor landing and jumped to the first. He burst out the door and found Freddie the doorman on the floor, rubbing his head. Black had pistol-whipped him and run through the lobby and out the front door.

Berenger rushed outside and saw Black sprinting across West End Avenue toward Riverside Park. The sirens now filled the air, for two patrol cars screamed into view and pulled over in front of the building. Berenger ignored a policeman's command to halt and he took off after Black.

Black ran west on 103rd Street and bolted across Riverside Drive, straight into heavy traffic. The scream of brakes and the sudden dull *thump* accompanied the horrific sight of a taxicab slamming into the running man. The impact flung Black into the air and he landed hard on the hood. More cars screeched to a halt. Berenger ran into the avenue, prepared to grab the guy and disarm him, but Black rolled off the cab and continued to run—with a pronounced limp—toward the park. His pace was much slower now and Berenger had no problem decreasing the distance between them.

Black hobbled onto the grass, causing a group of carriage-pushing mothers to scream. Berenger stopped at the edge of the park to examine his S&W. There was one cartridge left. No time to reload.

"Black! Stop now!" he shouted, but it didn't do any good. The man kept limping away.

Berenger took aim at Black's lower body and squeezed the trigger. The S&W coughed loudly and Black dropped to the ground.

"You! Throw down your weapon! Now!"

Berenger turned to see three policemen, guns drawn, running toward him. He immediately dropped the S&W and raised his hands.

"I'm a PI!" he shouted. "I have a gun permit!"

"On your knees! Now! Hands on your head!" one of them shouted as they reached him.

Berenger did as he was told. "I can show you my ID, fellas. The guy you want is over there." The cops looked up and saw Black attempting to crawl across the grass. He moved like a wounded bird, unable to fly to safety.

Two patrolmen left Berenger in the care of the third and ran over to intercept Black. At that moment, a familiar voice yelled from the edge of Riverside Drive.

"Let that guy go!"

It was McTiernan. He and two other patrolmen ran across the avenue to Berenger. "This man's on our side, Officer," McTiernan said, addressing the patrolman. "Get up, Berenger."

Berenger stood and picked up his S&W. "Thanks, McTiernan. I tried to tell 'em I was one of the good guys but they didn't listen."

One of the two policemen with Black shouted, "Sir, the suspect has a gunshot wound in the right leg. We've cuffed him and he's ready for an ambulance."

"That's fine, Officer!" McTiernan yelled back. "Keep him under wraps!"

"McTiernan, have you been upstairs to Joshua's apartment?" Berenger asked.

"The paramedics are up there now. They'll be bringing him down any minute."

As the police took charge of Black, Berenger followed McTiernan back to Duncan's apartment building, where a sizable crowd had gathered. Four patrol cars and two ambulances were parked in front, lights blazing.

Eventually the paramedics brought Duncan out on a stretcher. They were about to load him into one of the ambulances when the young man opened his eyes and saw Berenger. The paramedics paused a moment to get the gurney ready to slide in.

"How ya doin', kid?" Berenger asked.

"I'm . . . sorry," Duncan whispered. Tears streamed down his face. "I didn't mean . . . for it to go this way . . ."

"Save your breath, Joshua. You can tell us all about it when you feel better."

"All I wanted . . . was a chance to prove myself. I could be something . . . in the music business . . . too. Patton . . . Patton promised to help me . . . after I got control of Flame Productions . . . if I'd let him release . . . if I'd let him release . . ."

"I know," Berenger said. "Hush now. They're gonna take you to the hospital and fix you up. Don't worry about a thing. We got Black and we're gonna get Patton, too."

Duncan coughed, spitting blood.

"Back away, please, sir," one of the paramedics said as they shoved the gurney into the ambulance.

Berenger stood and watched it speed away, and then he turned to McTiernan, ready to give the police detective his statement.

32

Watching the Detectives

*(performed by Elvis
Costello and the Attractions)*

Three hours later Berenger walked into Lightning Rod
Studios at the appointed time and could hear smoking
jazz-fusion coming from the monitors in the reception
room. He recognized the signature sound of Blister
Pack, formerly known as Flame's Heat, but without
Flame. Berenger told the receptionist he was there to
see Dave Bristol. She shrugged and gestured toward the
studio access door. Security was unbelievably lax in
some recording studios.

When he walked into the control room, Al Patton
looked up and was momentarily unable to conceal the
expression of surprise on his face. He quickly recovered,
smiled, and nodded.

"Hey, Spike, how'zit goin'?" he said.

"Hello, Al. I'm fine. How are you?" Berenger asked.

"Good." Berenger turned toward the plate glass win-
dow that separated the control room from the studio.
Dave Bristol was banging away on his Tama kit, Brick
Bentley was slapping his Rickenbacker bass, and Moe
Jenkins was pouncing on his array of Yamaha and
Roland keyboards. Bristol noticed Berenger and their
eyes met in collusion.

"I didn't expect to find you here," Berenger said to Patton, but he was lying. He had spoken to Bristol by phone two hours earlier. Berenger explained what was going on and Bristol agreed to help with the private investigator's plan.

"Yeah, I'm working with Dave on their new stuff," Patton said. "I'm hoping to make Blister Pack a bigger household name than Flame's Heat ever was. What are you doing here, Spike? This is supposed to be a closed session, my friend."

"Oh, Dave told me I could come by."

"He did?" Patton frowned. "That's weird. Dave usually doesn't like *anyone* but essential personnel in the studio when he records. I mean, I know you guys are friends and all . . ."

Berenger shrugged. "He's never said anything to me. I've always been welcome."

Patton didn't respond. He fiddled with the mixers and focused on the music.

"You know, Al, I've been trying to get hold of you," Berenger said. "We never did have that talk you promised me."

"Yeah, I know. I've been super busy, Spike. You know how it is."

"Your assistant says you're on vacation."

"I am. This is how I spend it!" He laughed unconvincingly.

The music continued for another minute and then Bristol abruptly stopped playing. He got off his stool and shouted, displaying his famous temper.

"This is crap, Al! I hate it! We sound like *shit!*"

Bentley and Jenkins stopped playing and looked at their partner as if he were crazy. "What do you mean, Dave?" Brick asked. "We were cooking!"

"Fuck this!" Bristol said. "I'm going out for a smoke." He threw his sticks on the floor and stormed out of the studio. Bentley and Jenkins exchanged expressions of bewilderment. Jenkins addressed the control room, "What the hell was that all about, Al?"

Patton punched the intercom and spoke. "I don't know. Sounded good to me."

"So what do we do, take a break?" Bentley asked.

"I guess so. Let him cool off a bit."

Patton leaned back in his chair and shook his head at Berenger. "That bastard Bristol. You never know with him."

Berenger chuckled. Of course, Bristol's little act had been prearranged. It was just what Berenger needed.

"So let's go get a cup of coffee or something, Al. I can't let you put me off any longer. Now you have no excuse," Berenger said good-naturedly.

Patton knew he couldn't get out of it easily. "All right. Let's go downstairs to the diner."

He stood and Berenger opened the control room door. They walked through the reception room and down the stairs to the street.

Just as Patton opened the front door, Berenger said, "Oh, by the way, did you hear that your big brother was arrested a few hours ago?"

Patton froze. "Shit," he muttered under his breath when he saw what was waiting for him on the sidewalk. Lieutenant McTiernan, two other plainclothes detectives, and four police officers stood with weapons drawn.

"Mr. Patton," McTiernan said. "I'd like you to turn around, place your hands against the wall, and spread your legs."

"What is this?" Patton growled. He looked at Berenger. "You fuck!"

"Sorry, Al," Berenger said. "You gotta pay the piper."

The two plainclothes cops "helped" Patton turn and face the wall. As he was being frisked, McTiernan began the litany.

"Mr. Patton, you are under arrest. You have the right to remain silent. If you give up that right, anything you say . . ."

Berenger walked away. He had heard the Miranda warning too many times in his day. It was music you couldn't dance to.

Everyone but Suzanne gathered in the Rockin' Security conference room the next morning for a debriefing. Remix had put on Elvis Costello's "Watching the Detectives" as a joke to start off the meeting but Berenger told him to shut it off.

"Ringo, what's the word on Suzanne?" he asked.

"The doctor says she's doing great," Mel announced. "She had some solid food for breakfast this morning. That's four days ahead of schedule."

Bishop, Briggs, and Remix applauded.

"You mean she actually kept that hospital shit down?" Remix asked.

"Her prognosis is excellent and the doctor says she'll make a full recovery," Mel continued.

"That's good news," Berenger said. "I hope everyone finds the time to go visit her once a day. It really lifts her spirits."

He got nods all the way around.

Briggs raised his hand and asked, "Are the Patton brothers gonna confess?"

"Ron Black—er, Paul Daniel—already has. It's probably only a matter of time before Al Patton breaks. He's wise enough to cop a plea. A judge would be a lot harder on him if the city has to go through a lengthy trial and he's found guilty."

"How did you know it was Ron Black and Al Patton that was behind it?" Remix asked.

"It was a culmination of things, Remix," Berenger explained. "I was really leaning toward the Messengers as being the culprits until I learned of the connection between Al and Flame's driver, who of course was Al's estranged brother. Tommy provided us with the story on Paul Daniel Patton's background and how he was a hit man for the mob and eventually found himself sharing a jail cell in Jamaica with Theodore Ramsey."

"Reverend Theo," Mel said.

"Right. Theodore Ramsey was in the Jamaican drug racket since he was a kid and could be a pretty nasty character. But while he was in prison for a number of drug charges, old Theo became religious. But he's got a warped mind, you see, and he twisted the religion to suit his needs and his drug-soaked little brain. He formed the fundamentalist Messengers as a means to make money and control people. It's the same kind of syndrome you see in guys like Charlie Manson. They have charisma and intelligence and can influence the weak-minded. That's what 'Reverend' Theo managed to do.

"Theo got out of prison in 1987. He had known Paul Patton for a year inside but they kept in touch. Theo knew he could use some muscle like Paul Patton. So Theo arranged for Patton to have a completely new identity when the guy was released, finally, in 1990. That's when Paul Patton became Ron Black. With the help of Reverend Theo's special mixture of Ecstasy and Sodium Pentothal and other tropical hallucinogens, along with Messenger mumbo jumbo, he was able to turn Paul, now Ron, into a devoted convert. And whenever Theo needed some dirty work performed, it was Ron Black who did it. Are you with me so far?"

The group nodded. They were spellbound.

"Okay. Back in the good ol' USA, Flame was battling drug addiction and trying to keep Flame's Heat together. By now it was the turn of the millennium. He was committed to a rehab center and there he met Brenda Twist. Brenda was a runaway teen from Seattle who was also an addict. She had met Reverend Theo and his wife here in New York shortly after they moved from Jamaica. By 1992 they had begun the Messengers branch over on the West Side, and Ron Black was their first employee. Brenda was in New York at the time and she somehow found herself at their services. She, too, became a convert—but she hadn't kicked her habit. We're still not sure how she ended up in rehab with Flame, but she did. And she and Flame fell in love. I guess. It turns out she was also having an affair with the good reverend but we're not sure how long that's been going on.

"Anyway, Brenda and Flame both got out of rehab in 2000 and Brenda convinced Flame to give the Messengers a try. Reverend Theo saw a prize convert in Flame— a very rich one—and used all the powers at his command to make Flame a Messenger. Flame was in a very vulnerable emotional state at that time in his life. So suffice it to say that converting Flame turned out to be pretty easy.

"Okay, now let's cut to Al Patton, Flame's manager. He was here in New York, running his business, making lots of money. But guys like him, they always want more. You see, he knew about the lost recording that Flame and John Lennon made with the help of David Bowie, Harry Nilsson, and Dave Bristol. Flame and Lennon thought the material was crap and agreed not to release it unless both of them were dead. They even signed an agreement to that effect. I confirmed this with Bowie and with Yoko Ono.

"So Al Patton had been after Flame for years to let him release the recordings. Adrian Duncan also knew about the tapes and had once asked his father to let *him* remix and release them to help him make a name for himself in the music business. Flame refused. So, Al Patton started to think. The only way he could get his hands on those tapes was for Flame to die. The idea came to him when he went with Flame on a Messengers retreat to Jamaica. You see, when he got there, he ran into none other than his long lost big brother, who was going by the name Ron Black. Well, after a few nights of that special Messengers wine, old Al and Paul had something of an emotional reunion. They pledged to be brothers again but they knew they had to keep Paul's true identity a secret. Al was well aware of his brother's violent reputation but ultimately he was the one who arranged for 'Ron Black' to become Flame's personal driver in New York.

"Last night Black confessed that the murder plan was hatched less than a year ago. Patton, sick and tired of Flame's recent musical direction, wanted to drop him as a client. But if Patton released Flame from his contract, then Patton would never get the Flame/Lennon album. So he had to keep Flame and humor him over his music."

"So Patton paid Black to kill Flame and make it look like a suicide?" Mel asked.

"Yep. Only he went a step further," Berenger said. "He made it look like a *murder* that was *staged to look like a suicide* and in doing so *framed* Adrian Duncan. You see, when he was convicted in the seventies on a murder rap, Paul Patton had made some mistakes and the cops saw through the suicide staging. So this time, Paul—Ron Black—planted evidence to make it look like it was *Adrian* who had murdered Flame and staged the suicide. For example, Black retrieved Adrian's after-show pass the night of Flame's last concert at the Beacon Theater. Adrian had ripped it off and tossed it on the floor, backstage. Black found it and kept it, then later stuffed the pass in Flame's hand after he'd killed him."

"Wow. Was Reverend Theo in on it?" Bishop asked.

"Nope. The Messengers knew nothing about it. Brenda, Reverend Theo . . . none of them was involved. Just Black. This was between Black, Al Patton . . . and Joshua Duncan."

"Joshua Duncan!" Bishop cried. "Why was he in on it? He's Flame's son!"

"Patton had apparently enticed Joshua with coproduction credit on the Flame/Lennon album, as well as a percentage of the royalties. You see, Joshua, like his half brother, Adrian, really wanted a career in the music business. His father had squelched his dreams, just as Flame had done with Adrian. This was Joshua's big chance. And I'm sorry to say that Joshua was an accomplice in his father's murder. You see, Joshua could do a perfect impression of Flame. Carol told me that, but it didn't click with me at the time she said it. It was *Joshua* who got Adrian to come to Flame's town house that night after the concert by phoning Adrian and impersonating Flame's voice! Over the phone Joshua convinced a drunk Adrian that he was Flame and that he wanted to talk to him. So Adrian went down there and walked into the trap."

"So *that's* why Joshua is facing some charges," Remix said.

"Yep. But after Flame's murder, Patton blew it. He couldn't wait for Joshua to become president of Flame Productions. He got greedy. He wanted that album *now*. So he arranged a meeting with Carol Merryman the day of Flame's memorial service. He told her he wanted those tapes and that she was going to release the album to him. Carol refused."

"So she had to die," Remix said.

"Right. Patton paid his brother to throw her off the roof. And with that one, Black tried a different MO. He apparently offered her a ride home from Al Patton's party the night of Flame's memorial service. No one saw them get into the limo. He drove her home and accompanied her inside. He must have overpowered her and taken her to the roof. He made it look like her death was a suicide, too."

"And did Joshua know about that?" Bishop asked.

"According to Joshua, no. That murder was a surprise to him. That's when he realized he had made a deal with a couple of devils. Joshua spilled the beans in the hospital last night."

"So what about Suzanne?" Mel asked. "Why her?"

"Because Black knew she was on to him. He had recognized *her*. He knew she was following the limo that day and couldn't take a chance on her exposing him and his brother. And it turned out that after she was dealt with, Joshua was next on his list."

Briggs nodded at Berenger. "And what about you? The business with the Jimmys wanting to kill you . . . ?"

"That was Ron Black and Al Patton. It wasn't the Jimmys at all. They wanted me to *think* the Jimmys were after me, but Black and Patton wanted me out of the way. They didn't want me snooping into the case for fear that I'd discover that Adrian was really innocent. It was Black disguised as a Jimmy those nights when I was shot at."

"So, Spike, what about the Messengers?" Remix asked. "All this time we thought they were the primary suspects. Do they get off scot-free?"

"Yes and no," Berenger said. "It's true they had nothing to do with the murders. But as you know, it's come out that they're involved in a huge fraud. The drugs, the brain-washing of congregates, the taking of their money... Reverend Theo is gonna face some serious charges. You can be sure the Messengers will cease to exist as an organization. Theo, and maybe others in his little sect, will certainly do some time. But not for murder."

Bishop shook his head. "This is unreal. Only in the crazy music business, huh, Spike?"

Berenger nodded and said, "You should have heard what Billy McTiernan had to say about it."

"Yeah? What did he say?"

In his best impression of McTiernan, Berenger bellowed, "You mean to tell me that all this was because of a goddamned fucking hippie-shit rock 'n' roll record?"

For the first time in days, the employees of Rockin' Security had a good laugh.

33

A Hard Day's Night

(performed by The Beatles)

"I *love* banana splits. They were always my favorite," Ann Berkowitz said.

At first she hadn't been able to remember what they were called. "That ice-cream dish with the banana," she had said.

"You mean a banana split, Mom?" Carl Berenger asked, winking at his brother.

"Is that what it is?" she asked. "I just can't remember things like I used to."

"I think we can arrange a banana split, Mom," Spike said. "Carl, what do you think?"

The three of them were in her room in the Neighborhood at Franklin Village. She had been brought home from the hospital the night before and was now comfortably tucked into bed at 7:30 in the evening. But she had insisted on a bedtime snack and demanded to have a banana split. Carl, who had been in New York since his mother's stroke had occurred, stood and told Berenger that he'd go to the kitchen and see what they could whip up. Requests of that kind were not unusual at Franklin Village. As long as the kitchen was still open, they could normally handle just about anything.

Berenger watched his brother leave the room and admired how well Carl looked. His brother had avoided gaining the extra weight that Berenger had put on. He didn't know how Carl did it. Carl seemed to eat a hell of a lot more and claimed that he never exercised. Berenger, on the other hand, worked out constantly and tried to watch what he ate, but he still retained that annoying excessive twenty-five pounds. Carl seemed to lead a charmed life. He had a happy marriage and three terrific kids. As an entertainment lawyer, Carl Berenger was successful and managed to enjoy the benefits his work had brought him. Berenger considered the guy very lucky.

"So, Mom, is it good to be back in your room instead of that smelly old hospital?" Berenger asked her.

"The hospital? I wasn't at the hospital," she said. "You're trying to fool me."

Berenger smiled. "If you say so, Mom."

His cell phone rang, so he retrieved it from his belt clip and checked to see who was calling. The ID told him it was Gina.

"Excuse me, Mom, I need to take this." He walked out of her room and into the hallway to answer the call. "Gina?"

"Hey, handsome."

"What's shakin', sugar?"

"I'm calling to say good-bye."

Berenger sighed. He knew that was coming. They had spent a glorious last night together at her hotel and taken full advantage of each other's bodies while they still could. Both of them admitted using the other person to perform selfish acts of hedonism but also acknowledged that if those acts couldn't be done with a good friend, then they shouldn't be done at all.

"What time is your flight?" he asked.

"I have to be at LaGuardia in thirty minutes. The cab will be here in a minute."

"Well. I guess it sounds silly to say 'I hope to see you again soon.' "

"No, it doesn't. I hope to see you again soon, Spike."

"Me, too."

"I told you this last night, but I'll say it again. You made my time in New York a lot more interesting than it would have been if you hadn't been around."

"Aw, you say that to all your flings," he countered.

"Oh, shut up."

There was a slight pause. "And how's Adrian doing?" he asked.

"I guess all right. He's been a hermit since his release. I can't blame him. He's also in shock, I think."

Berenger understood why, too. Joshua Duncan, in a moment of extreme guilt and self-pity, signed away all his rights in Flame Productions to his half brother. As part of his plea bargain with the DA, Joshua would serve six months in prison in exchange for testimony that would nail Al Patton and Ron Black. Joshua figured he had no business running his father's estate and that Adrian was more suited. His half brother was, he felt, more entitled.

"Well, he's got his work cut out for him, too," Berenger said. "It won't be easy handling Flame's affairs."

"Tell me about it. I just hope he can hire some good legal advisers. He told me today that he's going to hire Joshua when Joshua gets out of jail."

"That's wonderful," Berenger said. "I doubt Josh will serve the full six months. I'll bet he's out in three or four."

"Mmm. And Adrian says he's giving up dealing drugs. I hope that's true."

"Me, too."

There was another awkward silence. Finally, Gina said, "Well, hell, I guess I have to go."

"Gina."

"What?"

"Take care of yourself."

"We probably won't see each other again for a while, will we?" she asked.

"I don't know, Gina. It's hard to say."

"Yeah. I know. You take care, too, Spike."

"Bye."

"Good-bye."

After she hung up, Berenger felt a slight pang in his chest. He knew, though, that it would be gone in an hour. Gina was a great woman but she wasn't what he needed or wanted for any kind of serious entanglement.

She probably felt the same way about him.

Berenger went back into Ann Berkowitz's room and found that Carl had returned with the patient's requested delicacy. Their mother was greedily slurping on a spoon that contained samples of the oversized banana, the ice cream, and the three toppings the kitchen staff had put on it.

"That's a really big banana," Berenger commented.

"It's huge," Carl agreed. He winked at Berenger again, which was a habit he had developed when they were kids in Texas.

"So what time is *your* flight?" Berenger asked.

Carl looked at his watch and said, "Too soon. I have to go, kiddies. Sorry, but that's my story and I'm sticking to it." He leaned over to his mother and gave her a hug and kiss. "You take care of yourself, Mom. I'll be back out to see you in a couple of months, okay?"

She kissed him back but immediately continued to work on her dessert.

Berenger gave his brother a big bear hug and said, "Give one of those to Sarah and the kids, okay?"

"You bet," Carl said. "You're doing a great job with her, Spike." They looked at their mother, who was enjoying the treat so much that she was oblivious to what they were saying. "I'll send you that check we talked about."

"Thanks, bro'."

They slapped each other on the back and Carl finally left the room. Berenger sat in the chair closest to his mother's bed and watched her eat. He suddenly felt that it was too quiet in the room, so he reached over to her dresser and turned on the radio. The station was playing a Beatles song.

"Hey, Mom, listen—it's 'A Hard Day's Night,'" Berenger said.

Ann Berkowitz looked up and smiled. "I remember that song." She began to rock back and forth a little in her bed as she mouthed some of the lyrics. Berenger knew that a person's love of and familiarity with music was one of the last things to go in an Alzheimer's patient. He was glad to see that his mother could still rock 'n' roll.

"Hey, Mom, do you remember when we sat in front of the television and saw the Beatles when they were first on *Ed Sullivan*?" he asked.

She stopped singing and looked at her son with a gleam in her eye.

"You silly boy," she said. "How could anyone forget when the Beatles first came to America?" She shook her head and made a "tsk tsk" sound. "Even *I* remember that!"